Moving Is Murder

Sara Rosett

KENSINGTON BOOKS
KENSINGTON PUBLISHING CORP.
http://www.kensingtonbooks.com

KENSINGTON BOOKS are published by

Kensington Publishing Corp.
850 Third Avenue
New York, NY 10022

All Kensington titles, imprints and distributed lines are available at special quantity discounts for bulk purchases for sales promotion, premiums, fund-raising, educational or institutional use.

Special book excerpts or customized printings can also be created to fit specific needs. For details, write or phone the office of the Kensington Special Sales Manager: Kensington Publishing Corp., 850 Third Avenue, New York, NY 10022. Attn. Special Sales Department. Phone: 1-800-221-2647.

Kensington and the K logo Reg. U.S. Pat. & TM Off.

ISBN-13: 978-0-7582-1337-2
ISBN-10: 0-7582-1337-9

First Hardcover Printing: April 2006
First Mass Market Paperback Printing: March 2007
10 9 8 7 6 5 4 3 2 1

Printed in the United States of America

Chapter
One

Light bled across the horizon, but it was still night below the towering pines where the figure in black slipped up the driveway toward the slumbering house and slithered under the parked minivan. A small flashlight beam illuminated the engine and its hoses. The beam found the right hose and followed it until it was within reach. Metal glinted in the light. A small prick, not a slash, produced a drop of brake fluid that bubbled out and dripped to the ground. The figure twisted around and repeated the procedure on the other hoses. The person allowed a small smile as tiny puddles formed.

With a backward push, the dark form emerged from under the van, grabbed the knife, and shoved it into a deep pocket before joining the early morning joggers trotting through the still neighborhood.

* * *

Nothing had gone wrong—yet. It made me nervous. Something always went wrong when we moved. There was the time our mattress became a sponge in the mover's leaky storage unit and another time our handmade silk rug vanished from our shipment but, so far, our move to Vernon in Eastern Washington State had been uneventful.

I set down a box brimming with crumpled packing paper that threatened to spill over its edge like froth on a cappuccino and watched the moving van lumber away. Its top grazed the leaves of the maple trees that arched over Nineteenth Street, making the street into a leafy tunnel. Sweat trickled down between my shoulder blades.

My fingers itched to get back inside our new house, rip open the butterscotch-colored tape on the boxes, and bring order out of chaos, but inside the heat magnified the smells of fresh paint, floor wax, and dusty cardboard from the boxes that were stacked almost to the coved ceiling.

The heat wasn't as bad outside because there was a breeze, but it was still ninety-nine degrees. Since we didn't have air-conditioning, stepping outside was like moving from inside a heated oven to the fringe of a campfire.

I pushed my damp bangs off my face as a black pickup slowed in front of our house. The driver draped his arm over the open window and called to my husband, "Mitch Avery, is that you?" A bright shoulder patch contrasted with the olive drab of the driver's flight suit. "I didn't know you were moving into Base Housing–East," he continued.

"Steven?" Mitch trotted down the sidewalk. I followed slowly. I'd probably heard him wrong. We were miles from base housing.

Mitch's friend parked his truck on the curb beside a pile of wardrobe boxes that needed to go to the shed since our bedroom closet was roughly the size of a matchbox. Patches on our visitor's chest and upper arms identified him as Captain Steven Givens, a member of the 52nd ARS, or in real language without the acronyms, the 52nd Air Refueling Squadron, Mitch's new squadron. They did the guy equivalent of air kisses: a handshake and a half-hug with slaps on the back.

Mitch introduced Steven.

"This is my wife, Ellie," he said. "And this is my daughter, Olivia." He patted Livvy's head, barely visible in the BabyBjörn carrier I had strapped on my chest.

Steven smiled and shook my hand in a firm, eager grip. "This is great that you're moving in. We live on Twentieth." He had thick burnt almond–colored hair cut neatly to regulation above sincere hazel eyes. His smooth complexion made him look young, even though I knew he had to be older than Mitch.

I glanced at Mitch. His smile was relaxed, so apparently he didn't mind that Steven lived one block away.

"So what do you think of Base Housing–East?" Steven asked, gesturing to the empty street.

Mitch and I looked at each other blankly.

"You didn't know half the squadron lives up here?" Steven asked.

"Here? In Vernon?" I asked.

"Right here, on Black Rock Hill. Most everyone lives within a few blocks," Steven said.

So much for our flawless moving day. Mitch and I exchanged glances. This was much worse than damage to our household goods.

"Well, it won't be like living on-base. We're not next door to each other, right?" Mitch asked.

"No, but Joe, our 'C' Flight Commander, and his wife live across the street from you. The McCarters are on Twentieth with us. There're too many to count, probably ten or fifteen couples, now that you're moving in." Steven beamed like this was the best news he could give us. Why hadn't my friend Abby, who had also just moved here, mentioned this?

"At least the squadron commander is still on-base," Mitch joked.

"No, with the remodeling going on in base housing they don't have many houses open. Colonel Briman lives down your street." Mitch looked like he'd been punched in the stomach.

Steven thumped him on the shoulder. "Welcome to the neighborhood." Steven hoisted up a box, spoke around it. "Where do you want this? I can help you out for a few hours. I was coming home to meet Gwen," he glanced at me and explained, "that's my wife, for lunch. But she's tied up at work. She's the manager at Tate's and has a heck of a time getting away from there."

"So the old bachelor finally got hitched?" Mitch seemed to have recovered from Steven's bombshell. A smile tilted up the corners of his mouth as he kidded with Steven.

"Yeah. I gave in." Steven shrugged.

Mitch's smile widened as he transferred his gaze to me, but spoke to Steven. "It's great, isn't it?"

"Sure is. Now, where do you want this box?"

Mitch pointed to the shed. "Over there. Anywhere inside."

I touched Mitch's shoulder to hold him back from following Steven. I kept my voice low. "I can't believe we bought a house in the wrong neighborhood," I said. "I mean, we've moved how many times? Four?"

"In five years," Mitch confirmed. I felt a sigh bubble up inside me. I squashed it. When I married Mitch I knew we'd have to move. After all, he was a pilot in the Air Force. Moves came with the job. We'd talked about our next assignment and I'd pictured somewhere exotic and foreign, Europe or Asia, Germany or Japan. Not Washington State. And certainly not Vernon, Washington, during a heat wave. And my vision of our next assignment *definitely* hadn't included living next door to everyone else in the squad.

I needed chocolate. I dug into my shorts pocket and pulled out a Hershey Kiss. Chocolate makes even the worst situation look better. It was mushy from the heat, but I managed to peel the foil away and pop it in my mouth. I felt as weak as a wet paper towel.

I lifted Livvy out of the BabyBjörn and transferred her to the bouncy chair in the shade of the pines beside Mitch's makeshift table, a wardrobe box, where he'd checked off each box or piece of furniture on our inventory as the movers unloaded it.

I surveyed the quiet street and came back to what was really bothering me. "Four moves and we make a mistake like this."

We'd researched everything. At least, we thought we had. To avoid living with Mitch's coworkers twenty-four hours a day, we'd decided to live off-base. We wanted privacy and Vernon, Washington, the major city thirty miles from Mitch's new assignment, Greenly Air Force Base, seemed like the perfect place to buy our first home.

We picked an arts-and-crafts-style bungalow on Black Rock Hill, a "regeneration area," our realtor, Elsa, had called it. As the original owners retired and moved to sunnier climates, young professionals moved in and updated. Apparently, everyone else from Greenly AFB had picked Black Rock Hill, too.

"This is one of the best neighborhoods in town." Mitch wiped the sweat off his forehead with the back of his arm. "Great schools, there's a park one block down the road, and it's only thirty minutes from the base."

"I know. I know. You're right," I said. "But it's not our property values I'm worried about. Well," I amended, "I certainly don't want them to go down." My stomach flip-flopped every time I thought of the money we'd plunked down on the house. Buying a house was kind of risky for us. Unlike corporate America, there weren't any moving packages for military folks. Either we sold our house when our three years at Greenly were up or we took the financial hit.

"Buyer's remorse?" Mitch asked. "You look a little sick."

"No. It's the thought of people from the squadron dropping in at any moment or watching us."

Mitch stepped on the paper in a box to flatten it. "At least they can't make us shovel our sidewalk or mow the lawn."

"You're right." I removed the Björn carrier and pulled my sweaty T-shirt away from my back.

"Come on," Mitch said. "It won't be so bad. Everybody's so busy that most people won't even notice us."

"I don't know. Ten or fifteen couples. And the squadron commander," I said, thinking of nosy neighbors checking our driveway for Mitch's car to see if he knocked off work early. "You can park in the empty side of the garage," I offered. "But only until it starts to snow. Then I get it."

"Deal," Mitch said. "You'll have the boxes on the other side of the garage sorted out in a few weeks. How's it going inside?"

"Great, if I want to do some baking. So far I've found the placemats, cake pans, and measuring spoons and cups, but no plates or silverware. Or glasses."

I'd made sure the boxes we needed with our essential things were the last items loaded on the truck, so they'd be the first off. I hadn't counted on the movers unloading our stuff, storing it for two weeks, and then reloading it on another truck in random order.

Mitch considered the seven empty boxes stacked by the curb. "You know, it's not too late to move again. Almost everything is still in boxes."

I was tempted for a moment, but then I looked at the neighborhood and our house. Bungalows with broad porches and sturdy pillars rested in the shade of towering maple and pine trees. A few houses, like ours, had an English influence. Its steep A-line roof sloped down to honey-colored bricks, leaded-glass windows, and an arched front door. It was a gingerbread cottage out of a fairy tale and I loved it. A warm breeze stirred the trees and lifted the strands of hair off my sweaty neck. "No way. We'll just have to be mildly friendly and keep our distance."

Three hours later, I plodded along, gritty with dried sweat, mentally running down my Day One Moving Checklist while I pushed Livvy's stroller. We'd found sheets, but towels were still a no-show. No sign of plates, silverware, and glasses either.

Livvy let out a half-cry, more a squawk, then fell silent to study the dappled sunlight and shade as it flicked over her stroller canopy. She'd been content most of the day to watch the parade of movers, but half an hour ago her patience ran out. I'd fed, burped, and changed her, but she still squeezed her eyes shut and shrieked. She didn't like walking, humming, or singing either. I used to rely on a quick car ride to soothe her, but her enchantment with the car seat evaporated during our road trip from Southern California to Washington State. That meant I had to resort to the big guns, a walk.

Where else could the towels be? We definitely needed showers tonight. We'd unpacked all the boxes labeled BATHROOM. Maybe LINEN CLOSET?

"Ellie, did you hear me?"

"Sorry. I was wondering where the towels might be packed," I said to my friend Abby, the one person I didn't mind dropping in on me. She was such a good friend I put her to work as soon as she had showed up this afternoon even though her style was a shotgun approach compared with my more methodical way. She tore open the boxes and pulled everything out.

Her curly black hair, pulled back in a ponytail, bounced in time with her steady stride as she motored down the sidewalk. "I'll bring over some of our towels for you. I'm so glad you're finally moving in," she said. "You can run with me. I go every morning." Her white sleeveless shirt and jean cutoffs showed off her tanned, toned arms and legs. She claimed her figure tended toward stockiness, but with her energy and huge smile she looked great to me. I couldn't get into last summer's shorts because of pregnancy weight still hanging around, especially on my tummy and thighs.

"Yeah, right. I can't stand running, remember?" Before my pregnancy I ran a few times with Abby, but it reminded me of how much I hated it. Abby and I met two years ago in one of those prefabricated friendship opportunities that arise in military life. Mitch and Abby's husband, Jeff, were friends at the Air Force Academy. More than once, I had found myself straining to carry on a conversation with another wife over dinner while Mitch and his friend caught up. But Abby and I hit it off right away, except for her love of jogging.

"Why didn't you tell me there were so many people from the squadron in this neighborhood?" I asked.

"I didn't realize until we moved in and started unpacking." Abby bounced along beside me. "It'll be great—just like base housing, only better because these houses are newer."

Before I could argue with this overly optimistic view she pointed to a gray stucco house with black shutters. Blooms of roses, hollyhocks, and mums layered color and texture around the base of the trees and house. "That's Cass and Joe Vincent's house," Abby said. A spade and pruning shears had been tossed on the ground beside a bucket sprouting uprooted weeds and grass. "He's Jeff's flight commander, 'C' Flight. She's into gardening and ecology—the environment and all that. She writes about it." Abby's voice had an edge to it.

"You don't like her?" Abby's bubbly personality blended with most people's.

"She's all right," Abby said.

"Cass, from that gardening column in the newspaper, 'Clippings with Cass'?"

"Yes. And she writes articles for environmental Web sites and magazines. A few months ago she headed up a crusade to keep Wal-Mart from building a supercenter on Black Rock Hill. You know, the usual—local neighborhood versus big retailer. But she found some restriction and she was on that news show, *24/7*, as the local environmental expert. I think it went to her head." Abby waved her hand, shuffling the subject away. "Enough about that. How about going to the spouse coffee with me tomorrow night?"

I felt Abby look at me out of the corner of her eye to gauge my reaction before she said, "I know you just got here, but please go with me tomorrow night."

"Abby." My voice had a warning tone.

"I know you don't like the coffees, but I need you to go with me. The times I've gotten together with the spouses here it's been strained, or, I don't know, tense."

"Sounds normal."

Abby sighed as I maneuvered the stroller onto the bumpy walking path of the park down the block from our house. "I know you don't want to go, but I really want to make a good impression. And I want to get involved, too," she added, almost defiantly. "When I finally got to Hunter, they announced the base closing and the coffees just sort of fizzled out."

"Thank God," I muttered.

"You can sneer all you want. You've done it, but I want to give it a shot."

"Abby, they're boring. No fun." This was the most convincing argument I could think of to persuade Abby not to go. She always wanted to experience new things, but she wanted them to be fun and exciting. "It's just the wives of the higher-ranking officers and enlisted trying to outdo each other."

"Well, I don't care if it is boring. We'll make it fun. I want to support Jeff and if it can help him, I'm doing it."

"Slow down," I pleaded. She'd picked up the pace

and we were nearly running around the rolling path that circled the playground and duck pond of Windemere Park. "Mitch says if his career depends on how many cookies I bake, then he doesn't want an Air Force career."

"Jeff supports me in my teaching," Abby countered. "He doesn't say a word about the extra time I put in getting ready for school. And last year I bought so many school supplies I thought I should just stay in line at Wal-Mart, but he didn't mind. I want to support him, too."

We left the park and crossed Birch Street to head back down Nineteenth Street. "How much is the Vernon Public School District going to ask of Jeff? Monthly meetings? Two dozen cookies?"

I knew that set look on Abby's face, so I gave up trying to argue with her and looked down the street to our new house. Even from this end of the block I could see it. Warm yellow light shone from every window. Why hadn't Mitch closed the curtains in the growing dusk?

I did a quick mental tour of the house, then groaned. "Look. The sellers took every curtain and we didn't even notice during the walk-through before we signed the closing paperwork." Yep, we were first-time home buyers, all right. No wonder our house glowed like a birthday cake for a retiree.

"I guess we'll have to do some shopping," Abby said. I nodded, wondering if our budget could stretch to include curtains.

As we paced along the twilight sounds were loud in the silence between us: the racket of the crickets, the swish of sprinklers, the yells of the kids on their bikes as they took one last ride down the sidewalk.

A burgundy minivan backed out of the Vincents' driveway. "That's Cass," Abby said. Cass slammed on the brakes to let a kid swoop across the street on his bike, then she zipped down the street toward us.

Instead of making the slight adjustment to follow the gentle curve of the street, the van stayed on its current track with its nose pointed straight at us. "What's she doing?" I quickened my steps and steered the stroller away from the street.

"I don't know—" The blare of the horn cut into Abby's words. The stroller wheels caught on the uneven sidewalk and the handle slammed into my stomach. "The yard," Abby said. We wrenched the stroller back, shoved it across a driveway. I stumbled. The cement bit into my knee.

Abby steadied the stroller. "Are you all right?" The headlights closed on us.

"Yeah—" We rushed into the grass.

My vision turned to glaring white. I blinked in the black that descended, but I was aware of the solid mass of metal and glass as the van swept past us. I turned and my eyes adjusted. The van's front wheel bounced onto the curb of the driveway we'd just ran across. It bumped along the sidewalk a few feet, then dropped back onto the street before barreling into the intersection next to the park. My shoulders tensed.

Brakes screeched and a crunch of metal sounded as the front of a car grazed the back bumper of the van. The car stopped beside the park. Cass's minivan jumped the curb and sped across Windemere Park, its tires kicking up little branches and pinecones. The van jolted along the walking path, headed up a slight rise near the playground, and took out a wide section of low bushes, which slowed it down. It rolled to a stop on the next rise of ground, then settled back into the little gully.

My fingers trembled as I pushed back the stroller awning to check on Livvy. Her eyes were closed and she had her thumb tucked in her mouth. I guess she'd liked the bumpy dash across the neighborhood.

The driver of the car beat us to the van. My knee stung with each step. A woman in a turquoise tank top and brightly flowered capri pants sat on the grass. She ignored the driver of the car, who muttered about reckless drivers and the crushed headlight of his Volvo.

"Cass, are you all right? What happened?" Abby bent over her, touched her freckled shoulder.

Cass's voice trembled. "No brakes."

An Everything in Its Place Tip for an Organized Move

Create and label an "Open First" box with:
- Sheets
- Pillows
- Towels
- Shower curtain
- Paper plates, cups, utensils
- Alarm clock
- Phone
- Answering machine

Chapter
Two

A female officer with a thick twist of braid handed Cass a paper. "Looks like your brakes failed."

Cass snatched the form. "No kidding. The steering wasn't working either. It was hard to turn."

"We'll check with your repair shop tomorrow. Want it towed up to Bob's?"

"Might as well. He's the closest." Cass seemed recovered from her earlier shock. She moved toward Abby and me as the police called for a tow truck. Abby introduced me.

Cass gripped my arm. "I am *so* sorry. I can't believe it. No brakes! I don't know what happened. Joe's always so paranoid about taking the cars in for the whatever-thousand-mile checkup that I can't imagine what happened. Please say you'll forgive me for nearly running you down."

I blinked. "It's okay."

Before I could say more Cass said, "Look at your knee. I saw you fall. That scared me so bad."

"You should have been on the other side of the steering wheel," I said. "I'm fine. Just a scraped knee. It isn't even bleeding."

Cass leaned down to peek under the stroller's awning. "Who's this?"

"Olivia. We call her Livvy," I said.

"She's gorgeous," Cass said. "My Chloe looked just like her when she was a baby. Pale fuzz for hair and a cute little rosebud mouth."

"How old is your daughter?"

"I have two. Chloe's four and Julie is three." She brushed a loose strand of honey brown hair away from her face. Her smile faded as she rubbed her lightly freckled arms. "They live with my ex-husband."

I took in her smooth face, slim body. She couldn't have been more than twenty-five years old. Pretty young to have two kids and be divorced and remarried. She spoke so quietly I had to strain to hear, "I made some mistakes. I miss my daughters so much." Abruptly she came out of her reverie and focused her attention on me. "So did you get the Hansons' house for less than they were asking?"

I tried to think of a way to divert the nosy question, but she rolled on, "I heard they had to move. That they were really desperate."

"We got a good deal." I hedged, glad for my stint in a PR office, which had taught me a few deflection techniques.

"Two thousand less? Or maybe five?" So much for deflection.

"So what time is the wives' coffee?" Abby asked.

"Spouse coffee," Cass corrected. "It's silly, but we have to be politically correct. Although I don't think we have any male spouses in this squadron. It starts at seven-thirty tomorrow night. Everyone will be here because this will be the first meeting since we broke for the summer. The food's going to be yummy. Diana's bringing her raspberry torte." Cass leaned toward me and said in an undertone, "It'll be perfect, of course. Everything Diana does is perfect." Then she switched back to her normal tone. "But the rest of us are bringing brownies and cookies."

"I'll see. Nice to meet you. We've got a lot to do . . ." I turned toward our house.

Cass changed gears and rolled on, "I write the 'Squadron Spotlight' column in the newsletter. It introduces the new spouses. I'll spotlight you next month. So where were you stationed before you moved here?" Cass's hazel eyes fastened on me with the intensity of an investigative reporter.

"Hunter, in California." She extracted my minibiography before we could escape. She didn't write anything down, but I had a feeling Cass was filing away every word and wouldn't forget a single detail.

A tow truck rolled into view. "I'd better get back to unpacking," I said and escaped before she could ask any more questions.

"Good grief, she's nosy. And all that breathless energy. It makes me tired," I said.

Abby's forehead crinkled. "I didn't know she had kids. I thought they were newlyweds." Abby was a people person. Within a few minutes of conversation she knew most people's life stories. I could tell she was wondering how she missed knowing about Cass's kids.

"I knew living in the same neighborhood with most of the squad wouldn't be good." I was half-joking, half-serious. "Look what happened on our first day. We almost get run down by a van."

Abby said, "Don't be so dramatic. We're fine. Livvy's fine. It was an accident."

"FP Con: Bravo," declared one sign at the main gate to Greenly AFB. Another sign announced, 100% ID CHECK. I shoved the diaper bag aside with one hand and pulled my billfold out of my purse. Some women have a weakness for shoes. I've got a passion for purses. I breathed a sigh of relief this morning when I found the box marked PURSES. I might look like a frazzled, sleep-deprived mom in my red T-shirt, jean shorts, and sandals, but my purse said I still had style. Today I had my patriotic purse, rectangular red and blue leather, with a short oval strap, an appropriate choice for a squadron barbeque.

I extracted my pink photo ID and cranked down the window of the Jeep Cherokee. Everything on the Cherokee was manual—windows, seats, locks. I'd scraped together the money to buy it in college and I was quite fond of the Blue Beast, as Mitch called it. He preferred his sporty Nissan. He'd almost convinced me to sell the Cherokee, but when we got our northern-tier assignment there was no way I was parting with four-wheel drive.

Livvy gurgled in her sleep as a blast of hot, dusty air tinged with gasoline fumes swept into the car. I came even with the young security policeman in fatigues toting an M-16 on a shoulder strap. He skimmed the card. "Thank you, ma'am." He stepped back and I eased down the wide, flag-lined boulevard to Mitch's squadron. I sent up a quick prayer of thanks that we were out of Lodging and into our house. The two weeks we'd spent in the small hotel room waiting for our household goods had seemed like two months.

We were in our house, but so much for my intention to not get too deeply involved in the squadron. Abby had guilt-tripped me into going to the spouse coffee where I'd somehow volunteered to help with the garage sale fund-raiser. And here I was, two days later, going to the squadron barbeque. I had boxes to unpack, crumpled packing paper to flatten. I still needed to find the answering machine. I'd be polite for the shortest amount of socially acceptable time and then get home.

I heard Cass as soon as I pushed open the heavy door to the squad. Frigid air hit my bare arms as I followed her excited voice down the stairs.

"So, I was practically pressing the brake through the floorboard with trees whizzing past me. In the park!" Cass's voice rose and her eyes widened as she mimed driving without brakes. She pulled the energy and attention of the room to her. "Can you believe it? I barely missed Abby and Ellie. And the baby! I was terrified when I saw that stroller and I couldn't move the steering wheel. Anyway, I finally remembered to put it in neutral. Joe showed me how to do that last winter, if it was icy. I took out a whole row of azaleas." A group of people holding paper plates piled with hamburgers and chips gathered around Cass.

The squad was built into a man-made hill. The steep sides at the front dropped away in the back so the basement had doors that opened outside to picnic tables with a view of the flight line. Usually we'd be outside at the picnic tables, but today everyone was inside the squadron, which had air-conditioning, something I realized I had taken for granted all my life. Now I was thoroughly appreciative and wouldn't dream of eating outside in the 100-degree weather.

A few bursts of color, the spouses, broke up the monotony of the green flight suits that dominated "The Hole," the name of the basement break room. In every job I've ever had the break room is a little plain space no bigger than a cube with a few sticky tables, painfully uncomfortable chairs, a vending machine, and an ancient microwave that makes you wonder if you should wear protective gear when you hit the "on" button. Unlike the civilian workforce, the military takes rest and relaxation seriously. The Hole took up the entire basement of the squad. It had a bar at one end, scratched tables and worn chairs spaced throughout, and a ratty earth-toned couch in front of a large TV.

The bar was stocked and in full swing. I'd been surprised at the first barbeque I'd attended. What employer hands out beer in the middle of the day? To people flying multimillion-dollar aircraft, no less? Of course, if you were flying you weren't supposed to be drinking. The whole atmosphere was part of that tradition of being a flyer—virility and masculinity personified. The mystique of doing a dangerous job and then partying hard, reinforced in movies like *Top Gun*.

Despite the increasing presence of females, the military is still a rather masculine profession, at least in the flying squadrons. The Hole was a case in point. The walls were covered with beer posters featuring bulging breasts and long legs. I wondered how much longer they would be able to get away with it before someone made them take the pictures down. Not much longer, I hoped.

Various trophies covered the walls, ranging from the more normal baseball type to the rather risky "souvenirs" people brought home, such as beer mugs from bars, signs, and even rugs. This practice, also known in more crass terms as "stealing," was now officially frowned on, but I thought new souvenirs probably showed up regularly.

Cass's voice broke into my thoughts. In her hot pink T-shirt and shorts she was a flash of color amid a crowd of olive drab. "It's just a good thing I had to go to the store and I wasn't going down Rim Rock Road like I usually do. I don't know what I would have done." I shivered when I pictured the steep curving road that hugged the escarpment of Black Rock Hill. Without brakes Cass would have been in serious trouble.

I waved to Mitch across the room. He motioned that he would get our burgers, so I set the diaper bag and my purse in the pile of purses and backpacks by the door.

"Vandalism." Cass's voice carried across the room as she replied to a question about what happened to her van. "The police say they've had some 'incidents' in our neighborhood."

I took a seat off to one side of the group surrounding Cass with another wife that I had seen at the spouse coffee, but hadn't talked to, Friona Herrerras. I thought she might be lonely. She had dark chocolate hair smoothed back into a French twist, olive skin, and gorgeous dark eyes with thin arched brows. She was from New York and had moved to Vernon after her wedding to Senior Airman Herrerras. I introduced myself and asked, "So how do you like Vernon?"

For an answer, she raised her shoulders in a languid shrug and took a drink of her Diet Sprite. She wasn't eating. Her sleek, sleeveless blue-green dress accented her thin figure and contrasted sharply with the dented folding chairs, frayed carpet, and crinkled beer posters. She looked like an exotic sea creature grounded on a beach. I could see her mentally counting the months until they were transferred. I recognized that look; I'd had it myself right after the first 5.0 earthquake rocked our California apartment. One good thing about the military: if you don't like your assignment, you know you'll move soon.

She scratched a few red welts on her forearm. Her lips twisted in distaste as she explained. "Poison ivy. God, people out here are crazy. Everyone has to be outside. Hiking, yard work, rollerblading. It's like they're in love with the trees or something. What I wouldn't give for a skyscraper.

"A couple from the squad said, 'Let's get together.' I'm thinking, like—you know—dinner, right? Wrong. We went on a *hike.*" From her tone, I could tell she thought hiking was as crazy as walking on hot coals. She set the Sprite can on her arm, covering the spots.

Okay, she didn't want to talk about the great outdoors, so I searched for another topic. "What do you do? Are you looking for a job?" Or going to school? She looked like she was about nineteen.

She examined the strap on her sandal and waved her hand vaguely. "I shop." I revised my opinion of Friona from lonely to aloof. Not an exotic sea creature. More like a bored mermaid. She twisted around, inspected the room. "What's taking Keith so long? I swear." She stood and said abruptly, "See you."

Mitch arrived with two plates and we moved to the tables to sit with Abby and Jeff. They were easy to spot because Jeff's tall figure topped with red hair cut in a crew cut towered over everyone. I popped the top of my Diet Coke, poured it into the clear plastic cup of ice Mitch had brought back, and took a bite of hamburger. No efforts to be supermodel thin for me. Livvy babbled away in her car seat near my chair, a combination of gurgles and murmuring.

Abby pulled a key out of her pocket and slid it across the table. "I brought a copy of our house key. I locked myself out last week and Jeff had to drive all the way home to let me in. At least he wasn't on a trip or I'd have had to fork over fifty bucks for a locksmith. Do you mind keeping an extra key for me at your house in case it happens again?"

"No, of course not. In fact, it's a great idea. I'll leave one with you, too." I worked my key off my key ring and gave it to Abby. "I'll get Mitch's key before I leave. I'll be there to let him in."

Livvy's gurgles merged into a few gulps. I checked her face. Tomato red. A storm of crying was about to break. I looked at Mitch and he smiled and shook his head. "Right on cue." He picked her up and walked. I ate fast.

"Hello, everyone," boomed a man up front. "I'm Colonel Briman. I want to welcome all the new arrivals." He whipped off his hat and set his flight bags down. He must have come straight from the flight line. "Everyone who has transferred here within the last month, please stand up, stand up. Welcome to Greenly AFB.

"We're a team here and we want everyone to join in and be right at home. If you need anything, anything, just let me or my wife, Jill, know." Briman had wiry brown hair, a tan face, and green eyes made greener by the flight suit he wore. There was a round of half-hearted applause and we sat back down. "Now some of you know we have to pick up an additional rotation to the sandbox in December, but I'm going to make it as painless as possible."

No one made a sound, but the temperature in the room seemed to drop about twenty degrees. The "sandbox," the deserts of the Middle East and Southwest Asia, are the bane of everyone's life in the Air Force. It didn't really matter where, Iraq, Qatar, the UAE, or another small but strategic country. It would be a hot, dry, and lonely time away from home. Mitch had been there last year over Christmas. It was something almost everyone hated, but you didn't complain, at least not in front of the squadron commander. "We're glad to have you new folks here and I know we'll work together and make a great team," Briman concluded. "Now I've got a meeting, but my door is always open to anyone at Team Greenly." He picked up his flight bags and headed out.

Team concept was big right now. Briman must be brushing up on it, I thought cynically. Then I felt bad. It wasn't his fault there was a deployment over Christmas. I met Mitch's dark eyes and he said quietly with a minimal shrug of one shoulder, "I'm low man on the totem pole here." I sighed. He would be gone over Christmas this year, too.

Diana, a thin woman with straight blond hair cut in an androgynous "little boy" style, slid into a seat, moving with a fluid, catlike grace. I'd met her at the coffee. She hooked her short hair behind her ears and introduced her husband, Brent. His thin blond hair fell across his forehead as he leaned over to shake my hand. "So nice to meet you." He held my hand in both of his, looked directly into my eyes. Diana and Brent looked like a magazine ad for expensive perfume; both were blue-eyed blonds and attractive. But I realized Brent was handsome in the blond Nordic style while Diana merely made the best of what she had. She compensated for a pointy nose with a short haircut that emphasized her translucent blue eyes. She adjusted her rings to centered positions on her fingers, then cut her hamburger exactly down the middle. With her eyes, pale hair, and fastidious ways, she reminded me of Abby's Himalayan Persian cat, named Whisk. Brent's arm bumped mine as he reached for his beer. "Sorry," he said with a charming smile.

I took Livvy to give Mitch a turn to eat and scanned the room. Gwen, Steven's wife, paused in the doorway. I'd met her at the coffee, too. She held up a stack of paper cut into small slips. "Tickets for the Christmas party at the Aurora Mansion," she announced in a sultry voice. "I know it's still months away, but there's limited seating, so get yours today." Sunglasses pushed up on her head held back her shoulder-length wavy brown hair, showing her excellent bone structure. Gwen was a dark-haired Kathleen Turner, complete with the husky voice. But instead of Kathleen Turner's air of sexiness, Gwen exuded confidence and power. She was in charge and she liked it that way.

She spotted Steven and strode confidently across the room, her silky navy dress fluttering around her legs. I was sure if I checked the latest Tate's catalog, the upscale women's boutique she managed, I'd see her stylish dress. She joined Steven and he slipped his hand into hers. I smiled when I thought of Steven. He'd moved boxes and hooked up our washer and dryer for us that first day. They looked mismatched, Steven with his boyish good looks and smooth face and Gwen with her wrinkles around her eyes and her finesse and style. But they looked incredibly happy together.

"Excuse me, El," Brent said, abbreviating my name. He bumped into my shoulder as he leaned across me to reach for a napkin. I hate it when people shorten my name. I scooted my chair half an inch away as unobtrusively as I could. There was something unidentifiable that made me want to avoid any casual contact with him.

Cass plopped into a chair on my other side. Her hazel eyes fixed on Gwen across the room. She leaned close and dropped her voice: "You aren't going to believe what I found out about Gwen. It's just so . . . not Gwen."

I didn't want to know anything about anyone, so I pretended I hadn't heard her. I wanted to stay out of the squadron gossip, so I asked the table, "Does anyone know a good pediatrician?" Or dry cleaner, or hair stylist, or Mexican restaurant, I added silently to myself. One of the best and worst things about moving is starting from scratch. It's exhilarating and difficult at the same time. Cass leaned back, but she still had an air of barely suppressed excitement.

Diana brushed a few crumbs off the table and placed her plastic cup of water back exactly in the wet ring it had left on the table. She seemed as finicky as Abby's cat, Whisk. Her clothes today were as immaculate as they had been at the coffee. No wrinkle marred her cream silk tank top or her red and blue floral tapestry skirt. "We go to the hospital here," she said.

"Dr. Williams at Family Health is excellent. She's in family practice," said Cass. "In fact, I saw her this morning. I've had this awful sinus infection."

A wife down the table offered, "Dr. Henry on Fifth Street is good, too."

I should write this down, but my hands were full with keeping Livvy balanced and happy.

"Anyone else want another beer?" Jeff asked as he stood up with his plastic cup in his hand.

Abby said, "I'll take another Snapple." Jeff unzipped a pocket on his flight suit and pulled out some quarters. A folded, rectangular piece of paper fluttered to the table.

Cass picked it up. "Jeff, here—" She glanced at the writing on it as she held it out. Her posture went from casual to tense and her arm froze, halfway extended. "You're mixed up in this?" She crushed the paper in a tight grip and pulled her arm back.

I could see the faint gray lines on the paper and the perforated edge along the top. It was a check. Jeff swiped it from her hand, shoved it back into his pocket. "Now, Cass, I know you've got some strong opinions, but—"

"Strong *opinions*?" Cass stood up. The chatter around the room died away. "Well, my *opinions* are right." Cass gestured at the pocket where the check had disappeared and groped for words. "I-I'm shocked you'd do something like that."

"Listen, Cass. This is going to be great. If you'll just calm down and listen—"

Cass's expression hardened. "I can't believe what you're doing. It's disgusting. Who's in it with you?"

Jeff's already ruddy complexion transitioned to fire engine red and his tone went from positive to sarcastic. "Just because you've been on TV doesn't mean you know everything. There's lots of ways of doing things. There's other opinions, other options besides yours."

Despite Jeff's height and sturdy build, Cass wasn't intimidated. "Don't try to change the subject. Who? Who's in it with you?"

He leaned over the table and opened his mouth to respond, but Abby said, "Jeff." He glanced around the room and realized everyone was focused on him and Cass. He brushed his hand over his crew cut and blew out a breath. Then he turned and walked away. Abby followed.

"Don't think you can just walk away," Cass shouted at his back. "You can't keep it quiet, keep it hidden. I'll find out and everyone will know." Jeff rammed the bar to the outside door and it swung open. He didn't glance back. Abby caught the door before it closed and slipped outside.

Cass shoved her chair out of the way and stalked out of the room into the hallway. In the silence that followed her departure, I could hear her stomp up the stairs.

Conversation rolled into the quiet like water flowing into a dry gulley after a sudden storm. I raised my eyebrow and turned to Mitch. "What was that about?" I'd never seen Jeff that angry. In fact, I realized, I'd never seen Jeff angry. He was usually even tempered.

"Beats me."

"Do you think we should check on them? Make sure Jeff's okay?"

"No. He'll cool off in a few seconds."

"You've seen him like this before?" I asked.

"Sure. Jeff's got a long fuse, but when he does get mad, he blows up, then it's over. He'll be fine."

Livvy hiccuped, waking herself up from the minuscule nap she'd taken during the tense conversation between Cass and Jeff. I checked my watch. About time to go. I had just enough time to get home before Livvy's next feeding. I slid out of my chair and gathered baby paraphernalia—car seat, diaper bag, and rattles—while Mitch pitched our plates and cups in the trash. He took my keys and went to start the Cherokee and let the air conditioner run to cool it off while I packed up everything and headed down the hall after him.

I turned a corner, expecting to find a door to the parking lot, but instead I saw a corridor of offices. I wandered around until I saw Diana come in a door. She let in a swath of sunlight and glided down the hall, her blond head barely visible above a stack of paper plates, napkins, a small cooler, and plastic packages of hamburger and hot dog buns. "See you later," she said and passed me. I headed for the door. At least it would get me outside.

Hot air gushed over me when I pushed open the door with my shoulder and hip, balancing Livvy's car seat in the crook of my left arm and the diaper bag and purse on my right shoulder. "Here, let me help you with that," said Diana's husband, Brent, from right behind me. He must have come down another corridor because he wasn't behind me until that moment. He reached around me to give the door a shove with one hand. His other hand snaked up my right arm, his fingers lingering against my arm and shoulder as he removed the diaper bag from my shoulder. "I forgot how much these diaper bags weigh." He stepped into the parking lot.

My arm felt like it had a slimy trail from his touch. I resisted the urge to wipe it down and said shortly, "I could survive in the wilderness for three days with that bag." Mitch was walking across the parking lot with another man. We met in the middle of the lot. Mitch introduced the small and wiry man moving impatiently from foot to foot as Nick. He shook my hand and then quickly headed for the squad.

I thought Brent was a flight commander, so he carried some weight in the squadron. I should be careful here and not do anything stupid for Mitch's sake. "Brent helped me with the diaper bag." I looked at Mitch, trying to convey: "This guy is a jerk."

Mitch took the bag from him. "I think I can manage from here."

Cass passed us on the way to her van with a wave that jangled her keys. Brent gave Mitch a fake little salute and strolled away with a self-satisfied smile. Like he enjoyed that whole thing.

"I don't like him," I said to Mitch as we walked toward the Cherokee.

Mitch gazed out over the flight line to the flat land around the base. Unlike Vernon, which was rich with texture since it perched on a hill and spilled down into a valley, the base was located several miles farther west, on the flat plains that stretched out to make the central valley of Washington between the Rockies and the Cascades. His eyes followed the undulating curve of the distant foothills of the Rockies. "He's not well liked in the squadron."

I clicked Livvy's car seat into the base inside the Cherokee. Mitch tossed in the diaper bag. "I think Briman's just waiting for Brent to mess up. Briman'll hammer him." I stood uncertainly by the driver's door. Should I tell Mitch? But what was there to tell? His fingers brushed against my arm? That wouldn't interest Colonel Briman.

Cass eased out of her parking space, pulled through the empty one in front of her. I watched her burgundy van lumber away around the curve toward the back gate until an adjacent building blocked it from view. I explained about the key swap Abby and I had made and Mitch gave me his house key. I said, "Well, see you in a little while," and climbed into the Cherokee. Before I shut the door, Mitch kissed me rather fiercely and smiled.

"Love you," I said.

"Love you, too." It was a little superstitious, but I always told him I loved him when we parted. I didn't think about it much, but with his job we never knew what might happen.

The burgundy minivan stood out against the dull brown soil and cloudless blue sky as I rounded the last curve before the turn to the back gate. Why was Cass pulled over on the side of the road with both front doors open? I passed the van, but I didn't see Cass. I pulled over on the shoulder, a narrow strip of hard-packed dirt that dropped off steeply to a drainage ditch. I left the Cherokee running with the A/C blasting for Livvy, who was sleeping, then I made my way back to the van.

The sun scorched my shoulders. Only the hum of bugs and the faint whine of the van's engine broke the silence. No cars passed on the road. In the distance, I could see the building that blocked the squadron from my view. Strange to think people were still there cleaning grills, picking up trash, talking. Faintly, the engines of a plane droned. Someone preflighting or doing maintenance. I checked the driver's seat of the van. Empty. I waved away a bug buzzing near my ear and glanced into the back of the van. No one.

Cass's purse, a large woven bag, tilted sideways on

the passenger seat with its contents strewn across the seat and console: lipsticks, pens, paper, a plastic sleeve of wallet-size pictures, checkbook, and a sunglass case. The glove compartment hung open. Maps, a flashlight, cassette tapes, and napkins littered the floorboard. I glanced back at the Cherokee, unsure what to do. Even though Livvy was asleep, I'd need to feed her soon.

But I couldn't just leave.

I walked around the hood to the passenger side and barely avoided a pool of vomit. I saw her, a bright splash of pink against the monochrome brown, about five feet down at the bottom of the drainage ditch.

"Cass? Cass? Are you all right?" I slithered down feet first, one hand behind me for balance. My sandals kicked up small pebbles and dirt that rained down on her arms. She wasn't moving. CPR. How many compressions? How many breaths?

She was on her stomach in the ditch, like she'd tried to climb up the hill, but crumpled back with her knees bent and her arms outstretched. One espadrille twisted almost off her foot. I touched her shoulder. "Cass?" She rolled away from me. Dirt matted her face and hands. Red, lumpy patches of raised skin dotted her arms and legs. I remembered the dirt and her swollen skin later. Mostly, I saw it in my dreams. At that moment, I could only focus on her hazel eyes that blindly faced the sky.

An Everything in Its Place Tip for an Organized Move

Recruit friends to help you pack and unpack. Here's how to make the most of the additional help:
- Situate people in rooms and have them com-

pletely pack out a room so the contents of the room stay together. For instance, instead of having several boxes labeled "Lamps," pack the lamps from the living room in the living room boxes.

- Encourage specific labels on boxes. Instead of "Storage Closet," use "Games."
- Devise a code to help prioritize unpacking, such as #1—items needed everyday, #2—decorative items that can be opened later, #3—out of season items.
- Station one person at the door and have them make a master list of every box.
- Whether your movers are professionals or helpful friends, buy everyone lunch!

Chapter Three

Simplicity is making the journey of this life with
just baggage enough.
—Charles Dudley Warner

Oh, my God." It was a prayer. I scrambled back up
the hill to check on Livvy. Of course, she was fine
and still sleeping. Death hadn't touched her. I dropped
into the driver's seat and opened the console with shaking hands. I flipped open the cell phone and turned it
on, but no answering beep or lights greeted me. I took
a shaky breath. It was one of the things on our lengthy
list: activate cell phone.

"Ellie, are you okay? Do you need some help?" Gwen's
husky voice sounded loud in the stillness. Her brown
hair curtained her face as she leaned across the leather
seat of her sleek white Camry to talk through the open
passenger window.

"It's Cass." My voice was breathless. "In the ditch," I said more strongly.

"She's hurt?" Gwen reached for her purse and drew out a cell phone. "Damn, the battery's not charged and I don't have the power cord. It's in Steven's truck."

"Dead." I whispered the word. I hadn't needed to check for a pulse to know.

Gwen looked up, shocked. "I'll go to the gate. They can get . . ." her voice, raspy now, trailed off and she accelerated away.

I rested my head on the steering wheel. Should I go back down? There was nothing I could do. I thought of Joe. Someone would have to tell him and her family. Tears gathered in my eyes when I thought of her little girls. I prayed silently for them. It was the only thing I could think of to do.

"Ma'am? You found a body?" I started. A man wearing fatigues and a beret stood in the "V" of my open car door. Security Forces was printed on the car parked across the road from me. I hadn't heard him drive up.

A body? "You mean Cass?"

"You knew her?" He asked.

"I met her a few days ago. Her husband's in the same squadron as my husband. She's down there. In the drainage ditch."

"Wait here." He was gone for a few minutes, then returned.

"What was her last name?" he asked.

Was. Cass was dead. I felt cold and clicked the air conditioner down to low. I paused and eventually came up with it: "Vincent."

"Your name?" He had out a notebook and waited pen poised.

"Ellie Avery."

"Address and phone number?"

I looked into his dark eyes in his coffee-colored face as numbers jumbled up in my mind. 14486 East Palm Drive. No. That's the old address. I dredged up our latest address. "Umm, 3415 West Nineteenth. We just moved here. I can't remember my phone number," I said helplessly.

"You're in shock. Do you have a blanket or a jacket?"

I nodded. "In the back." He went to get it, unhooking my keys from the ring and handing them back when he returned with the green blanket. He put it around my shoulders and said, "You sit tight. Put your head between your legs if you feel dizzy. I'll be right back."

His words seemed to prompt the foothills to spin around me. My stomach clenched. I slid out of the car, sat down on the ground, and put my head down, intently studying the cracked dirt and clumps of tiny grass. Dirt. Dirt caked on Cass's face and hands, like she was clawing her way up the slope. My stomach heaved. *Stop it.* I concentrated on the stubble of green blades growing out of a split in the dirt.

Gwen dropped down beside me and talked to me, her words flowing like water from a faucet, but I didn't take any of them in. Cars arrived and parked at odd angles. Traffic crept through the narrow opening in the road. An ambulance arrived. It was quiet. No lights. I felt detached, as if I were watching a movie.

At some point Gwen left and I climbed back into the driver's seat. I repeated what happened to different people. I pulled out my ID card and handed it over. Borrowing a cell phone, I called Mitch, but he wasn't in the squadron. I finally found my phone number on a slip of paper in my wallet.

A government-issue four-door car with a squared,

finlike attachment on the trunk drove up. One of the bigwigs from the wing. I vaguely remembered Mitch saying something about it being for radio communications between command post and various base VIPs. I didn't know exactly how the slender rectangle worked. But when I saw a car with the attachment I knew it was someone from the elite leadership ranks of the base and I steered clear of the car and occupants, like a swimmer avoiding a shark.

Livvy's cry split the air and, instantly, I was grounded and out of the fog.

I glanced at the Cherokee's clock: twelve forty-three. Only thirty minutes since I left the squadron, but it seemed endless. Livvy would definitely be hungry now and there was no way I was going to feed her here, where this awful thing had happened, not to mention the people milling around. I motioned over the Security Police officer who had arrived first. His name tag read NOTT.

I reached backward and shook the car seat gently. Sometimes that motion lulled her back to sleep. Her screams intensified, basically conveying, "Nothing doing, Mom. I'm seriously hungry."

"I need to go," I said to Nott.

"Sorry, ma'am, but Colonel Witson has to talk to you first."

"I've already told three different people what happened."

"I'm sorry, but he says he will get over here ASAP."

"What caused her death?" I hadn't seen any obvious wound, just swollen, inflamed patches of skin. Did she have some sort of medical problem?

"Couldn't say, ma'am."

I slouched back in the seat and rocked the car seat,

not so gently this time. After thirty seconds of continu-
ously escalating screaming I muttered, "This is insane."
I jerked a notepad out of my purse and scribbled my
name, address, and phone number with only the slight-
est of pauses before the zip and phone number. I
slammed out of the Cherokee, jerked open the back
door, and with greater care, extracted Livvy from her in-
fant seat. Her screams went down a notch when she
emerged into the open air in my arms, but then, like
the future opera star she could be, she hit her previous
high note and carried it as I wove my way through the
crowd in the direction Nott indicated when I demanded Colonel Witson's location.

Colonel Witson watched my approach with a smile
on his beefy face. He was bulky with black hair going
gray. His comb had left furrows in his hair styled with a
poof over his forehead, à la Elvis Presley. He wiped his
forehead with his hand and replaced his beret.

"Colonel Witson"—I thrust the note page at him and
shouted over Livvy—"I'm Ellie Avery. Obviously, I need
to leave. Here's my contact information. I'll be happy
to talk with you later."

"And who is this?" He leaned toward Livvy's face,
smiling, but antagonizing at the same time. She gulped,
studied his face, and then squeezed her eyes shut and
cried again.

"This is Livvy. She's tired and hungry."

"Well, then, you'd better get her home, Mrs. Avery."
I marched back to the Cherokee and drove home with
sweaty hands. What had gotten into me? I had heard
about the fierce mother-bear-protecting-her-cub syn-
drome, but I'd never acted like that before.

I pulled in our driveway, which sloped down to our
basement two-car garage. I got out, heaved open one

door and drove in. Then I dragged myself and Livvy up the stairs and left the door unlocked for Mitch. My burst of angry adrenaline had burned off, leaving me drained. I picked up my huge water cup that the hospital had given me after Livvy was born. I guzzled the water. In Livvy's room, I changed her diaper and then fed her. After a few cries to let me know she was still not happy, she latched on and gulped down the breast milk. After I burped her, I cuddled her on my chest and ran my chin back and forth over the soft fuzz of her hair. She wasn't a baby who liked to cuddle, but she only wiggled for a few seconds and then fell asleep. I closed my eyes, rocked, and stroked her back. The even rise and fall of her back steadied me. I held that bundle of life tight in my arms.

Mitch arrived home as I reluctantly settled Livvy in her crib. For once, she didn't awaken. She must be exhausted from her crying. Mitch dropped his gym bag on the hall floor and waited until I closed her door. I went straight into his arms.

"You heard what happened." I could tell from the tight look on his face. His usual relaxed smile was gone.

"Colonel Briman told me they found Cass dead on the road to the back gate and you were there."

"I called you."

"I know. I got your message. I wish I hadn't gone to the gym. What happened?"

"I found her," I said as we walked back into the living room and I told him what happened. "But it seems surreal, it couldn't have really happened." It didn't seem real, except when I thought of her vacant eyes.

Stop thinking about it. But the vivid mental picture didn't go away.

* * *

Okay, focus, I told myself as I surveyed the living room later that day. Mentally, I shut the door on Cass's death and concentrated on our mountain range of boxes.

It has to get worse before it gets better, I told myself. Flattened boxes sagged drunkenly against the dining room wall. A few had slid under the table. Piles of crumpled paper in the corners of the living room almost reached the windowsill.

I'd just switched the fan dial to high and angled it to blow right on Livvy in her crib during her late afternoon nap. I'd paused, watching her sleep while I wiped the sweat off the back of my neck. I wanted a shower, but I'd be soaking again five minutes after I toweled off.

Slanting the bedroom door half closed, I moved stealthily down the hall on my tiptoes. When the golden oak floor creaked, I held my breath. Blessed silence. I relaxed and walked normally through the shoulder-high maze of cardboard boxes. With Mitch on a run to the store for diapers and batteries for Livvy's swing, I had about forty-five minutes, an hour, at the most. Where to start? I rewound my sagging hair and replaced the clip in it. Immediately, half of it slipped out. In a fit of optimistic prenatal time management I had cut my shoulder-length hair to a bob at my ear lobes. It was growing out, but I couldn't do a thing with it. I tried to tuck it back up into the clip as I looked around the room.

A sense of strangeness assailed me, like the feeling of waking in a hotel room and seeing the doors and windows in the wrong place. I was off kilter. Everything was changing, from the trivial things like my hair and my body to the more significant things like our marriage and where we lived. I felt this way every time we moved, but this time it seemed magnified. I tried to shrug off the sense of strangeness and told myself to get to work. It just takes some time to get adjusted. And I knew I was shaken from finding Cass in the drainage ditch.

I dragged my mind back to our unpacking. We'd found the silverware, but no plates or glasses. So, I'd look for plates. And the rest of the towels, I reminded myself. I was ready to have more than a few emergency towels. And the answering machine.

In the kitchen, I grabbed a few Hershey Kisses—for energy, of course—then I found the utility knife and slit the butterscotch-colored packing tape. The box contained only one thing, our DVD player, well cushioned in layers of spongy padding. I closed my eyes briefly. How can someone be so vividly alive one day and gone the next? I pulled the DVD player out of the box and twisted it around. It looked great, not at all like Cass's. At the coffee, she'd glanced down at the DVD player to check the time and then made a disgusted sound. "I can never remember that the movers scratched it so bad that I can't read the clock."

"Wow," I'd said, "I hope our DVD player doesn't look like that when we find it."

I slid the DVD player into its slot under the TV and took a deep breath. Then I moved on to the next box. Focus. I had to concentrate or I wouldn't get anything done. After opening three boxes marked "Kitchen— Dishes," and finding only placemats, napkins, and couch throw pillows, I grimly decided whoever packed and labeled the boxes had a warped sense of humor. I ripped into the next box, taking out my frustration on the tape. I removed Mitch's cordless drill case and pulled out a heavy bundle wrapped in blank newsprint. Now we're making progress. I yanked the paper back. It crackled like a gunshot. A soft whimper answered from down the hall. I sighed. The plates would have to wait until after Livvy's nap.

I grabbed the utility knife and hurried into the living room, checking my watch. Only fifteen minutes had passed. As I heaved boxes around, the sweat trickled down my forehead.

Elsa, our realtor, had stood in this room on an overcast day two months ago and waved her hand dismissively. "Oh, you don't need air-conditioning in the inland Northwest." I'd raised my eyebrows and looked at Mitch. Air-conditioning was a must-have where we came from. But it seemed Elsa was right. We looked at thirty-one houses during that whirlwind home-buying weekend and none had air-conditioning, even the new construction. In realtor-speak, houses here didn't *have* air-conditioning so you didn't *need* it. Until a freak heat wave smothered the city in August, it was fine.

Lowering a box to the floor, I found the thermostat. It was pegged out at eighty-five degrees. How could Livvy sleep? Her room was at the back of the house and shaded, but it was still sweltering. I gave up on the boxes and chipped at the fresh paint on the dining room windowsill. If I could get one window open below the decorative leaded glass there might be a cross breeze through the kitchen screen door.

I leaned against the wavy, aged glass and sliced the globs of dried paint around the lock. The rest of the neighborhood was quiet. In our side yard, the pine branches swayed in the breeze beyond the window. Where was everyone? Sweltering inside their houses?

More likely, they were at work in frigid offices, I decided, after studying the closed windows on house after
house.

The lock finally released and I pulled, but the case-
ment wouldn't budge. I went back to work with the
knife, searching for seams of paint that hadn't been cut.
I tried the window again without success. I needed a bar
of soap. In the kitchen, I started another list on a scrap
of packing paper. Livvy whimpered, breathed huffily,
and then transferred to a wail. I glanced at my watch.
An hour was gone and what had I accomplished? Nothing. I closed my eyes and rested my head on the cabinet. Don't cry. It's just the postpregnancy hormones.
And the move. But I still started sniffling.

When Mitch came in the kitchen door, I wiped my
eyes with the backs of my hands. I tried to pretend I was
just wiping the sweat off my face, but Mitch put a plastic
grocery sack on the one square foot of open counter-
top and asked, "What's wrong?"

I gestured vaguely at the boxes. My throat tightened
again. "Livvy's been down for an hour and I didn't get
anything done, except open a few boxes and try to
open a window that was painted shut. And now she'll be
hungry again. How are we going to get anything done?"

Mitch went over, examined the window, and heaved
on the sill. "You need some soap."

"I know I need soap," I said sharply. "I don't have
any." Now I was wailing, too.

Livvy's cries went up another notch. Mitch crossed
the room and enfolded me in his arms. "Hey, it's okay.
We'll get it done. We'll buy some soap, too. Don't
worry. I can work my schedule for the next few days to
be here and unpack most of the day."

I pressed my face into his sweaty white shirt and nodded. "I know. I'm just stressed." I leaned back in his arms, and he kissed my forehead. "You're too hot to hold." He waggled his eyebrows suggestively.

I laughed. "Too stinky, you mean." I broke out of his arms, found a roll of paper towels in the grocery bags, and blew my nose.

"You're probably hungry, too. I brought dinner. It's in the Cherokee. I know how cranky you get when you need to eat." He smiled. It was a little joke between us. I always wanted to eat.

"There's nothing wrong with eating every few hours. It's called having a meal, you know. Just because you can go for days without eating, there's no need to rub it in," I retorted, but I was smiling, too.

"I'll get Livvy and distract her for a few minutes while you eat," Mitch said.

After I found the Wendy's sack and two large drinks, I pulled out the blanket we kept in the back of the Cherokee and spread it on the grass under the pines in our backyard. The breeze wasn't cool, but it was enormously better than in the house. I left Mitch's grilled chicken sandwich in the bag. He eats such healthy food it makes me feel guilty sometimes, but not today. I unwrapped my crispy chicken sandwich, thought briefly about whether it would upset Livvy later when I breastfed her, but then I decided I was starved and it was the only food in sight. Livvy had done fine so far with whatever I ate. I took a big bite and hoped the trend would continue. I felt a little better after a few bites.

It was great Mitch would be off, but his idea of unpacking was to pull everything out of a box and toss it in a closet or a drawer. If I let him unpack I might never find the Christmas decorations, much less the juice glasses. I grabbed a handful of fries. How would I take care of Livvy, feed her every two or three hours, and unpack several thousand pounds of household goods?

A brown grocery bag thudded onto the blanket.

Chapter
Four

Abby plopped down across from me. "Hi, there. You doing okay? Jeff called me and said you'd found Cass. That she'd died?" Her voice made it a question. I nodded. Abby's face was a mixture of puzzlement and concern. "Wow." She pointed to the bag. "I was finishing up dinner, so I brought you some. Grilled chicken pasta salad, bread, and some cookies for dessert. And"— she reached in the bag and pulled out a Mason jar filled with a thick gold liquid—"honey. Straight from Jeff's mom in Oklahoma. She FedEx-ed it." A portion of the honeycomb tilted inside the jar. "I figured you wouldn't feel like cooking, but it looks like you've already got dinner right here," Abby said as she replaced the jar and scooted around to grab a few fries.

"Thanks, Abby." I felt the tears gathering in my eyes again. She waved away my thanks. "Since I'm breast-feeding, I'm always hungry. I'll be ready to eat again in a few hours."

"It's too hot to cook all the time, so I made a big batch. Jeff and I will be eating it for a week. So what happened? The squad's buzzing, but no one seems to know anything."

"That was fast."

"Well, you know how it is. The grapevine in the squad is as good as the one back home in Erick, Oklahoma. And just about as accurate, too."

I recounted the story while she nibbled on my fries. A touch of genuineness set in every time I told what happened. Like a mist clearing, the edges of reality were bleeding into the unreal experience of finding Cass's body. "She was the center of attention just a few minutes before and now she's gone." I shrugged.

"God. This is terrible. And now I feel kind of bad. I mean Jeff was furious with her, but it seems so insignificant with her dead. Dead. I can't really believe it. You know?"

"Yeah. I know. What was going on between him and Cass? What were they arguing about?"

Abby dusted the salt from her fingers and plucked a blade of grass. She concentrated on the blade. "I don't know. He said it was a misunderstanding. No big deal." Abby tossed the blade away and looked at me. "We hung our last picture yesterday."

"You're done?" She didn't want to talk about the scene between Cass and Jeff, so I went along. A determinedly blank expression had replaced her usual transparency. It wasn't like Abby to keep anything back.

"Pretty much, except for a few boxes of odds and ends in the basement." Abby and Jeff had moved one month before us when the military began closing Hunter

AFB. Remembering Abby's walls at their last apartment,
I knew the picture hanging must have been a job. Photos,
paintings, quilts, display shelves, and decorative plates
covered her walls, but somehow her house didn't look
cluttered, just artistic.

"It was quite a night. Jeff out with his tape measure
and you know me, I just want to slap some nails in the
wall and hang the stuff." She looked me over critically
with her blue eyes. "So, what have you been doing this
afternoon?"

"Making a tiny dent in the mountain of boxes."

"You're doing great. I felt that way a few weeks ago,
too. And I don't have a new baby. We'll have you unpacked in a few more days. How about I watch Livvy
while you unpack? You've got a knack for seeing where
everything should go. I do draw the line at poopy diapers, though."

". . . though I walk through the valley of the shadow
of death, I will fear no evil, for you are with me. . . ."
The words from the church service were still in my
thoughts as we drove home. Livvy kicked the rattles suspended from the car seat handle, glad to be released
from what she obviously considered a prison, the nursery. Mitch drove with one hand on the wheel, the other
holding my hand as we took the sweeping curves up
Rim Rock Road.

The Sunday worship service had been formal with
hymns, readings, responses, and a rambling series of
tear-jerking stories for a sermon, but no real inspiration
or wisdom. One elderly couple greeted us, the wife with
her nose crinkled like she smelled a bad odor and the
husband speaking to us but searching the faces behind

us. It certainly wasn't an improvement over the previous
Sunday when we had visited a small church where the
worshippers had converged on us with eager smiles,
clinging handshakes, and reassurances that they were
"so glad to see some new faces" and we "*had to come back
again.*" I'd felt like bait dropped into shark-infested waters. Looking for a church was only slightly less exhaust-
ing and frustrating than looking for a home, I decided.
The road emerged from the neighborhoods and clung
to the edge of Black Rock Hill. I studied the tops of the
pines marching down the escarpment that fell steeply
away from the road.

"I haven't seen that sign before," I said. Perched on
the edge of the drop-off, the large sign with a pinecone
logo shouted, WILDE CREEK ESTATES. EXCLUSIVE GOLF COURSE
COMMUNITY WITH LUXURY HOMES STARTING IN THE LOW
$300,000S. CONTACT: DIANA MCCARTER. A phone number
filled the space under the name.

A switchback road cut down into the trees. In the flat
valley at the bottom of the escarpment, yellow construction equipment parked in a freshly cleared patch of dirt
looked like toys in a sandbox.

"Wow. Can you call anything in the three-hundred-
thousand-dollar range low?" I asked.

Mitch grinned. "Way out of our league."

"I know Vernon needs more housing, but I don't
think many people from the base will be able to afford
anything down there. Diana McCarter. Isn't she one of
the spouses? Petite, blond?"

"I think that's Brent's wife. He said she was a realtor."

As I studied the river winding through the valley I remembered a phrase from the reading at the Sunday service, "valley of the shadow of death." Cass's husband, Joe,
was certainly there. I knew I had been introduced to

him, but I couldn't remember him. Was there anything I could do besides pray for him? There was always the old standby of taking food.

That afternoon I pushed the stroller up our steep driveway. I balanced a dish on the cover of the canopy over Livvy, who was dozing despite the roar of the lawn mower. I wondered how Livvy could sleep through the racket when other times a sneeze could wake her. I caught Mitch's eye, held up the dish, and pointed to Joe's house. He waved and pushed the mower he'd borrowed from some neighbor in front of a line of bushes I'd trimmed. Or tried to trim. They looked fine until I stepped back for a wider view. Definitely sloping like a playground slide.

Despite the shade from the maple and pine trees, I already felt sticky. It was a different heat from Southern California's dry, scorching heat. There was a touch of humidity in the air here. I looked up at the pines, almost surprised that I missed the fan palms and yucca. I heaved the stroller up the steps to the bungalow's wide front porch, then paused between the sturdy porch piers, reluctant to ring the doorbell. I couldn't decide why. Was it just the proximity of death I was avoiding? Maybe I knew it would make me reexamine what happened. I'd tucked that event away in my mind and I didn't want those images and feelings pulled out again.

I didn't really know Joe, I'd argued with myself, but in the end my upbringing won out. My mother, so relaxed and easygoing in so many ways, was adamant about certain things. If there was a death, you took food and later you went to the funeral, regardless of how much that person's life had intersected with yours. If you knew them well enough to know they had died, you knew them well enough.

I pushed the doorbell and looked over Cass's yard. Already yellow patches pooled in the grass and her roses needed deadheading. Joe opened the door. His thin black hair receded at the temples gave him a large forehead. He was tall, probably six-three with a rectangular face and rough skin, the kind with easy-to-see pores. As soon as he opened the door, I remembered him. He had carried a black trash bag around after the barbeque cleaning up. Today his brown eyes were pink rimmed and his skin, instead of being the olive tone I remembered, looked pale and washed out. He gazed blankly at me. A brown and black rottweiler stood, solid and alert, beside him. Joe automatically rubbed the dog's ears.

"Hi. I'm Ellie Avery." I angled the stroller away from the dog. "We live over on the corner." I gestured to our house across the street. "My husband is in your squadron."

The only advice I had heard about talking with grieving people had come from my mother after my grandfather died when I was twelve years old. She had said go ahead and say you're sorry and say the person's name. "For God's sake," she had said, "can't they remember his name? I'm not going to burst into tears if they say it." So I plunged in even though I felt awkward. "We're sorry about Cass." He still stared at me. Was he taking any of this in? "I brought you some minestrone soup and bread." I held out the container topped with the foil-wrapped bread, which the dog sniffed appreciatively but Joe made no move to take.

"Um, if you've had supper already you could freeze this," I said. He didn't say anything. I asked, "Have you had supper?" I felt like I was talking to a three-year-old, prying out a few words.

His gaze transferred from me to my house, "Ah, some cereal this morning," he said vaguely.

"You haven't eaten all day?" If I could get him to take this food, odds were he'd leave it on the kitchen counter and forget about it. "How about I warm it up for you? You can eat some right now. You need to eat."

His eyes focused on me and he seemed to see me for the first time. "Ellie Avery? That's your name?" he asked as he opened the door wider and called for the dog to follow him. "I'll just put him out. Kitchen's over there."

Dark and silent, it felt like a different house than the one that had been filled with women's voices and energy just a few days ago at the spouse coffee. I pushed the stroller past two suitcases standing near the door and went to the kitchen. In the living room, the remote rested on the couch beside a blanket. A twenty-four-hour news channel silently flickered blue light on the furniture.

I deciphered the microwave and looked for silverware. Joe called out, "I think the Security Police mentioned your name." I paused with a spoon in my hand. Did he want to ask me about finding Cass? I closed my eyes and frantically tried to think of what I could tell him. Not the truth. She had obviously died in pain and terror, frantically clawing dirt to get up the hill. My mind froze on that image, the microwave beeped, and Joe returned to the kitchen. He paused over Livvy's stroller and she yawned, stretching her hands and feet. He gave a small, automatic smile and turned to me.

I hastily set the steaming bowl on the table in the breakfast nook and searched in the refrigerator for a drink for him. "Be careful. It's hot." Cass's refrigerator was crammed with haphazardly stacked containers: a block of cheese, an apple, and a stick of butter sat on top of wrinkled whole wheat tortillas wedged in beside soy milk. I found a pitcher of tea and poured him a glass. I'd tell him as little as possible and let him talk.

"I found her on my way home." I sat down at the other end of the table and pulled Livvy's stroller over. I fiddled with her Pooh bear.

"I just can't believe it happened. That she's gone." He ate his soup and bread unconsciously, but his eyes searched my face. "Did she say anything?"

"No. She was . . . gone when I found her. It must have happened fast because she left just a few minutes before me." I offered this information, hoping the speed of her death would gloss over the terror of it.

"I told her and told her . . ." his voice trailed off and he pinched the bridge of his nose with his fingers. After a moment he sighed, rubbed his high forehead, and took a drink of the tea. "I always hounded her to keep the EpiPen with her. Her last reaction to a wasp sting was so severe she almost died. That happened last year at the squad's pool party. But she wasn't like that, cautious. She used to tease me that she wanted to live life without worrying about every little thing, like I did. She was impulsive and fun and full of energy."

To keep him from asking me anything else, I asked, "Is that what happened, she had a reaction to a sting?"

"Anaphylactic shock." The syllables rolled off his tongue with ease. It was a familiar term. He drained his glass. "A wasp got in the van. It stung her several times. Her whole body reacted to the venom. That's what the medical examiner's office found. She must have stopped the van to get out, away from the wasp, then she went around the passenger side to get her EpiPen. But she got queasy and dizzy. They think she slipped and fell down the slope. She must have lost consciousness before she could get back up. At least, that's what the medical examiner and the Security Police think. They're releasing her body today. I'm flying home to Houston tomorrow."

"Her family lives there?" Livvy started to fuss, so I pulled her favorite red and blue clown rattle out of the bin in the bottom of the stroller.

He nodded. "Mine, too. We knew each other in high school." He took his bowl over to the sink, rinsed it, and put it beside the lone bowl in the dishwasher. He refilled his glass and looked embarrassed. "Can I get you something to drink? Sorry, I'm kind of out of it."

"No, thanks. I'm fine."

"That was great minestrone. Thanks for bringing it over."

"Look, if it makes you feel any better, she might have been trying to get her EpiPen out when she slipped down the slope. Her purse was open on the passenger side."

He nodded. "There was an EpiPen in the glove compartment, too. I always made sure she had one there and one with her." He shook his head. "It doesn't matter, though. She's still gone."

I gathered up the toys Livvy had flung out of the stroller and pushed the stroller to the door, mentally kicking myself for bringing the conversation back to Cass's death.

On the porch, I paused. "Do you need anyone to water your plants or take in your mail while you're gone? Mitch and I could do that for you."

Joe studied the hanging baskets of petunias like

someone had placed them there this morning. "Ah, yeah. I hadn't thought about that. The plants were Cass's department." He swallowed, fighting down emotion. "Let me get you a key." He disappeared back into the kitchen and then returned with a smiley face key chain with two keys on it. "Front and back doors. Just put the mail on the kitchen counter. Thanks."

I walked back across the street as Ed and Mabel, our next-door neighbors, drove their town car into their neatly shelved and spotlessly clean garage, not even an oil spot on the concrete. Mabel carried her purse and a small Styrofoam "to-go" container into the house while Ed, finger-combing his fringe of white hair, ambled over to talk to Mitch. Mitch saw him and cut the power on the mower.

"You've been busy." Ed Parsons stood on his side of the hedge that divided our front yard from his. Ed nodded to me as I joined them at the hedge. "Good to see you working so hard on the place. That last couple that lived there didn't do a thing, never mowed or picked up pinecones. Just blasted their music until we could hear it in our bedroom, that's on the other side of the house. You about unpacked?" I looked over their flawless carpetlike lawn and pristine flower beds. No way we would be able to measure up to that standard. And I thought we were leaving the "Lawn of the Month" competition to on-base housing.

"Almost. It's just too hot to work inside today, so we decided to get started out here." My frenzy of activity coupled with Abby's help had been productive. Our essentials were unpacked. Our home was emerging from the chaos. Mitch had hung our new miniblinds and curtains. I was thinking about where to hang pictures.

"Figured as much," Ed said with a satisfied smile. He removed his toothpick from his mouth and gestured to the street. "I saw that moving van yesterday picking up empty boxes, so I knew you were making progress."

Mabel crossed the driveway and ran a critical eye over the hedge, but didn't say anything when she joined us. "They're almost unpacked," Ed told her with triumph in his voice. "Knew it, seeing that truck."

Mabel nodded. "You had the blue carpet removed." Her voice was flat and I couldn't tell if she approved or disapproved.

"Yes, we did." I was glad Mitch had hung those mini-blinds. Were these people watching us instead of television for entertainment? "We didn't like the color," I said. It was an awful shade of turquoise and full of dirt.

"Hideous." Mabel said. She wore a white shirt, khaki pants, and a blue-and-yellow plaid vest. Did she always wear plaid? I saw her gardening a few days ago wearing orange and yellow plaid shorts.

Mabel nodded her head in the direction of the Vincents' house. "How's he taking his wife's death?"

"You knew the Vincents?"

"Of course. They're part of the neighborhood. We make it a point to meet everyone and keep an eye on things."

I'm sure you do. Mitch and I exchanged a glance and I knew he was thinking the same thing I was. He hid a smile and I said, "He's still in shock, I think."

"Not surprising," Mabel agreed. She squinted down the street at the plain white house next to the Vincents'. "I wonder if she ever met her neighbor—the one in the white house."

"I don't know."

Mabel leaned toward me and said confidentially, "Cassandra spent hours gardening in her yard, but I think she worked outside so she could watch that house."

"Now, Mabel, you don't know that," Ed cautioned.

"Well, she watched it and she asked me if I knew anything about the people who lived there."

Ed harrumphed and drew Mitch over to examine a patch of lawn that wasn't as verdantly green as the rest of his grass.

Mabel said, "I think Cassandra suspected it was a drug house."

"What?"

"Strange comings and goings at night. Lots of activity after dark. I'm watching it."

"Oh. Well. That's good." I think. At least it might keep her gaze off our house.

Mabel changed the subject. "How do you like your new house?"

I smiled. "We love it. Now if it will just cool off we can really start enjoying it. It's like an oven in there right now."

"You don't have a window cooler?" Mabel asked, glancing at Livvy in the stroller.

"No. We didn't know we needed one." How could they miss knowing that? They seemed to know everything else.

"Ed, find that window unit we got at the garage sale last year and help them put it in." Mabel started back to the house. She tossed over her shoulder, "Got a good deal on it. Use it until it cools off."

I stood for a few seconds with my mouth open before I shut it. Abrupt, generous, and nosy. What a combination for our next-door neighbors. I glanced back at

Joe's house. I hoped he was doing something else besides staring at the TV with the sound turned down. But
bluish light flickered in his front windows.

An Everything in Its Place Tip for an Organized Move

- You don't have to move everything. In fact, don't move everything!
- Sift through your belongings and lighten the load. If you've had something stashed in your closet for years, think about why you hang on to it.
- Purge old records from your files.
- Eliminate items you won't need in your new location. For instance, if you won't have much of a yard pare down lawn equipment. No fireplace? Give away fireplace tools.

Chapter
Five

Simplicity, clarity, singleness: these are the
attributes that give our lives power and vividness
and joy.
—Richard Halloway

With Livvy's cries ricocheting off the windows, I adjusted the angle of the mirrors and shoved a jum-
ble of paper cups, tissues, and a Snickers wrapper aside
with my foot to make room for my feet on the floorboard. Then I nosed Cass's van out of the Security Police's holding area. Joe had called early this morning to
ask me if I could pick up the van.

"The funeral's tomorrow," Joe had said. There wasn't
any inflection in his voice. I tucked the phone between
my ear and shoulder so I could hold Livvy in one arm
and pick up her plastic book from the floor with the

other hand. We had been up three times with Livvy during the night. She didn't seem to know what she wanted.

"I'm going to stay out here for a few more days. The Security Police at Greenly are releasing the van. Could you please pick it up for me?"

I did a quick mental scan of the day's events. Mitch had training in the flight simulator, or the sim, as the guys called it. I'd planned on going to the Comm, the grocery store on-base called the commissary. "Sure. I'll have Mitch drop me off on the way to his sim. I'll drive your van back and leave it in your driveway."

Hopefully, Livvy would sleep during the drive to the base.

That morning, I'd gone through the whole routine—feeding, burping, diaper changing. I'd hoped a car ride would soothe her. It didn't. She cried during the twenty-five-minute drive. As I stopped for a light, I reconsidered my grocery shopping plan. I didn't think I could handle it with Livvy's fussiness. I drove past the chapel, the gym, and the Comm, each painted pastel yellow with mud brown trim. The government must have gotten a huge discount on that paint. It's the standard exterior paint at every base I've ever seen. The color is probably called Pale Blah.

A military base is almost like a college campus, a self-contained world with everything a person could need: a gas station, credit union, banks, grocery stores, a base exchange, which is similar to a Wal-Mart only smaller, a recycling center, and a movie theater. Theoretically, a person never had to leave. Of course, if a person never left the base, theoretically, that person would go insane.

I rolled to a stop at the next intersection, tapping the steering wheel with my thumb, unsure what to do. I could tough it out and do our grocery shopping, but

Livvy's cries, although not as insistent as they were at the beginning of our drive, were still shrill and loud. Just the thought of navigating the Comm's aisles with Livvy crying made my head hurt.

I flipped on my blinker and turned right for the car wash. Sometimes loud noises soothed Livvy. She loved the roar of the vacuum cleaner and the gush of water into the tub. The van was dusty on the outside and gum wrappers, dead pine needles, and paper napkins and cups littered the floor mats. I doubted Joe would want to even see the van, much less clean it up, so I could do that for him. Livvy went silent in midcry.

I could feel my eyebrows wrinkle together as I tried to figure out why she stopped crying suddenly. Then she grunted. I knew exactly what that noise meant: urgent diaper change. I sighed and pulled over to the side of the car wash parking lot.

I hated changing diapers in the car, but this was the worst I'd ever seen. Without a second thought, I tossed her overalls and shirt embroidered with a gardening theme of flowers, pails, and shovels in the trash. There was no salvaging that outfit. I fished a worn onesie from the depths of the diaper bag. It fit like a surgical glove. She was growing every day. I put her back in the car seat. As soon as the buckle clicked, she squished her eyes shut and cried.

I found several quarters in the bottom of my brown leather backpack purse and slipped them into the machine. I sat back in the dim light as the water pounded the car. Livvy gave a few more gulping sobs, then a shaky sigh tapered off into silence. Thank goodness. My nerves were stretched to the limit. Mitch could ignore her crying or tell himself that she was fussy and would be all right in a little while, but my natural mother re-

sponse system couldn't take much more of Livvy's un-
ending crying. Shouldn't she quiet down when I com-
forted her? Shouldn't I be able to figure out what was
wrong?

I sighed again and glanced around the interior of
the van in the dim light. Cass sat in this same seat right
before she died. I got that creepy feeling I always get in
a car wash, the gloomy half-light and the sense of enclo-
sure. A fine layer of soap bubbles coated the van and intensified my uneasiness as it cut off my view of the
cinderblock walls. I flipped the wipers on to open a
small clearing. Get a grip. I sat up straighter. Cass didn't
even die inside the van. There was no reason to feel so
uncomfortable. I glanced around the interior. Someone had cleaned up the personal items that were scattered over the passenger seat and floorboard the day
she died. Probably returned them to Joe.

I opened the glove compartment and shifted the
maps, flashlight, tapes, and napkins around. Where was
the EpiPen? Joe said he kept one in the van. Had the
police returned it to Joe with Cass's purse? I flipped the
compartment door shut and eased the van slowly
through the dryer. Then I hit the accelerator hard,
knowing that without the loud water noises the motion
and tire noise of the van might keep Livvy asleep.

It worked. It was a blissfully quiet drive home. I was
even able to think about Livvy's crying with a little per-
spective. She had always cried loud and often. Livvy was
not one of those babies who slept for twenty hours
every day. My books said she fell into the "high maintenance baby" category. But, this was extreme, even for
her. Was she getting sick? I dreaded her first cold. I
knew she wouldn't be able to tell me what was wrong,

where it hurt. I decided to call a doctor when we got back home or, I amended, find a doctor.

"I'm sorry, but Dr. Henry isn't taking new patients," the cool voice said without a hint of regret.

I hung up and looked for Dr. Williams in the phone book. I finally found it under Northwest Family Health in the Yellow Pages. She was taking new patients and could see Livvy in six weeks. "You can try our Urgent Care Department. I'll transfer you," the receptionist said. I took their first opening, Friday at 10:30.

I sat on our kitchen steps with the thick phone book splayed open on my lap, hoping our neighbors wouldn't call Child Protective Services. Faintly, I could hear Livvy crying in her crib. I had done everything I could think of: feeding, burping, diaper changing, playing, cuddling, singing, and rocking. She seemed to want to eat, but after a few moments, she'd jerk her head away and cry.

I felt like crying myself. So I put her down in her crib and shut the door. I was amazed that Livvy, so small and powerless, could almost push me to my limit. When I was pregnant a friend told me, "You have to have a place where you can put your baby down and walk away when you get so frustrated you can hardly stand it." At the time I thought she was crazy. How could a sweet, helpless baby push someone over the edge? Now I understood.

I rubbed my forehead and tried to think of something to do outside. I looked over at the van still parked in our driveway, where I had left it as I hurried to get inside, feed Livvy, and put her down for her nap before I ran it across the street to Joe's driveway.

"If it's worth doing, it's worth doing right." My dad's steady voice sounded in my head. It was a hot spring day when he showed me how to wash a car. He unlooped the vacuum cleaner cord and said, "Doing it right includes vacuuming the inside and cleaning the tires, too."

I found the handheld vacuum and the extension cord. Sliding back the door on the passenger side, I tossed paper cups and a discarded newspaper into the trash, then I vacuumed up pine needles, lint, dried grass, pebbles, and tiny paper scraps. Neatness hadn't been high on Cass's priority list. When I turned the handheld vacuum off to close the sliding door and move up to the floor mats in the front, I knew something was wrong, but I couldn't place what it was. I stood still and listened.

Silence. I put the vacuum down and trotted up the steps. It was quiet inside the house, too. An article I had read about SIDS at one of my prenatal appointments leapt into my mind. Could she really be asleep? Of course, she was fine, but I'd just check on her. I tiptoed down the hall and struggled to open Livvy's door as stealthily as a spy breaking into a foreign embassy. Peeking in the crack in the door, I saw Livvy, her blanket twisted in a knot beside her, her hands loose and relaxed. I watched her little chest rise and fall and let out my breath, silently. And Mitch said I worried too much. Ha!

I went back to the van and worked my way around to the driver's seat, throwing away the trash, then vacuuming. I was thinking about what I would have for lunch when I pulled a cup from under the gas pedal. It was wedged, so I gave it a good jerk. I glanced in it as I turned to toss it in the trash can. I dropped it on the ground like it burned me, jerking my hand backward.

After a second, I poked it with my toe. When nothing happened I grabbed one of the sticks that littered our driveway under the pine tree. I gently slid the stick into the squished opening and angled the cup until it stood up. Then I peeked in, still ready to dive for cover. I wasn't wrong. I'd seen it right in that first glance. Black and yellow smears and a few wings circled the inside. At the bottom of the cup there were a few fairly intact bees or maybe wasps. Stinging things, anyway.

I stood there the hand-vac dangling in my hand, looking from the cup to the van. The cup was a generic, medium-size cup with the red and white Coca-Cola lettering. It didn't have a lid on it and I didn't see one inside the van. The cup had been wedged under the gas pedal. How long had it been there? How did it get there in the first place? The back of my neck felt prickly. This had to be a bizarre coincidence. Slowly I put the vac down and rubbed my forehead. Thoughts were skittering through my mind that I didn't even want to examine. What I was thinking was impossible. I squatted down to look at the cup again.

I felt a presence beside me and turned. A brown and black dog stood beside me, his face only inches from mine. I could see each sharp white tooth in detail as warm doggy breath engulfed me.

"What's up?"

I jerked around. Mitch, still in his flight suit and carrying his gym bag, stood behind me. I hadn't even heard him drive up. The dog trotted back to him, paused with his head under Mitch's hand. I took an uneven breath to calm down.

"Isn't he great?" Mitch rubbed the dog's ears. "Sit, Rex." The dog obeyed. His brown eyes fixed on Mitch adoringly.

"Where . . ." my voice trailed off. "That's Joe's dog."

"Yeah, Tommy was watching him for Joe, but Tommy had to go TDY, so I volunteered to keep him. I figured he could sleep in the garage. Rex, that is."

Tommy was gone on a trip, or Temporary Duty, as the Air Force referred to it. I'd never understood why the acronym for Temporary Duty was TDY instead of TD, but there's a lot of things I don't understand about the Air Force. What mattered now was Tommy was gone and Mitch had Rex. "Mitch," I paused, unsure which objection to voice first. "We don't know what that dog would do around Livvy. It might be dangerous. And does it shed?" I stood up to gain a better bargaining position.

"Oh, he'll be fine. Joe says he's great around kids." Rex's gaze bounced back and forth between us, like he knew he was being talked about.

"What kids has he been around?"

"Look, it's just for a few days. I thought he might get lonely, but if it will make you feel better he can stay over at Joe's house and we can go over and feed him and take him for walks. We're already going to be over there getting the mail."

Mitch wanted a dog. I'd held out. We moved so much that we never knew if we'd have a place to put a pet. But beyond that little difficulty, we disagreed on what kind of dog we would get, if we got one. Mitch wanted a big dog; I wanted a cute, little dog. A cuddly dog I could handle. Ever since a German shepherd chased me home from school when I was eight I'd kept my distance from large dogs. Rex eyed me with his solemn brown eyes.

"Okay," I said reluctantly. "You take care of the dog.

I'll take care of the plants and the mail. Are you done for the day?"

"Yeah. I decided to skip my workout since Livvy was so fussy. How is she?"

I listened for a moment. "Still sleeping." I pointed to the cup on the driveway beside Mitch's foot. "I found that in the van. Wedged under the gas pedal. Look inside." He peered in and then let out a low whistle. "We'd better call the Security Police."

"Then you think this means . . ." I didn't want to say it. If I didn't say it, it wouldn't be real.

"Someone wanted Cass to die. And made sure she did."

Chapter
Six

Aand you found this in the driver's seat after you drove the van home?" Nott looked at the cup now encased in a sealed plastic baggie on the desk between us. "After you vacuumed it. After you ran it through the car wash."

"Well, yes. I didn't notice it right away."

"Didn't notice it." Nott's dark eyes bored into mine. So far he had repeated everything back to me. Shouldn't he be taking notes?

Nott leaned back, studied the ceiling tiles for a moment. Then he stood. "Be back in a moment, ma'am." He took the baggie with him, casually swinging it back and forth, like it contained a ham sandwich and he was on his way to lunch.

What was I doing? Nott obviously thought I was crazy to bring in a cup of squished insects and claim they were a murder weapon. I rummaged through my bag until I found a Hershey Kiss. I popped it in my mouth. Who would kill someone with bees? You'd have to know how to handle them, that's for sure. Not something I'd want to mess with. A memory teased at the edge of my thoughts. Something about bees? No. Honey? I crushed the foil wrapper. Abby brought me honey the day Cass died. It was from Jeff's mom.

Oh, no. I closed my eyes and leaned back. Jeff's parents had a hobby that, to me, was slightly bizarre. They were beekeepers. Jeff couldn't be involved in this, could he? He didn't have a hive, but he knew how to get bees and handle them.

And Cass had threatened him. Then he'd gone outside. What had I done?

I watched Nott return without the baggie. He escorted me out of the large room with scattered desks into a private office with a faux cherry–finished desk and a window overlooking an empty parking lot. Colonel Witson sat behind his desk, turning the plastic bag around in his hands. "Nice of you to bring this in, all bagged up and everything. You must watch a lot of TV." Witson grinned and tossed the bag on his desk.

I felt my face heating up. I'd been trying to help, but Witson made me feel like I was some kind of bungling police groupie, a big joke.

"I thought you might need it. It might help," I said tersely.

"Was this"—he looked at a file on his desk—"Cassandra Vincent a friend of yours?"

"Not really. I'd just met her a few days before." I wished I had changed out of my shorts and T-shirt into something dressier. I felt a distinct disadvantage here.

Witson picked up the baggie. "And now you think

someone placed this in her car so she'd be stung and die?" His smile was wide.

"Look, I don't know. That's why I brought it to you. It sounds too crazy to be true to me, too. But I thought you would want to know."

"Yes, we do always appreciate any help we can get. Thank you for coming in, Mrs. Avery. We'll look into it." He closed the file and stood up to shake hands with me.

I tossed a load of tiny clothes in the washing machine. How could someone who weighs twelve pounds generate three loads of laundry? Upstairs, I heard the gentle splash of water and the murmurs of Mitch's one-sided conversation with Livvy as he bathed her. I closed the washing machine lid and looked at the cabinets without seeing them. The supper dishes were done and I'd started the laundry more to keep busy than anything else. I couldn't seem to focus on anything tonight. Despite Colonel Witson's apparent lack of interest, two Security Police officers arrived at our house shortly after I returned from the base. They left with the van and my hand vacuum, so Witson was more interested than he let on. Although I didn't like his attitude, he seemed to be following up on what I had found.

I felt a surge of anger and shook my head at myself. My time-delayed anger, which I experienced over and over again, didn't do me any good. I wished I'd spoken up and defended myself instead of being embarrassed.

I couldn't do anything about that now, but I could do a little research. I climbed the stairs from our basement garage/laundry room. In our bedroom, I punched on the computer. It was too big for the secretary desk that my dad had made, so the computer was squished into our already crowded bedroom on a tiny pressboard desk. While the computer whirred through its warm-up routine, I plucked a chocolate Kiss out of the dish on the desk. Chocolate helps you think, I'd told Mitch. It was logical to have Hershey Kisses beside the computer. I logged on to the Internet and searched for information on bees.

Even though Witson had the van at the base, there was no guarantee he would do anything. Cass had died an awful, untimely death and whoever planned it was getting away with it.

The confrontation between Cass and Jeff worried me. That scene combined with Jeff's knowledge of bees really worried me. I chewed the inside of my lip. Did I want to do this? I scooted the chair closer to the computer. The truth had to be better than not knowing.

After pointing and clicking my way around a few sites, I found several color pictures on a university education site and realized I had seen wasps, not bees. Wasps! I felt a little better. But if you know how to handle bees, you'd probably know how to handle wasps, too. I scanned the text. Yellow jackets are fairly aggressive wasps, especially if their nest is disturbed. If the hive is crushed it will provoke a fierce response, with wasps stinging repeatedly, instead of only once, as in the case of bees.

I scrolled down and clicked on the heading "Allergic Reactions." It described the symptoms of a reaction. If the reaction was severe, death could occur within half an hour, but sometimes within five minutes.

I bookmarked the sight and continued exploring the other hits. The emergency room on-base had closed last year. That info was part of Mitch's in-processing brief and he'd told me, so I'd know in case I ever had to get Livvy help when we were on the base. The nearest hospital was at least fifteen to twenty minutes away. I shivered, thinking of Cass. Even if she had been stung in the parking lot with people around, she might not have reached a hospital in time to help her. Whoever had placed the wasps in her car must have known it would be difficult for her to get to a hospital or emergency room.

But where was her EpiPen? Had it been in the car and she was too overwhelmed to find it and use it? I'd ask Joe when he called again. I wondered if the police would call him and ask about the wasps and the EpiPen.

I left the computer and went outside. Mitch joined me in the backyard a few minutes later. He carried Livvy. He'd dressed her in her pajamas dotted with violets. She grinned and gurgled at me. I kissed her fuzzy head and inhaled the scent of baby powder and lotion. "Are you feeling better?" I asked her.

She punched out her legs in a kick for an answer.

"What are you doing out here?" Mitch asked.

"See that?" I pointed to our trash cans in the alcove behind the shed. Two wasps dipped and dove around the cans and then disappeared under the rim of the lid. "Yellow jackets. The same thing I found in the van." I described the information I'd read online. "If we've got two in our yard, they must be pretty common. Anyone could attract them and then put them in the van."

"Yeah, but how would you do it? Wasps aren't the most cooperative things around," Mitch said as we watched one wasp emerge and fly to our neighbor's yard.

"A site online sells traps for bees. Apparently some people want to catch them. Or a bowl of water with sugar or rotting fruit attracts them. They're less active at night when it's cooler. They can even be refrigerated. And smoke calms them down, too."

Of course, if you grew up with beekeepers for parents you'd already know this stuff. I didn't say my thoughts aloud. Jeff and Mitch went way back. My worries could be coincidences.

I hoped they were coincidences. "The murderer could have trapped the wasps, cooled them down, and then moved them to Cass's van at the last minute. It would take a little time for them to warm up, but when they did . . ."

"She'd be on the road to the back gate, which is usually deserted." Mitch finished the thought for me.

"Whoever did it picked the base because it was farther from medical care," I said.

"And I suppose, if you weren't allergic, a sting or two wouldn't bother you," Mitch said. His words stirred a memory, but it flitted away before I could pin it down.

"Let's go inside." I felt cold even though the night was still warm.

I logged off the computer. Mitch placed Livvy in the middle of the bed and propped himself up beside her with his head resting on his arm. I settled on the bed on the other side of Livvy.

"Look, she's finding her hands," I said. Livvy stared intently at her right hand. She pulled it closer and closer to her face until she bumped herself in the nose and we laughed.

He looked at me over Livvy's flailing arms. His eyes turned troubled as he put his finger out for Livvy to grab and said, "It was probably someone from the squadron."

I thought back to the day of the barbeque. "There

was a one hundred percent ID check at the gate that day. It is possible that someone could have gotten on base with a visitor's pass or as a passenger in a friend's car, but I'm sure the Security Police will check it out."

Mitch said, "It's much more likely that it was someone from the squadron."

I sat cross-legged, Indian style, on the bed and rubbed my arms. I just couldn't seem to warm up. I was chilled from the thought that someone we know, maybe someone we had talked to that day, had purposefully put an end to Cass's life. "What kind of people are you working with up there?" I asked.

Mitch didn't answer. Instead, he said, "It could be someone I don't work with." Livvy started huffing, so I picked her up and moved to the chair in our room to breast-feed her. Once I was settled I realized what Mitch was saying. "You mean one of the spouses!"

Mitch rolled onto his back and crossed his arms behind his head. He looked relaxed, he usually did, but I could tell from the wrinkle between his eyes he was troubled. "There *were* plenty of spouses there."

I shook my head. What could drive a person to kill another?

Jeff had been angry with her. Angry enough to kill her? As soon as the thought formed, my mind skittered away from it. Not Jeff. Please not Jeff. Who else could have done it?

"Cass had a big argument with Diana at the spouse coffee. She was hot," I said.

"Who?" Mitch asked. "Diana was mad?"

"No. Diana was pretty subdued. That new subdivision came up after the meeting."

I saw Mitch's puzzled look and said, "You know, the really expensive one that'll have a golf course. Anyway,

Cass and Diana started out being extremely polite to each other. Cass gave Diana a compliment, but her smile was fake, kind of plastic. But Diana just said thanks. I thought she didn't notice. Then Cass started needling Diana about Wilde Creek. Diana's a realtor and I guess she's got the listings in there. Cass said something about how Diana must be raking in the bucks and that there wouldn't be one wild thing left when the development was finished. Cass started to simmer. I saw her flush and I thought the chips and salsa were going to vibrate off her plate because her hands were shaking so much.

"Diana just wiped her mouth with a napkin and explained the subdivision was going to maintain open space and preserve natural beauty. She talked about large lots and keeping trees. They have an arborist on retainer."

"What did Cass say?" Mitch asked.

"It was like the calmer Diana was the madder Cass got. She was flaming by then. She said, 'Don't give me that. You care more about your manicure than the environment. Don't kid yourself.' I could picture her at those anti–Wal-Mart rallies, appealing to the crowds, when she said, 'Acres of trees will be razed for the fairways on that golf course. And the chemicals, the pesticides and fertilizers. Wilde Creek will be as natural as one of those casinos on the Las Vegas strip.'

"That finally got Diana going. She stood up and said, 'You think I don't care about the environment? Then why would I take half my normal commission to handle the sales in Wilde Creek? Because I care.' As she said that she jabbed her drink at Cass and a few drops of water sloshed onto the coffee table. Then she said, 'But, unlike you, I'm practical.' She thinks controlled development with open spaces and upscale homes is better than a strip mall or condos covering every inch of the valley. She even challenged Cass and said, 'You fought that Wal-Mart with everything you had. You should be on my side.'

"Cass stepped closer to Diana and said, 'What're you saying? That keeping the valley unspoiled is an impossible dream?'

"Diana snorted. I had to smile at that because Diana seems so particular. She looks like the kind of person who wipes down the grooves in the jelly jar or the ketchup before she puts the lids on, you know? Snorting didn't quite go with the image, but she didn't back down. She said, 'More like a fantasy.'

"Jill ended it when she told them to stay on squadron-related topics if they couldn't be civil."

Mitch said, "It sounds like they were arguing more over philosophy than anything else."

I had to agree with him. "Diana did say the houses are already under construction, so their whole argument was kind of pointless anyway."

"The way you describe it Cass was the volatile one, not Diana," Mitch added.

"I know. She was passionate about the environment." I thought back over my interactions with Cass. "You know, Cass wanted to tell me something about Gwen. I had the feeling it was some juicy gossip, but I cut her off."

"That's kind of far-fetched, isn't it? To kill someone over gossip."

I murmured an agreement, but I still wondered what Cass had been about to say about Gwen. Who would go to such an extreme to murder another person? "Who hated her so much?"

"If we knew that we might know why she died and who killed her," Mitch said.

We didn't talk about it anymore because Livvy pulled away and cried, as if she didn't want to eat, but then she latched on again and gulped the milk. A few seconds later she pulled off again and cried. After a few minutes of that routine I was so frustrated I wanted to cry, too. Finally, I put her to bed and she fell asleep with a sigh of relief.

An Everything in Its Place Tip for an Organized Move

Stay in Touch

- Buy a small address book or notepad to carry with you to farewell get-togethers. Pass it around to get contact info, especially e-mail addresses.
- If your friends are military, exchange permanent addresses of parents or a relative who can forward mail in case you lose touch with friends between moves.

Chapter
Seven

How do I get myself into these things? There were about a hundred boxes left to unpack while Livvy napped, but instead of unpacking, I clutched a utility knife, masking tape, a black marker, and the baby monitor. I almost headed down the stairs to our basement garage, but the creaky steps might wake Livvy, so I changed direction. I eased the back door open, ready to sort and price things for the squad's garage sale.

As I turned toward the steps, my feet skidded across the tiny porch. I reached for the iron porch railing with my free hand, but it swayed under my weight. I let go of it.

And everything else. The utility knife, pen, tape, and baby monitor rained down around my feet as I flailed my arms like a novice ice skater. The railing fell away from the porch in a slow dive to the grass a few feet below and I thudded down on top of it with an impact that jarred me.

I took a few deep breaths and looked around. Had anyone witnessed my solo rendition of a scene from the Three Stooges? Apparently not. No walkers or joggers and—thank goodness—Mabel's house was on the opposite side, so she hadn't seen what happened.

I stood up and propped the railing against the porch. I'd leave it for Mitch. I had to sort boxes. I walked down the sloping driveway to the garage, shaking my head. If I'd been carrying Livvy, one of us would've been hurt for sure. Our house was old, but I didn't expect parts of it to break off in my hands.

In the garage, I opened a box and shifted through a mixer, paperbacks, and scuffed shoes. I closed it, scrawled "Garage Sale" on the side, and shoved it to one side of the garage. The cool of the concrete floor pressed against my knees and seeped through me. The garage was still the coolest place in the house, even with the window unit. I should have said no at the coffee. But I hadn't. How had I lost control of my vocal cords and volunteered for garage sale duty? I realized I was clenching my teeth and forced my jaw to relax.

I felt a surge of guilt. After all, Cass was dead and here I was mentally whining about a few boxes. Not a big deal compared to what Joe and their family were going through. It was hard to believe that lifeless body I saw in the ditch was Cass because she'd been so energetic at the coffee. Pushy, too. But vibrant.

She was the first person I noticed that night, as she flitted around the room like a hummingbird as she performed introductions and pulled little clumps of people together or broke up other knots of conversation. When Jill Briman, the squadron commander's wife, called the meeting to order, Cass hurried in from the kitchen with a huge bowl of punch. She subsided a little and lingered by the buffet table, but she still seemed to hum with barely suppressed energy as she twitched a napkin into place and readjusted a row of forks.

I had refocused on Jill as she snapped, "Sign-in sheet," and held out a clipboard. "Here's a list of dates for the monthly coffees." Jill was petite and pixie-like with short dark hair, pale skin, and gray eyes, but she ran the coffee with quick efficiency and an authority worthy of Patton. "Sign up to host one at your house." She passed another clipboard sharply toward the spouse on her left, who was still fumbling with the first one. Jill's steely eyes ran over the group and commanded we follow through or risk—what? Demerits? The bad spouse award? I felt a case of the giggles coming on.

"I feel like I'm in junior high," Abby said in an undertone.

"Or boot camp."

"All right. Fund-raising," Jill barked from the front of the room in her staccato voice. She absently rubbed her sunburnt nose and consulted her agenda. "We have an account at the thrift shop. Drop off things there and the proceeds go to our squadron account. That's an easy way for all of you to help raise money."

"What are we raising money for?" Abby asked quietly.

"I have no idea."

"The garage sale is the first fund-raiser. Clean out your closets. Bring your items to Cass." Jill's commands were beginning to annoy me. I wasn't in the military and didn't have to do one thing for the squadron if I didn't want to. Jill motioned that Cass had the floor. She stood up and waited until all eyes were on her. She soaked up the attention like a sponge.

"You've been great about bringing your things over, but don't stop there. We need you to sign up to work the checkout table. I think Jill has a sign-up sheet? Oh, good, it's already going around. I really need someone to help me organize everything." I'd only been half-listening to Cass. I longed for the meeting to be over. How was Livvy doing? Had she taken her bottle? Of course, the measly four ounces that I'd been able to pump, one of the most frustrating experiences of my life, wasn't exactly a bottle.

"Oh, you'd be great for that job!" Abby exclaimed.

"What?"

Abby turned to the curious heads that had swiveled toward us. "Ellie is a professional organizer. She helped lots of people in our squadron in California get organized. And she's worked with businesses, too."

I suppressed a groan. I had worked as a temp doing office work after my PR job was downsized. In every office I filed, straightened, and generally cleaned up. I had said to Mitch I should do it for a living as a consultant and he said, "Why don't you?" So I'd helped a few people organize their offices, helped a pregnant mom from the squadron get ready for her baby, and cleaned out a home for the children of an elderly woman who had to move to a nursing home. When I got pregnant all ideas of owning my own business flew out the window when I began to throw up every day.

"Ah, I don't know. With just moving and . . ."

"Do you spell your name with an 'ie' or a 'y'?" asked Jill, squinting at the scrawl on my nametag.

A little one-syllable word and I couldn't say it. I'm not good at saying no. It must be my quasi-southern upbringing, but I feel rude and selfish when I turn people down. I gave up and spelled it.

My feet were beginning to feel tingly so I stood up and stretched, then moved to the next tower of boxes. "No. I can't." I practiced saying it aloud. I could have at least said I didn't have any storage, but I caved on that, too. Abby and I were leaving the coffee and had almost tripped over some boxes in the entryway.

"Wait a minute," Cass had said, "let me move these. Someone must've brought them tonight for the garage sale and just dumped them here. That's the problem with these older houses, not much closet space. Hey"— she must have suddenly remembered my role as garage sale assistant—"do you have anywhere you could put a few extra boxes?"

"Sure," I said resignedly and we lugged the extra boxes to my garage.

"I have a few more in the van. I'll just grab those, too." Cass was already walking back to her house. She headed down the single driveway leading to the one-car detached garage. Abby and I followed. I whispered, "How did I get into this? I don't have time for this. And if anyone saw the inside of my house right now, I'd never get another organizing job again."

"I know. I'm sorry," Abby said. "My big mouth— sometimes I don't think. Look, I'll help you all I can." Cass passed her van and opened the front of the garage, which set off her dog alternately barking and whining inside the chain-link fenced backyard that ran along-side the garage.

"Hi, Rex. I'll let you inside when everyone is gone. You've been such a good puppy." Her voice was squishy but then changed abruptly as she called back to us, "I've got a dolly in here. It will go so much faster." I rolled my eyes at Abby and looked over the fence. The little puppy was a rottweiler with a dash of lab thrown in. I backed away from the fence.

Cass wheeled the dolly back to the van. She jerked open the passenger side door, brushed aside crumpled envelopes, an empty paper bag from Burger King, and an old newspaper before she loaded boxes onto the dolly. I was surprised she didn't lock her van since it was parked outside and not in the garage. I looked around the peaceful neighborhood of bungalows, minivans, and tree houses. Living in Southern California, where carjacking and murder headlined most newscasts, had made me a bit paranoid. But I wasn't going to stop locking my car doors.

On our third trip with her dolly loaded, Cass said, "You know, your garage would probably be a better place for the garage sale. You're on a cross street and you have a two-car garage."

"Ah, well, if I can get the moving boxes cleaned out, maybe . . ."

"Great!" Cass shifted the dolly from under the boxes with an expert twist. "Thanks. I didn't know where I was going to put it all."

I inched another box out of the pile Cass had deposited that night. Not much I could do about it now. I was stuck with all this stuff at least for a few weeks. "No, I'm sorry. I can't," I practiced with a new inflection. A cloud of dust hit me in the face when I opened the next box. I heard Mitch's Altima pull into our driveway. I gave a quick wave and checked the box. But instead of old clothes or broken toys, papers and folders filled the box. I ran my fingers down the folder tabs. Armed Forces Insurance. Carson FCU—statements. Nevis Bank. Pay Stubs. Tax return—last year. Utilities. Definitely not garage sale material.

I wrestled one of the folders out of the tightly packed box. Brent David McCarter. Ugh. I'd drop this off on their porch when they weren't home so I wouldn't have to see Brent again. As I closed the box and shoved it aside, I heard a clatter of claws and then felt heavy breathing on the back of my neck.

An Everything in Its Place Tip for an Organized Move

Three Ways to Lighten the Load
- Trash it—quickest and easiest way to cut down on clutter.
- Donate it—This is a good option if you feel guilty for getting rid of something that isn't broken or falling apart. If you never use your juicer, why keep it? Donate it to charity and you'll have the mental bonus of knowing someone else, maybe someone who couldn't afford a new juicer, is happily pureeing strawberries for a smoothie. Some charities also pick up large items, so there's no excuse for keeping that decrepit couch.
- Sell it—More time-consuming, but a garage sale or consignment shop lets you make a few bucks.

Chapter Eight

Before I could stand up, I was licked, sloppily, behind my ear and knocked onto the cool concrete.

"Rex. No," I snapped and struggled to my feet. He loped back to Mitch.

"I think he likes you," Mitch said.

"No, he likes you. He's being friendly to me to make a good impression on you."

Mitch grinned and I could have sworn he and Rex exchanged glances.

"See, I'm on to you," I said. "You think you can get me used to him and then work around to getting a big dog of our own. No way." I picked up the box. Mitch grabbed one side and helped me carry it to the Cherokee. Rex trotted along and waited while we shoved it inside. I slammed the hatch and sat down on the bumper.

"Maybe. Maybe a little dog. Someday. One that won't overwhelm Livvy."

Mitch sat down beside me. "But a big dog is protection. No one is going to even think about messing with you if you've got a dog like this around. As often as I'm gone, it would be good." Rex sat down beside me. He moved his eyes and the brown spots over his eyes seemed to tilt imploringly at me. I patted him on the head.

"I'll buy big water and food dishes with 'Killer' on the side and leave them on the porch. No one will know the difference," I said.

"But then you miss the companionship." Mitch looked pointedly at my side. I'd been rubbing Rex's ears as we talked. I pulled my hand away. "Come on, let's start dinner." I headed to the house. "Watch out. The porch railing fell off today."

Mitch leaned over and examined the braces. "Fell off? You'd think that would have come up in the home inspection if it was loose. I'll grab a screwdriver and put it back."

I went up the steps. On the way inside the door, my feet skidded. I gripped the door frame.

"Whoa, there, grace!" Mitch said as he lifted the railing onto the porch.

I leaned down and ran my hand over the green artificial turf doormat, complete with a daisy in the corner. It was one of the few things that the sellers had left, but it didn't quite hit the decorating note I liked. I'd been meaning to buy a new one.

My fingers were glossy when I pulled them away from the mat. I sniffed. Butter?

"Hey, where did you put the screws?"

"Umm. Nowhere. I just propped up the railing. I figured the screws would still be in it, if they weren't rusted out."

"There's no screws." Mitch scanned the grass where I'd propped up the railing. "Anywhere."

Mitch and I looked at each other. Mitch's eyebrows scrunched together. "Do you think someone came along and unscrewed the railing?"

"And sprayed the mat with cooking spray?" I held out my shiny fingers. "Who would do a crazy thing like that? We could have been hurt."

Mitch rubbed the back of his neck. "Maybe it was a prank."

Later that night, I jerked the sheet across the tiny mattress and pulled with all my might. Why do crib sheets seem to be an inch smaller than crib mattresses? I struggled to work the edge down between the slats while Mitch walked with springy steps up and down the dark hall with Livvy. She had been very upset when she awoke with her pajamas and sheets soaking wet. We cleaned everything up and got Livvy back to sleep; then we stumbled down the hall and fell into our blessedly cool bed. The window unit pumped wonderful arctic air across our bed and down the hall to Livvy's room. I curled up on Mitch's shoulder with his arm tucked around me. Five seconds and Mitch was out, but I wasn't. We'd written off the railing incident as a teenage prank— or possibly a squadron prank. Mitch didn't buy this last idea, but I didn't think it was beyond the realm of possibility. Kind of a welcome-to-the-neighborhood initiation joke. I heard Livvy shuffle around and shifted my thoughts to her. She'd been fussy and hadn't wanted to eat. Maybe she was just coming out of a growth spurt and didn't need as much milk. I rolled over, smacked the pillow. Maybe she was fussy because she didn't get enough to eat. I read an article about babies that got dehydrated. Was it time to start supplementing with formula?

Mitch breathed deeply, on the verge of snoring. Down the hall Livvy moved restlessly, murmured a protest, and then was quiet. I'd been busy all day running errands, sorting out the garage, and fixing dinner. I had hardly played with her. She had spent most of the day strapped in her car seat, the bouncy chair, or napping. I shifted onto my back and felt a surge of guilt for not planning time to play with her. Mother guilt. No matter what I do, I'll always question if I'm giving my family the best of everything. Every mom feels like this, I counseled myself, so go ahead and get some sleep or you won't be awake enough to give Livvy or Mitch that quality time you're so worried about. Livvy cried again, this time with more force. I padded down the hall.

She settled down when I rubbed her back. In the dim light, I could barely see her plump arm, clenching the blanket, and her back rising and falling with the steady rhythm of her breathing. She tensed but didn't awaken when a string of sharp barks punctured the quiet night. It was Rex.

I lifted the edge of the miniblinds and a movement down the street caught my eye. A slender figure carried a small bundle and moved down the driveway of the house next door to Joe.

The person opened the driver's door of the car parked at the end of the driveway and tossed the bundle inside. The brake lights came on as the car rolled silently out of the driveway and then coasted down the slight descent toward the park. At the corner, headlights flicked on and I faintly heard the engine. Rex's barks trailed off to low growls and then stopped as the car turned the corner.

I absently fingered the plastic pole of the blinds. The car, a small white two-door car, was usually parked there, but it was odd that the person had left without using the engine or lights. Mabel said Cass had asked questions about the people in the house. Mabel thought it was a drug house.

At least they weren't messing with my porch railing. I checked Livvy one more time and ambled back to bed. I snuggled up to Mitch again, but it was a long time before I slept.

Late afternoon sun slanted through the windows when Abby knocked on the screen door and I motioned her inside. "Can you believe that the weather is finally cooling off?" Abby stepped inside. She wore a white T-shirt, purple shorts, and serious running shoes, although her shoes would be underutilized because we were going walking. As the first of my post-baby workouts, walking three nights a week, I intended to keep this walk sedate, a stroll really. Of course, Abby took her workouts very seriously. She plopped two sets of hand weights down on the kitchen counter. "And I was so envious of your A/C unit," she added with a smile.

I gestured to the weights. "I think pushing the stroller will be enough added weight for me," I said.

"Isn't Mitch going to watch her?"

"He's fixing the leak under our bathroom sink. I stepped on the throw rug in front of the sink this morning and it squished."

Abby wrinkled her nose. "Yuck. Big mess?"

"Not too bad. That's the good thing about hardwood

floors. We just had to mop up the water. I hope nothing else breaks. I'm tired of living the reality version of *This Old House*." I left the weights on the counter, put the happy face key chain in my shorts pocket, and hitched them up to retie the drawstring in the front. I was wearing Mitch's old blue workout shorts that had shrunk after years of washing. Mitch didn't give up his clothes easily. I'd practically had to arm wrestle these shorts from him. For a man so laid back about everything else, he was very particular about his clothes. "I've got to get some more shorts. Nothing fits anymore. My maternity clothes are too big and my regular clothes are too small."

I strapped Livvy in her stroller and we walked down the street to the park. The breeze was cool on my legs tonight and I almost wished I had brought a sweatshirt.

"I guess I'll just buy a few pairs of shorts because it feels like fall is almost here."

A few days ago a sweatshirt would have brought on heat exhaustion. But now I noticed the leaves on some of the trees were already fading to brown and gold. The wind whistled through the tops of the trees, whipping them back and forth. I tucked a blanket more snuggly around Livvy. I nodded to Joe's house as we passed. "I need to stop and take in their mail on the way back."

"Sure," Abby said as she pumped her weights.

Dark clouds sliding in from the north infused the day with an overcast tinge. I'd better wait on watering Joe's yard. It looked like it might rain. I made a mental note to find the box with our coats soon.

"Did you sub today?" I asked.

"Yeah."

I realized we were halfway around the park and Abby had said only a few words. "Abby, are you okay?" If she wasn't chatty, I figured Abby was coming down with something. She stopped, covered her eyes with her forearm, the hand weight pulling her hand down at an angle.

"Abby, are you crying? What's wrong?"

She dropped the weights to the ground and leaned over to wipe her eyes on the edge of her T-shirt. "I'm worried." She straightened up, blinking. "Jeff's been acting all strange. And then last night an investigator, a detective from the OSI, came to our house and asked a bunch of questions about Cass's death. It was awful."

"I'm sure it was routine stuff. They're probably talking to everyone." Even I could hear a hint of doubt in my tone. "What's the OSI?"

"If I understood it right, it's like the FBI for the Air Force. Office of Special Investigations."

Oh. Maybe not so routine. "What did they ask about?"

Abby swallowed and looked up at the gray sky. "About the barbeque and when Cass yelled at Jeff, and about bees. It was so weird."

"Okay. What did Jeff tell them?" This didn't sound good for Jeff.

"He said Cass saw the name of a deer lease on that paper and she was furious because she thought hunting was wrong. She wanted to know who else was in the lease with Jeff, so she could go after them, too." Abby took a deep breath. "Then they wanted to know where Jeff and I were every second of the barbeque."

"And you were together, right?"

"No. I followed Jeff outside. I tried to find out what was going on, but he was so mad he didn't want to talk at all. He was smoking! He'd bummed a cigarette off someone and was smoking."

"I didn't know he smoked."

"He did. A little in high school, to be cool, but then his uncle died of lung cancer and Jeff stopped. Scared Jeff to death. Or life, I guess. Anyway, I knew he needed to cool off, so I went back inside." Abby picked up the weights and we slowly resumed our walk.

So Jeff had been smoking and I'd read that smoke calmed bees down. It probably did the same thing to wasps. Great. A public argument, specialized knowledge of bees, and smoking. I bet the investigators were combing the trash cans around the squadron for wasps. How could there not be wasps with the food and trash from the barbeque? Now Jeff had motive, means, and opportunity. I hadn't wanted to even consider that Jeff might be involved in Cass's death. Jeff was a friend. He was nice. Despite his hefty build he was gentle and careful with Livvy when Abby insisted he hold Livvy "for practice."

But how well did I know Jeff, really? Weren't we all capable of doing shocking things to protect ourselves? The news was full of people saying they couldn't believe their nice, quiet, normal neighbor killed someone. The smidge of doubt grew into full-fledged suspicion.

Abby interrupted my thoughts. "Then the questions were all about bees. Did he have a hive? Did he have all the special equipment? Had he ordered any bees lately? They think he killed Cass. I mean, sure, his parents keep bees, but that doesn't mean he used them to hurt Cass."

"You know she died from an allergic reaction? To wasp stings. Joe told me."

"Right. Bees, wasps, what's the difference?" Abby's eyes were glassy. "The worst part is he's lying. I can tell."

She saw my shocked look and said, "Not about Cass. I know he didn't hurt her, but he's lying about something and it scares me."

Except for Mitch and the Security Police, no one knew I'd found the wasps. Even though no one from the Security Police had asked me to keep quiet, I felt compelled to keep the information to myself. I felt terrible. I wasn't about to tell Abby I'd set in motion an investigation that put Jeff in the role of prime suspect. I wanted to reassure her and tell her I knew Jeff didn't do it, but the words stuck in my throat. This was awful. I knew Abby needed to hear something encouraging. "Abby, I'm sorry. I'm sure they'll find whoever did it. Let me know if there's anything I can do."

Abby nodded, sniffed, and picked up the pace. "So you were asking about my class." She had a six-week assignment filling in for a teacher on maternity leave.

"It's going all right. Third grade. I don't think they get my jokes. But I need to go shopping, too. I need some pants. How about we go to the mall? Have you been there yet?"

"No. It's somewhere in the North Valley." We huffed and puffed, or more accurately Abby sailed around the park, while I huffed and puffed. She'd regained her quick stride and outwardly she looked fine, except for her puffy eyes and quiet manner. She wasn't her usually bubbly self. She said Jeff wasn't lying about murdering Cass, but she was so worried. Maybe she wasn't completely sure of Jeff's innocence, either.

I stopped at Joe's house, parked the stroller in the driveway with Abby, and ran the mail inside. The house had that closed-up-and-no-one's-home feeling. The only light came from the green glow of the DVD player clock. I glanced at it, but I couldn't read the time. A scratch distorted the numbers, reminding me of Cass talking about the moving damage. After I watered the ficus plant beside the TV cabinet, I did a quick check of the kitchen and bathroom. Then I locked up. Around the side of the house in the empty driveway, Abby cooed at Rex through the chain-link fence. Mitch had fed him and his bowl was half full.

"We should have taken him with us. I bet he would have loved it," Abby said. Rex sat at attention, his ears perked up, and his mouth open in a doggie grin. Or possibly snarl. I stopped short of the fence. Abby poked her fingers through a hole in the chain link and Rex licked them.

"Maybe next time." I wasn't sure I wanted Rex walking beside Livvy. I glanced around the backyard and garage, automatically. Something was off. I walked over to the single garage. The latch on the garage door dangled open. If there had been a lock, it was gone. Joe struck me as the type of person who would use a lock, but in his haze of grief maybe he forgot to put it on the door on his way out of town. I rubbed my arms. With my heart rate slowing, the crisp air chilled me.

I pushed back the old-fashioned folding door. It swung accordion-style back on its hinge. Musty, earthly smells filled the dim garage. Joe's car, a blue Civic Hatchback, squatted in the gloom. Boxes lined the walls. An assortment of garden tools, fertilizer, plant food, power tools, and antifreeze ranged over shelves near a lawn mower. A cool breeze fanned across my face.

"Abby, come look at this," I called.

An Everything in Its Place Tip for an Organized Move

Unpacking Strategies
- Focus on "high-use" rooms, like bathrooms and bedrooms. Bathrooms are usually small rooms with limited items to unpack, so you can finish the job quickly and have a sense of accomplishment in the midst of disarray.
- If you've got helpers, let several people work on the kitchen, the most time-consuming room to unpack.
- Kennel pets for a few days after arrival so you can focus on unpacking.
- Setting up appliances can be time-consuming. Concentrate on connecting the washer, dryer, and refrigerator first. Leave the DVD and computer for later.
- As you unpack, put things close to where you will use them. Store pans by the stove, plates and glasses near the dishwasher, spices and measuring cups with the mixing bowls.
- Eliminate the debris of moving, the boxes and paper, as you unpack. Flatten boxes and put them in the garage, an extra room, or the attic until the moving company returns to pick them up. Or if you've moved yourself and don't want to keep the boxes, check for a recycling center in the Yellow Pages. It may even pick up recyclables like cardboard.

Chapter Nine

I crossed the garage to examine the jagged hole in the windowpane above the shards of glass scattered over the floor and the boxes. The boxes looked odd, too. Most gaped open with clothes trailing down their sides like batter dripping down the side of a mixing bowl. A few were nearly empty with books or dishes stacked around them.

Abby entered the garage. She'd opened the gate and Rex pushed in front of her and scurried around, nose to the cement, sniffing and whining. "Wow, looks like someone broke in," Abby said.

"I know. Do you think anything is gone?" I gestured to the lawn mower and power tools.

"Doesn't look like it, but you'll have to call Joe, won't you?"

"And the police, too." Livvy picked that moment to

begin crying. She had decided it was time for her last feeding. She was like a parking meter, fine until the time expired and then that was it. Nothing else happened until she was fed.

By the time I fed Livvy and got her to bed, Mitch had shown the police the garage and tracked down a number for Joe. Mitch dropped into our favorite overstuffed chair and propped his feet up on the double ottoman.

"Was anything stolen?" I called from the kitchen. Mitch had walked around the garage, telling Joe what he saw.

"Right now, the only things he could say for sure were a cordless drill and a socket set. The police said they've had a lot of break-ins lately. Burglars like detached garages. Rex probably scared them away before they got much."

"Do you realize we've moved into a neighborhood with garage break-ins and possibly, a drug house?" I said as I filled my extra-large cup with water. "Not to mention practically your whole squadron right on our doorstep." Ice cubes crackled as I dropped them in the water. "Someone went through everything. That would take time." I snapped the lid into place and guzzled the cool water while I walked to the living room. I plunked down on the ottoman and untied my shoes. "Did you tell the police I saw someone drive away without lights last night?"

Mitch nodded and took a drink of my water. "They'll call you if they need anything else. But I don't think we'll hear from them. I got the impression that it was no big deal."

"Yeah, I read an article in the paper last week. Detached garages are easy targets. Oh. With all the commotion, I almost forgot. I think Jeff is a suspect." I summarized what Abby had told me on our walk.

"That's stupid. Jeff can't be involved," Mitch said, dismissively.

I pushed the straw around the cup. "You really think so?"

Mitch studied me for a long moment. "No. I know it. You don't go through all the"—he paused, amended what he was about to say with a glance at Livvy's door—"crap at the Academy for years and not get to know someone. I know Jeff and he couldn't have done anything to hurt Cass."

I kicked off my shoes and said, "But don't you think it's—" I broke off when I looked at his face. It had a tight, angry look.

"You think he did it, don't you? How can you doubt him?"

"How can I not? Everything says he could have done it. He's experienced with bees and could probably handle wasps, he was smoking, there were probably wasps at the squad, and he was alone right before Cass left the squad. He had time to trap some wasps in a cup and put it in her van. She didn't lock it."

"I can't believe this. You really think he did it?" Mitch stood up and paced the edge of the oriental rug.

"I don't want to believe it. I *hope* he *didn't*. How can you be so sure he didn't?"

"Because he's my friend and at times like this you don't doubt your friends. You support them." Mitch stalked off to the bathroom. I collapsed back onto the ottoman. Oh, man. I hadn't expected Mitch to be so defensive. A few minutes later I heard the shower.

When the water stopped flowing, I got up and walked down the hall. Mitch had left the bathroom door open a slit. I pushed the door open another inch and humid air oozed into the hall. Mitch, his towel wrapped around his waist, jerked the shower curtain into place.

"Mitch, you know I like Jeff. I don't *want* to think these things about him."

I couldn't see his face, but his stiff shoulders relaxed. "I know."

We settled into an uneasy truce. We didn't talk about Jeff, or really anything else for the rest of the night. The silence between us seemed like a tangible thickness. It weighed us down and separated us into our own quiet worlds.

"Ellie, where's the baby Tylenol?"

"What?" I pushed myself up on one elbow and rubbed the sleep out of the corners of my eyes.

"Where's the Tylenol?" Mitch repeated. His question penetrated my fuzzy brain. Livvy. Mitch was holding her, rubbing her back. I had fed her at two A.M. and she had gone right back to sleep. In fact, she'd been sleeping, except for a few sneezes. When I heard her crying a few minutes ago I had shaken Mitch's shoulder and said, "Your turn." I must have dropped right back to sleep. A hard, deep sleep because I felt like I had been sleeping for two hours instead of ten minutes.

I stumbled into the hall bathroom, our only bathroom. Most of the older homes in this area only had one bath unless someone had updated the house and added another. I opened the medicine cabinet and looked through it by the glow of the nightlight.

Mitch came in with Livvy and I felt her forehead. It was warm and her big blue eyes shined. I resumed my search through the medicine cabinet, wide awake now. If Mitch said she had a fever, I knew she did. I was the worry wart. He was the relax-don't-worry-about-it one in our family.

"I know we had some before we moved. But I don't remember unpacking it," I said. "I'd better go to the store and get some Tylenol. It might help."

Mitch nodded and went back to doing the baby bounce, a springy step to keep Livvy from crying. I yanked on jeans and a sweatshirt because it would be cool. Then I brushed my hair and left with one side flattened against my head and wrinkle marks from my pillow across my cheek.

I tossed my sleek black Kate Spade purse wallet into the Cherokee and backed out of our driveway. At least I had a doctor's appointment for Livvy in the morning. We could find out what she had and get her some medicine if she needed it. I paused, trying to remember which grocery stores were open twenty-four hours. To the right was Rim Rock Road, a quick route downtown. Something would be open there, but I didn't really want to go downtown at almost three in the morning. To the left was Birch, the next main street that led to a small shopping center with a Copeland's grocery store, but I didn't know if it stayed open all night.

A movement down Nineteenth caught my eye. A white car without lights eased out of the driveway next to Joe's house. I waited until it was at the corner and then I turned left and followed it. At Birch, I turned left just as the car had done. Well, it was the same direction as Copeland's, I reasoned with myself. I'd just see where it was going for a little way.

I cruised through the eerie, still streets. Widely spaced streetlights flickered over the car. At Sixteenth, I followed the white car into the large parking lot.

Copeland's squatted at one end of the strip mall,

with LaMont's, a department store, at the other. In between were a string of smaller shops, a pack and mail place, a beauty shop, a Chinese restaurant, a barbershop, and a dog groomer. The white car parked under a street light at the farthest end of the lot. I slid into one of the open slots in the front row and watched the car in my rearview mirror.

A woman got out of the car. She slipped a green apron over her head, wrapped the strings around her slender waist, and tied them at her back as she walked inside the store.

Automatically, I hooked the long strap of the purse wallet over my shoulder while I stared at the advertised specials posted on the bright windows. It couldn't have been her. Could it? I saw my eyebrows in the rearview mirror drawn together in a frown. It looked like Friona. But the bored newlywed I had talked to at the squadron barbeque wouldn't be working at Copeland's. All the employees wore green aprons. At the squadron, Friona had looked like a model with her long willowy body, and her sullen expression showed she was clearly bored. I couldn't picture her working nights at a grocery store.

I roamed up and down three aisles of glossy industrial-size floor tiles until I found the children's medicine. I bought two packages and checked out without seeing anyone who looked like Friona.

"Your receipt," the checker called. I turned back, took the receipt, and caught a glimpse of a trim, dark-haired young woman walking to the customer service center, where you could buy stamps or lottery tickets. She looked like Friona. She didn't notice me. I'd have to ask Abby where Friona lived. It was too strange. I could picture Friona working in an upscale trendy restaurant as a hostess, but at ordinary Copeland's? At three in the morning? No way.

An Everything in Its Place Tip for an Organized Move

Garage Solution
- Invest in heavy-duty plastic shelves for the garage. You can set up and break down these shelves quickly without any tools, so you can arrange items in your garage as soon as you unpack them. Then, when it's time to move again, your storage solutions will go with you.

Chapter Ten

Northwest Family Health was carved into the side of one of the hills that formed Black Rock Hill, the name of the neighborhood that had grown up over the large rock outcroppings that rimmed the southern side of Vernon. With its basement submerged in the rock, the rest of the red brick building stair-stepped up the hill.

I saw an open slot in the parking lot and twisted the steering wheel to slide into it, but a black Mustang cut me off. It barely squeaked past my front bumper and whipped into the opening. The Mustang had vanity plates that read AFPILOT. A short man hopped out of the car and trotted past me as I made another circuit of the lot. That's how pilots get a reputation for being arrogant, I groused. Finally, I found an empty slot and parked.

I filled out the paperwork and found Urgent Care in the basement. The lack of windows and dim lighting gave the waiting area a gloomy atmosphere. After checking in at the counter shared between Urgent Care and Lab/X-ray, I sat down on one of the cheap, streamlined couches. There were three clinics on this floor and they shared the same waiting area. I vacantly looked across at the Family Practice area as I rocked Livvy's blanket-covered car seat with my toe. Livvy was worn out. She had slept fitfully, either on Mitch's shoulder or mine, until five in the morning. Then she had slept in her bed from sheer exhaustion.

I watched the clock creep around from 10:15 to 10:30. This approach to health care was different from the base hospital, where we had been seen before moving to Vernon. At the base hospital the idea, as far as I could tell, was move patients in and out as quickly as possible. I'd never had to wait long. In fact, the appointment desk usually told you to arrive fifteen minutes early, so they could get your vital signs and get your paperwork done. Livvy was sleeping, so I'd give them a few more minutes before I checked on our appointment.

A man brushed past the car seat and dropped onto the far end of the couch across from me, the guy who'd beat me to the first parking space. He picked up a magazine, flicked through it, tossed it back on the table, then rattled a newspaper as he scanned the headlines. He lobbed the paper onto the table and leaned back against the cushions, one foot bouncing up and down. He looked familiar. I went through faces I'd met recently, trying to place him. Watching him made me feel more tired. I must have looked like I was moving underwater compared to his fidgety energy. After he checked his watch, he jiggled his change. I was still rocking the car seat with my toe. My eyes drooped as I focused on the rhythmic movement of the car seat.

"Nick Town," snapped a voice beside me and I nearly fell off the couch. The man seated across from me jumped up and followed the nurse through the door marked Lab/X-ray. The door on the other side of the counter opened and a nurse called Livvy's name. I followed the nurse through a maze of twisting corridors to a small examining room. I felt like I needed bread crumbs to sprinkle behind me.

After a few minutes, Dr. Stig arrived. The nurse's initial poking and prodding had awoken Livvy and she didn't like the doctor's exam much better.

"Looks like she has an ear infection." Dr. Stig whipped out a pad and scrawled a prescription. He was young with fair hair and pale skin. He wasn't wearing a white coat, just khakis and a knit shirt. He looked like he was ready to hit the golf course.

He handed me the slip of paper. "Here's an antibiotic for her. Bring her in next week for a recheck. Everyone should be getting more sleep in a day or two." He smiled and told me to give her Tylenol for the pain and was out the door before I could get Livvy back in her car seat.

With the help of a nurse, I found my way back to the waiting area, where I scheduled an appointment for the next Friday. As I signed my check for my copayment, a nurse hurried over from behind the stacks of medical records and said to the nurse who was waiting for my check, "Go on. I'll finish this. There he is." The newly arrived nurse, whose name tag read YVONNE, made shooing motions with her hands. The other nurse giggled, flicked her blond ponytail, and went to the other end of the counter.

I waited for my receipt, bouncing the handle of the car seat in the crook of my elbow. The fidgety man from the waiting room came out the door and pulled out his wallet. He wasn't one of our new neighbors.

Ponytail smiled and leaned over the counter. He shifted down to a lower gear and took quite a bit of time to hand over his money and get his appointment card.

"Good to see you again. Are the shots helping?" Ponytail held on to the appointment card, turning it over and over in her hands.

"Yeah, they seem to." He smiled, pulled out his keys, and flicked them back and forth.

"Have you been flying lately?" Ponytail asked, reluctantly handing over the card. I took my card, too, and looked at the man again. His car keys glittered in the low light. Then I had it. I'd met him on the way to the car at the barbeque. He had been talking to Mitch.

I'd missed his reply to Ponytail's question.

"See you next week," he said and jogged up the stairs.

Ponytail dropped his file in a bin. "Isn't he cute?"

"Too short for me." Yvonne, who was probably close to six feet tall, tossed Livvy's paperwork into the same bin.

"I thought you only saw dependents from the base," I said. Mitch might rather see a doctor off-base. But as soon as I asked the question I knew the answer. No way would the Air Force allow civilians to treat pilots. The Air Force would be out of the loop.

"Yes, just dependents. Unless we get a special referral from the base for something they don't handle. Usually specialty things," Yvonne replied. Nick must have been referred off-base for something, like the time Mitch pulled a ligament in his foot and had to see a physical therapist. But Nick looked healthy as a horse, a jittery thoroughbred racehorse.

I set the car seat on the table and scooted into the plastic booth with a sigh. My few hours of sleep were running out and I felt like I could put my head down on the table and sleep for hours. Mitch set down the tray with our sub sandwiches and drinks. The restaurant, Robin Hood's, in the Base Exchange was almost deserted. One-thirty was late for lunch around the base; most people ate at eleven-thirty, since they started work at seven-thirty. As we ate, I filled Mitch in on the doctor's visit and my trip to the base pharmacy.

Then he opened a shopping bag I hadn't noticed and pulled out a kid-size tennis racket. "I went shopping while I waited."

"Mitch, she won't play tennis for years. She's got to walk first."

"She can work on her grip."

Mitch can be almost as stubborn as I can, so I changed the subject. "So how's mission planning going?" I asked. Mitch had a flight the next day.

"We finished this morning. We're lead in a two-ship." He meant he was flying the lead plane. I could tell he was glad to have a flight. The work in the safety office was fine with him, but he'd fly every day if he could. Of course, everyone else in the squad felt the same way.

"Anything else going on?"

"Detectives from OSI are talking to everyone about Cass and the barbeque."

"Really?" Our truce held, mostly because we didn't talk about Jeff's possible involvement in Cass's death. I phrased my next questions carefully. "So they do think someone put the wasps there intentionally?"

"Who knows what they think? They're asking questions, not answering them."

"Did they talk to you?" I asked.

Mitch nodded. "Well, what did they ask about?" I prodded. Men can be so big-picture. I wanted the details and Mitch thought he'd covered everything with his blanket statement.

"About the barbeque. Who was in the parking lot, which was probably just about everyone. Did anyone dislike Cass?"

"What did you tell them?"

"I couldn't tell them much. We've only been here a few weeks."

"Did you tell them about the argument Jeff and Cass had?"

"They already knew. I told them it was no big deal. Why are you so interested?" He wadded up his napkin and threw it on the tray. His eyes challenged me.

I sipped my Diet Coke. "I don't know," I said slowly. "I guess because I found Cass and I found the wasps. I feel a little guilty, too, about washing and vacuuming the van. What if I destroyed evidence?" I set my cup back down and pushed my plate away. "I don't want whoever did this to get away with it." And most of all, I knew Jeff was a suspect and I'd started the whole thing, but I kept silent about that issue. I felt miserable. I hated being so guarded and careful in what I said to Mitch, but I didn't say anything. I knew how the whole conversation would go. I knew Mitch would defend Jeff and be hurt that I suspected Jeff.

"Ellie." Mitch hunched over the table, gripped my hand. "I know finding her was awful, but you're not responsible for making sure her killer doesn't get away with it, even if you did wash and vacuum the van. You were trying to help Joe. The police and the medical examiner thought it was a natural death, otherwise they'd have checked the van out better. You shouldn't feel guilty. If it weren't for you, there'd be a person out there who got away with murder." Mitch squeezed my hand, then said, "That worries me. Keep your distance from this thing, okay?"

"Sure," I said and smiled, but inside I knew it was a halfhearted promise.

Mitch studied my face without saying anything and then stood to carry the tray to the trash bin. That's the problem with being close to your husband. He knows when you're lying. But he knows how hardheaded I am, too, so I guess he decided not to try to press any more promises out of me. At least, not right then, anyway.

I hooked my elbow through Livvy's car seat handle, tucked my wallet purse into the diaper bag, and slung it over my shoulder. As I walked down the narrow aisle of tables, I noticed a familiar face from the squadron's orderly room, Airman Tessa Jones. Mitch was talking to a friend in the restaurant line, so I paused and said, "Tessa, how are you?"

Tessa put down her book. "Oh, you've got Livvy!" The book's cover had a bare-chested man embracing a woman in a nightgown. The background, a field of pink flowers, contrasted with Tessa's camouflage uniform, called Battle Dress Uniform, or BDUs. People's reading choices always surprised me. She smiled at Livvy. Tessa's white teeth shown brightly against her dark chocolate–colored skin as she said, "She's still gorgeous."

When we first arrived in Vernon we stayed in Lodging on base in a hotel room until our boxes were delivered. I could only spend so many hours in a hotel room watching TV and reading the local paper. It was too hot to do anything outside, so after I wandered around the Base Exchange and checked our mail at the post office, I'd head over to the squad where Mitch was already working. Tessa was Livvy's biggest fan in the squad.

"Want to hold her?" I asked.

"Nah. You've got her all buckled in. Leave her. I'll hold her next time you come by the squad. I haven't seen much of you lately."

"I've been unpacking."

"But you were at the barbeque. Can you believe that?" Tessa's soft southern drawl stopped abruptly. "Oh, I forgot. You . . ."

"Yeah. I found her."

Tessa's face turned sympathetic. "I shouldn't have said anything. I'm sorry."

"It's okay. Don't worry about it."

"It's just that everyone is talking about Cass nonstop. Especially with the questioning going on." Tessa shook her head. "Couldn't get any work done when she was alive and can't get any work done with her gone, either."

"What?" I slid into the chair across from her and put the car seat on the floor.

"Well, I don't want to speak ill of the dead or anything, but that woman was at the squadron all the time. Constantly in and out of the orderly room, looking for Joe or for Colonel Briman. She always had some 'issue' to discuss with Briman, but I don't know why she had to discuss everything draped over his desk. Like she was his top priority." Tessa usually had a stack of forms for

Briman to sign on her desk. I'm sure Tessa thought the forms took priority over Cass. "But she treated all the guys that way. Like on Friday. I saw her on my way to the barbeque. There she was practically glued to Captain McCarter, laughing and flirting."

So, Cass was snuggling up to Mr. Wandering Hands. "And I bet he didn't discourage her."

Tessa shook her head. "He certainly wasn't running the other way." Tessa leaned toward me. "Colonel Briman's had several complaints about Captain McCarter being too friendly to the ladies, if you know what I mean."

"I know exactly what you mean. What's going to happen?"

"Nothing, for now. No one wants to put anything in writing."

I asked, "Do you think there was anything going on between Cass and Brent?"

Tessa stirred the chicken noodle soup in her bread bowl before she answered. "You know, I don't think there was. I told that closed-mouthed detective that, too. I think she wanted, maybe needed, the attention. She had to have every man in the vicinity wrapped around her little finger. She was a flirt, but I don't think it went any deeper."

Mitch came over, said hello to Tessa, and then we left. As we stepped into the parking lot, I wondered if Cass had died because she was a tease. Or maybe she did have an affair.

"I'd better go. Got a meeting in ten minutes," Mitch said. He kissed me good-bye and headed for his car on the other side of the parking lot. I trudged down the row to the Cherokee. In the slot next to the Cherokee, a man sat on the open tailgate of his small white pickup truck, pulling on boots.

"Hi, Jeff." I waved and closed the last few steps.

"Hey, Ellie. Is Mitch around?" I'd wondered what Jeff's attitude would be when I saw him. Would he be depressed or angry? But his tone and open smile were so, well, normal that I found myself talking to him without feeling awkward. He patted Livvy's foot and scanned the parking lot for Mitch.

I said easily, "No. He's gone back to the squad."

Jeff pulled the laces tight on the last boot, a pale brown desert camo boot. I nodded at the boots. "Left over from your last deployment to Iraq?"

He yanked the laces into a tight bow, then tucked them inside the top of the boot. "Yeah." He hopped off the tailgate. Without his weight, the pickup rose several inches. "I'm going scouting. Best use of these dang boots, yet."

"Oh. Scouting. Like for a place to hunt?" Abby had explained that scouting out good hunting locations and obtaining the owner's permission to hunt on the land could take as much, or more, time than the actual hunting.

"Yep." Jeff stowed his shiny black boots that went with his flight suit in the bed of the pickup and grabbed a plastic bag with the AAFES logo, the company that ran the Base Exchange. He slammed the tailgate closed.

"I thought you were in a hunting lease." He eyed me for a second before he stripped the plastic bag off of a grid map of Eastern Washington.

"Abby told me," I explained.

Jeff smiled, his eyes crinkling and the second of tension I'd felt dispersed. "Yeah. Abby tells everyone everything. I'm in a deer lease. Today, I'm looking for a place to hunt ducks."

"Oh. So who else is in the lease with you?" To keep

the relaxed atmosphere, I quickly added, "Is there room for Mitch?"

"Sorry. We're full up. Got me, Tommy, and two other local guys. They won't take anyone else, but maybe someone will drop out and Mitch can join next year."

"Okay. I'll tell him. Is it close?"

"North of town. About an hour up 247," Jeff said, naming a state highway. "Okay, I'll let you go. Good to see you." He patted Livvy's foot again and got in his pickup.

I drove home from the base on automatic pilot. So Jeff really was in a hunting lease and I bet the guys at the squad would back him up. And his disposition was sunny, upbeat. He looked like his biggest worry was finding a pond full of unsuspecting ducks. I should have felt better after seeing how relaxed he was. He wasn't worried about a murder charge. But shouldn't he have looked a little worried? If detectives were asking questions about me, I'd be a nervous wreck. Of course, he didn't do it. Not Jeff.

I hoped he didn't do it. Okay, don't think about that. Who else could it be? Cass caused a lot of trouble. She was fired up about some housing development and had it out with Diana at the spouse coffee. But that was underway. Diana was selling lots and people were already building. Not much Cass could do there. Cass was spreading rumors about Gwen, and Cass was snuggling up to Brent.

I turned the corner at our street and saw Rex, lounging in the sun on our concrete driveway. He flipped from his side to his feet, then stretched, first his front legs, then his back legs. Finally, he trotted over to my car door, languidly wagging his tail.

"What are you doing out of the backyard?" I asked Rex

as I climbed out of the Cherokee. Mabel rounded the corner. She quickly strode along in a black shirt paired with black, red, and tan plaid pants.

"He's been there for about an hour." Mabel patted her shiny forehead with a tissue. "I saw him jump the fence when I started my walk. He's been very well behaved. Just sunning himself."

"But how did he get out of the Vincents' backyard? Does he get out a lot?"

"Oh, no. I've never seen him out before,"

I bet if Rex had gotten out before Mabel would have seen him.

Mabel continued, "He's really quite clever. Used that tree beside the fence with the low-forked trunk. He jumped on it and boosted himself over the fence." She tucked the tissue in her waistband and reached down to scratch Rex's ears.

"Why would he want out now?"

"Probably lonely." Rex thumped his tail. "Well, I've got to get on the Nordic Track. Good luck." She patted my shoulder. Livvy realized the Cherokee's rocking motion had stopped and started crying.

"I don't need this today," I muttered to Rex.

An Everything in Its Place Tip for an Organized Move

Hand carry essential paperwork. If you're driving to your new home, consider purchasing a small safe with a lock to store documents like:

- Financial records
- Marriage and birth certificates
- Shot records

Chapter
Eleven

Even though the North Country Mall was located in the relatively flat and treeless North Valley of Vernon, which had been cleared for the development of tract housing and strip malls, the interior of the North Country Mall combined the atmosphere of a log cabin and a northwest forest. Rough bark lined the walls between the shop entrances; planters with lofty trees stretched toward the second-story skylights and ivy twisting up their trunks. The centerpiece of the mall was the two-story waterfall cascading from the edge of the food court on the top floor. "So where is Rex now?" Abby asked as she took another bite of pepperoni pizza.

"In our backyard." I raised my voice over the rush of water beside our table near the waterfall. Last night Rex had decided he was tired of being by himself in the Vincents' backyard. "Mitch fed him and we walked him around the park before we went home. He barked and whined for two straight hours. We finally gave in around nine o'clock. I figured the neighbors would call the pound if the noise went on much longer. He slept in the kitchen last night."

"I bet Mitch is happy."

"Ecstatic." I took a bite of pizza crust. "Mitch loves having a dog. Now he'll want to get one as soon as Joe is back." I sighed and wiped my greasy fingers on a paper napkin, hoping Rex wasn't licking Livvy's toys or Livvy. Maybe Rex was even outside. No, as soon as Abby had called this morning Mitch said, "Go on. A break will be good for you." He had shooed me out the door and I'm sure he opened it wide for Rex as soon as I turned the corner. I decided not to think about it.

"When is Joe coming back?" Abby asked.

"We're not sure. He's staying at least until the end of this week. Mitch talked to him last time and said he sounded vague even about that. I'm sure he'll call us."

Abby's face still had that closed look and dark circles under her eyes indicated she wasn't sleeping well. As I opened my mouth to ask how she was doing, she said, "Hey, isn't her husband in the squadron?" Abby nodded to a woman weaving her way through the tables.

"That's Friona." She set her drink down a few tables away from us, then piled four shopping bags on one chair and flung a hanging bag over the pile. The hanging bag, stuffed with clothes, looked like a body bag. It slid to the floor.

"Oh, I meant to tell you I thought I saw her at Copeland's the night Livvy got sick. She was wearing one of those green aprons like she worked there." Friona picked up the bag by the hangers, flung it across another chair, and then sat down in the third chair.

Friona's black jeans emphasized her long legs and
her black short-sleeved turtleneck showed off the rest of
her figure. Today her dark hair hung thick, straight,
and shiny to her shoulders. With a pair of dark sunglasses, which she probably had in her oversized black
bag, she would look like a movie star or model dressing
down to elude the paparazzi. She took a drink of her
soda, then unzipped one ankle-length boot, kicked it
off, and rubbed her instep.

"It must have been someone else," Abby said.

"I know. It doesn't look like she spends her working
hours asking if it will be paper or plastic."

We finished our lunch and stopped at Friona's table
to say hello. When she recognized us, she put her boot
back on, slid the zipper closed, and stood up in one
smooth motion. "New boots. I had a wicked cramp."
She edged over to the pile of packages.

Abby smiled. "I know exactly how you feel. I love to
buy shoes, but I hate breaking them in. We're on our
way to the parking lot. If your car is on the other side of
the mall, we could give you a ride."

"No." Friona snatched the bags and smiled a shallow
smile to cover her sharp tone. "Nice of you, but I've got
more shopping." She tucked her hand with the shopping bags behind her and hooked the hanging bag over
her shoulder, her elbow extended out.

She edged away. "Bye." She hurried out of the food
court.

"She didn't want to spend an extra minute with us,"
Abby said as we stepped on the escalator.

"She told me she shops, but wow, she had a lot of
bags."

"Must have been a sale."

"You know, I think she lives on your street," Abby said

as she swung open the heavy glass door to the parking lot. "I talked to her and her husband when I was out on a run.

He was mowing the yard while she sat on the porch."

"My street? Are you sure?"

"Yes. Across the street from you. Next door to Cass and Joe."

I hooked my keys on the key hanger inside the kitchen door. "Hello?" I called softly in case Livvy was sleeping, but the house felt empty.

I found a note beside the phone. "Gone for a walk. Back soon." The hardwood floor creaked as I walked through the quiet house. I thumped down into our overstuffed chair and wondered what to do with myself, looking at the disarray of folded onesies on the couch and Livvy's favorite rattle dropped under her bouncy chair. Fold clothes? Take a bubble bath? Read? Start supper? I discarded the ideas as quickly as they came. I wondered where Mitch had taken Livvy for a walk. Probably to the park, but if I left now I might miss them. We walked several different routes to the park and back. I'd stay here and wait.

I realized I was anxious to see them, especially Livvy. I laughed at myself. Here I was with nothing to do and I was alone, a state I missed and longed for frequently now that Livvy dominated so much of my days, and nights for that matter. But now that I was alone and it was quiet, I was wondering where Mitch and Livvy were and if I could catch up with them. I shook my head at myself. I wanted something, and then when I got it I wanted something else.

I emptied my shopping bags on the ottoman, a pitifully small haul compared to Friona's purchases. Fall was on the way, so the stores were well into their winter clothes with coats, wool, and flannel dominating the displays. I had found one pair of shorts on a clearance rack and bought them. Then I paid way too much for the jeans, but I would need something when the weather turned cold. And everyone kept assuring me that it would be a long winter. Like I really wanted to dwell on those thoughts. I'd never liked driving on ice.

I found a pair of scissors and cut off the price tags on the clothes. Then I pulled out the purse I'd found at a kiosk in the mall. Patchwork-like squares of tapestry fabric mixed with denim covered the tote bag. A fuzzy black trim edged the top of the bag. It was just the thing to add some pizzazz to my sedate mommy wardrobe of jeans, shirts, and sweaters. I added it to the pile of clothes on the ottoman, then I leaned back and put my feet up. I'd do nothing. I gazed out the window across Ed and Mabel's perfect lawn and studied the Vincents' house. I needed to pick up their paper and take in the mail today. I wondered if the investigators would ever ask us for a key to the Vincents' house to check it out.

My eyelids were drooping when a white car slowed and pulled into the driveway next door to the Vincents'. I sat up and watched a slim woman with long dark hair get out of the driver's seat. It was Friona. She opened the trunk, pulled out her bags, and dragged them inside. So it had been Friona I'd seen going to Copeland's that night. I looked from Friona's house to the Vincents' house. Did Cass notice Friona leaving at night? Friona drove without lights, perhaps because she didn't want to be seen. I got that prickly feeling along the back of my neck. Cass's death and Friona's stealthy nighttime drives probably had nothing in common.

But then I remembered what had teased at the edge of my thoughts when Mitch said a spouse might be involved in Cass's death. Friona had red lumpy marks on her arm at the barbeque, like bug bites or stings.

I'd go take in the mail for the Vincents' and see if I ran into her again.

I moved the hose and turned on the water in the front yard before I unlocked the Vincents' front door. I tossed the newspaper onto the counter beside the growing mound of mail and rolls of newspapers encased in plastic covers. I glanced in the bedrooms, checked the bathroom quickly for leaks, and stuck my finger into the soil of a few potted plants. They were still moist, so I twisted the dowel to open the living room miniblinds. It was overcast and they needed as much light as they could get.

Something seemed off, different. I tilted my head sideways and thought as I retraced my steps through the house. I stopped at the pink bedroom. The closet door was open. It must have caught my eye when I checked the bathroom. I knew that closet door had been shut the last time I checked the house, because I remembered noticing the pastel poster of a ballet dancer on the door. Now the door was open. The eyelet bedspread and pink lamp on the nightstand were for Cass's daughters who visited a few times a year. Cass put in a lot of work to make their room special. During the rest of the year wouldn't it remind her everyday that her daughters weren't with her?

I walked around the end of the bed and closed the closet door. Everything else looked fine. I'd have to remember to ask Mitch if he opened it when he brought in the mail yesterday. As I stepped onto the porch, Mitch turned the corner down the street and waved. He pushed the stroller with Rex bouncing around him and the stroller like a basketball. I locked the front door and went to meet them.

I plunged the pan into the warm soapy water in the kitchen sink. I could hear Mitch talking to Livvy down the hall as he changed her diaper and dressed her. Livvy still had a runny nose, so we had opted for French toast, eggs, and bacon instead of church hunting this weekend. I dried the skillet and wondered if we would be able to get a dishwasher soon. I loved the charm of the older homes, but they lacked what I considered basic amenities.

When I put away the orange juice and butter, I saw Livvy's antibiotic in the refrigerator. I measured out her dose, using the syringe from the pharmacy. A lot of neat things had come out since I was a kid, like pacifier holders that clip on to the baby's clothes and small plastic boxes for carrying wipes in my diaper bag. How did my parents get along without this stuff?

Mitch was changing the liner in Livvy's diaper pail while Livvy kicked her feet and waved her arms on the changing table at Mitch's elbow. She took her medicine and then scrunched up her face. "Didn't taste good?" I said to her.

I wiped the dribble of pink off her chin and said to Mitch, "I'm taking her back on Friday, so they can recheck her ears. I saw someone, Nick Town, I think, in the waiting room when I took her in last week."

"You mean Nick Townsend?" Mitch said as he looked through Livvy's clothes hanging on miniature hangers in her closet. He pulled out a denim jumper and pink top with flowers embroidered around the collar. He took a pair of orange socks out of her sock drawer and changed her out of her sleeper. I took the orange socks back and got out a pair of pink socks. "Yeah, I guess so. I must have misunderstood the name. Short, restless guy?"

Mitch smiled. "That's Nick."

"I wonder why he's going downtown? Think he's seeing a specialist?"

"Only if it's something we don't have on base," Mitch said as he matched up the snaps on the jumper. "Maybe he got hurt worse than he let on." He picked up Livvy, tucking her up on his shoulder so she could see around the room. Her fuzzy head bobbed as she gripped his shoulder. "A few weeks ago he got into a fight at some bar. A guy said something to him and he flew at the guy."

"Isn't Nick kind of small to be getting into barroom brawls?" I asked as I replaced the hanger in Livvy's closet.

"Tommy was there and he said Nick more than made up for his size. Said he looked like a terrier attacking the postman. But Nick knocked the guy out."

"But don't they have a lab and X-rays on base?"

"Sure," Mitch said and led the way out of Livvy's room. Before I could say anything else, the phone rang and I went to get the cordless phone from the kitchen.

"Ellie. Glad I caught you. Jill Briman."

I said hello, while searching my mind for any friends named Jill. Then my brain clicked on: squadron commander's wife. I might have to start drinking coffee if my brain refused to work more quickly than this.

"The planning meeting is tomorrow night."

Planning meeting? "Well," I paused, trying to buy

some time. Don't sound stupid to the squadron commander's wife if you can help it.

Jill zeroed in on my silence. "Cass didn't tell you, did she?" Her tone made it a statement, not a question. "She was always so excited and got people involved, but she wasn't a detail person." Jill sighed with exasperation. Then seeming to realize that she sounded very critical of someone recently deceased, she added, "Of course, what happened is such a shame."

I murmured an agreement while checking my wall calendar. Monday's square was blank.

"Well," Jill said briskly. With a dribble of solemnity for an untimely death out of the way, she was all business now. "I still have the sign-up sheets for the garage sale volunteers." Her tone implied it was a good thing she had kept them instead of giving them to Cass. "We'll need to discuss publicity, setup, the bank deposit, and cleanup. Seven o'clock at my house all right with you?"

I thought about Livvy's feeding schedule. "How about six? But I thought we were postponing the garage sale." It seemed like the appropriate thing to do. And I hadn't given it much thought or planning.

"A lot of people have that impression. That's why we need to get right on it. We've got less than two weeks left. If we wait any longer, it will be too cold. Then we'll have to wait until spring."

I suppressed a sigh. It seemed we were having a garage sale whether anyone wanted to or not.

"I'll be there at six and I'll bring Abby with me. She'll be a big help." She'd better be since she got me into this volunteer job in the first place. I pushed the button to disconnect from Jill's call, intending to call Abby and tell her she had an appointment tomorrow night, but the phone rang again before I could dial.

"Hi, honey." The voice that came over the line had just a hint of a Texas drawl.

"Hi, Mom."

"How's Livvy?" I smiled. There had been a definite change in the pecking order since Livvy's birth.

"She's doing better. Getting over an ear infection," I said as I rinsed the tiny syringe and dried it on a paper towel.

"Oh, no! You should have called us. Was it bad?"

I skipped over the feeling of slight irritation I felt when she said I should have called. They were too far away to do anything but worry and sympathize. I thought we had worked out this calling-with-information business when I got married. They didn't expect us to call with every bit of news, even trivia in our lives, and we didn't hear from them that often either. But it appeared that things had indeed changed since Livvy's arrival.

Then I felt guilty for even feeling irritated. It was her first grandchild and she wanted to know everything. "We were only up one night and then we got her on some antibiotics." I gave Mom the full story of our marathon night and doctor's visit to make up for not calling her. Rex whined from outside the kitchen door. He knew we were finished eating and wanted inside.

When Mom was sure Livvy was on the road to recovery, she turned the conversation. "Well, we were just sitting here on the deck reading the paper." I could picture them at the glass-topped table under the tall cottonwood tree with the paper anchored with their thick cups of coffee. The climate in their part of Texas would, for the most part, stay warm for quite a bit longer, maybe even into November. Not like here. I opened the door just wide enough to let Rex inside. Somehow he'd become an inside dog. Rex trotted over to his basket and curled up, watching me. His eyes seemed to be saying, "See, I can be a good boy."

I shut the door on the wind and low clouds skimming across the treetops. The thought of coffee or breakfast outside made me shiver. But I could picture Dad reading the front page of the newspaper with the warmth of the sun slanting in through the tall limbs of the cottonwood. Then he would find the History Channel listings in the TV guide. Mom would read the travel section, the book reviews, the opinion page, and then who knew what she would do. She might sit and read the whole paper for another hour or two before they left for church, or she might make banana nut bread or she might balance the checkbook. Mom was always unpredictable. She moved in fits and starts of inspiration, enjoying each project to the fullest until she found a new one. And if she was in the middle of the last project, she'd just abandon it until later. Right now, her passions were yard sales and refinishing furniture. At least, they were last week.

"I was reading the birth announcements and it made me lonely for Livvy and, well, we're wondering if y'all have decided what you are doing for Thanksgiving and Christmas this year."

I leaned against the cabinet. Just thinking of airline travel with a six-month-old baby made me feel exhausted. The price of the tickets made me feel queasy. "Mom, I haven't even thought about Halloween! We've been so busy unpacking and getting used to our house and living here we haven't made any plans."

"No, of course not. But if you can't come here, maybe we could visit you. We'd need to check into it soon. So let us know."

We talked some more about Dad's sideline business

of making cabinets, desks, and hutches, which had grown so big it was about to crowd out his main job of teaching history and government.

After hanging up, I jotted some notes on the calendar: garage sale, holiday tickets? When was I going to find the time to organize and run a garage sale? I felt like I was a cartoon character with my legs spinning so fast they blurred, but I wasn't going anywhere. Taking care of Livvy, just feeding us, and keeping up the house, even though Mitch did work around the house, too, took all my time. Where would I find any extra? The holiday thing I decided to leave alone for a while, but I wondered how long it would be before we received a similar call from Mitch's parents. Kids changed all the rules.

An Everything in Its Place Tip for an Organized Move

You'll probably need some important papers to get started in your new location.

- Banks require bank statements and pay stubs to start loan paperwork.
- Schools need birth certificates, shot records, and transcripts, as well as the contact info of the child's prior school.
- Kennels may require proof of vaccination and shot records.
- State motor vehicle departments often need proof of insurance and title to your cars before issuing new tags or license plates.

Make a few phone calls and find out exactly what paperwork you'll need because requirements vary from state to state; then pull your documents and hand carry.

Chapter
Twelve

Our yard looked like a porcupine. A stiff wind during the night had blown the brown pine needles out of the trees. They stood straight up, poking up in the air, coating our lawn and our neighbor's lawn, which seemed a little unfair since Ed and Mabel didn't even have a pine tree in their yard.

I twisted the trash bag closed and dragged it to the pile on the curb. The crisp, cool air held the faint smell of wood smoke. Just a few days ago we were sweating and running the air conditioner. I pushed up the sleeves of my turtleneck and listened to the baby monitor. It broadcast static from the top porch step, not cries. I surveyed the other side of the yard and the tall trees overhead. Lots of dry needles still up there. I pulled a Hershey Kiss out of my pocket and popped it in my mouth.

Mitch shook his head. "You and your chocolate," he said.

"Energy boost. Do you think it will warm up again?" I called to Mitch as he tied up our latest bag. But it wasn't Mitch's voice that answered.

"Once the needles start to fall, that's it. Summer's over." Mitch waved and I turned to see Ed Parsons standing on his side of the hedge. He wore a sport coat and tie and Mabel had on a sturdy raincoat over a shirtwaist dress. They must have just returned from church.

Ed pulled a toothpick out of the corner of his mouth and used it to point to the trees. I wondered if he always had a toothpick in his mouth or if they had returned from eating out again. "We cut all of ours down. Had the stumps ground and everything. Can't even tell we used to have four in our yard."

"Such a mess. Needles and branches and pinecones everywhere," Mabel said with a tiny shake of her head.

I glanced at the unbroken lawn and thought it looked boring. Having grown up in dry west Texas, where trees were scarce, I thought our tall pines were beautiful, even if they were a little work.

"So you don't think it will warm up again?" I asked.

"Nope. It'll start to snow soon. Fall is our shortest season. But don't worry, I have a snowblower and I'll do your sidewalks and driveway. Do almost everyone's on the block, in fact."

"Does it snow that much?" I asked, dreading the thought of a long winter, especially driving on ice. After living in California, I was out of practice.

"Well, it depends. Sometimes we don't get that cold and we get more rain than snow, but other times . . ." He grinned and offered to show Mitch the snowblower. Mabel rolled her eyes as if to say, "Men and their toys." She waved and went inside.

Mitch returned in a little while and said, "It's huge. He could probably clear the whole street with that thing."

I shook my head. "But we don't need one, especially if Ed is going to snow blow our driveway for us." Mitch could be a rather impulsive shopper when he actually went inside a store. To change the subject I said, "We'd better leave the blinds open at the Vincents' since it's overcast. I opened them this morning. The plants need as much light as they can get."

Livvy's wake-up sounds reached us from the monitor. "I didn't close them." He frowned. "I wasn't even over there yesterday. You took the paper in."

I leaned on the rake. "I did?" What had I done yesterday? Oh, the mall and then I had taken their mail and paper inside. "Maybe I closed them because it was getting late the day before and I just forgot. I'll get Livvy." I propped my rake against a tree trunk.

Abby and I walked briskly through the park in the predawn haze. The air inspired us, or rather me, to keep up the quick pace and get back to my warm house, where Mitch was probably walking a fussy, hungry Livvy around from room to room. Of course, last week I'd returned home from our walk expecting Livvy to be crying for her seven-thirty A.M. feeding, but she was cooing at Mitch from her bouncy chair while he poured cereal. One look at me and she'd switched to crying. Did she cry when I was close because she knew I would feed her?

"I wonder when Joe is coming back from Houston," Abby said.

"I don't know. We haven't heard anything from him. Have you heard anything about the investigation?" I asked Abby.

"No."

Why hadn't Jeff been arrested? Don't get me wrong,

I was glad he hadn't been arrested, but he did have the big three against him: motive, means, and opportunity. I checked Abby's face. Her usually smiling lips were pinched tightly together. I wanted to talk to her, but I didn't know what to say. This was awful. Cass's death and the investigation had made my life into an emotional minefield. I tiptoed through every conversation with Mitch and Abby.

We were quiet as we crossed from the park back onto my street. Then Abby broke the silence. "I'm going to ask Rachel what she knows. She teaches first grade and her husband is in the Security Police on-base. She might have heard something. I've been debating whether I should call her or not, but this whole thing is driving me crazy."

I picked up the paper from the Vincents' driveway and said, "Sounds like a good idea. See you tonight. Six o'clock?"

"I'll be there." Abby headed down the street to her house.

I pulled my set of keys out of my sweatpants pocket and unlocked the door. I had put Joe's key on my key ring because I was always running something inside or checking the plants. I felt a small itch of irritation at Joe for being gone so long and not letting us know when he would be back. The good neighbor routine was getting tedious. Immediately, I felt guilty. He was grieving and I should be able to do a small thing like take in the paper and water the plants for weeks if it helped someone after a loved one died.

As I opened the door, a headline on the rolled paper caught my eye: NO ENVIRONMENTAL DEBATE FOR CLAIRMONT. I skimmed the first lines of the story as I flipped on the lights and walked to the kitchen. I knew this floor plan almost as well as I knew mine. I could walk and read at the same time.

"We're excited to have them moving in and we hope others follow," said Clairmont's Economic Development Coordinator, Terrance Brisbane. Unlike the Black Rock Hill neighborhood that opposed the development of a Wal-Mart Supercenter, citing traffic congestion and a decline in property values, smaller economically strapped Clairmont has welcomed the retailer with open arms. After a watershed regulation forced the retailer to abandon plans to build on Black Rock Hill, Clairmont aggressively pursued Wal-Mart.

I slapped the newspaper on the kitchen counter beside the mound of mail and papers awaiting Joe's return. I froze.

The kitchen looked like the video clips on the news after an earthquake—tumbled cans and broken glass. Cabinet doors gaped open. Canned food and silverware covered the floor. I poked a can of green beans out from under the lower cabinets with my toe. Pots, pans, and mixing bowls tilted in piles on the countertops and the floor. Sugar and flour trailed over the counter from upended canisters. I turned in a slow circle and surveyed the living room. Couch cushions ranged over the floor beside scattered DVDs.

I groaned and hurried down the hall to the bedrooms. Someone had not only broken into Joe's garage while we were "watching" the property for him, but now they had broken into the house itself. Lousy neighbors we'd turned out to be.

I glanced into the pink bedroom. Open boxes, shoes, wrapping paper, folders, and clothing tangled together on the pink and white rag rug. Mounds of clothes surrounded empty dresser drawers.

I stopped short at the door to the master bedroom. I didn't want to walk in the room. The devastation here had a violent quality to it. A vicious blow had shattered the mirror on the antique dresser. Shards of glass dotted the feathers from the white goose-down comforter and the slit pillows. The mattress, stripped of its sheets, tilted to one side of the bed. The closet door yawned open. I could see the upper shelves were empty. The clothes were in a twisted mess on top of open plastic storage containers. In the corner, beside a dented hard drive, spiderweb cracks spread across the computer monitor. Papers covered everything like leaves sprinkled across the ground in the autumn. I shook my head and took a deep breath. This was bad. This was more than a burglary. It was an attack. Even the plants had been knocked over and stepped on, grinding potting soil into the carpet.

A muffled thud sounded behind me.

An Everything in Its Place Tip for an Organized Move

When packing your belongings, keep a supply of plastic zip-top bags nearby. As you disassemble each piece of furniture, put all the screws in a bag, then tape the bag to the bottom of that piece of furniture so all the nuts and bolts will be together when it's time to reassemble.

Chapter Thirteen

Make everything as simple as possible, but
not simpler.
—Albert Einstein

I froze. The hairs on the back of my neck stood up.
What was I doing? Someone could still be here. Why
hadn't I thought of that when I looked in the pink bedroom? I couldn't move. The kitchen and living room
were fairly open, so there was probably no one in those
rooms, but the entrance to the basement was in the
kitchen. Had that door been open? What if I had interrupted the intruder and they were in the basement now?
These thoughts flittered through my mind in a few seconds.

I pivoted slowly. I could see a sliver of the front door,
the kitchen counter, and the back of the living room

couch. I tried to do my Lamaze deep breathing techniques, but just like during labor, they didn't seem to do much good. I took a cautious step, trying to make absolutely no noise, but the blood pumped through my body so quickly I was sure anyone within twenty feet would be able to hear it.

Another cautious step and I heard a faint sound. A magazine slid off the pile of mail and newspapers on the kitchen cabinet. It landed on the tile floor with a soft thud beside a newspaper. I shot to the front door and was on the sidewalk before the envelopes edging down the pile could cascade onto the floor.

"And nothing was gone except the DVD player?" Abby asked.

I tucked the phone between my ear and my shoulder so I could put Livvy in her swing. "I don't know. That's all I could tell. The computer was still there. Broken, but there. At least their DVD player was exactly like ours. I showed ours to the police, so they'd know what brand and model to look for." I rubbed my forehead. "I just can't believe someone broke into their house and only took the DVD player. It was odd. Like they were going through things, drawers and cabinets, but they didn't take anything valuable." I switched the swing on and picked up clumps of packing paper that were scattered around the floor.

"What about Joe? Did the police ask him?"

"They're still trying to get in touch with him. He went fishing with a friend. His mother said it was to get away from everything. Deal with things and think. He's at some remote cabin without a phone, but he's supposed to call her tonight." I shoved the paper into the box and dragged it over to the door.

"I thought everyone had a cell phone now," Abby said.

"I know. The cabin is out of range." I leaned against a box labeled DISHES that we hadn't unpacked yet. "Everything feels strange about this whole thing, these break-ins. And Joe can't be reached. He could be anywhere. The police seem to think whoever broke into the garage figured out the house was empty and came back again."

"Then why isn't more gone?"

"That's exactly what I'm wondering." I rubbed my forehead again. I was getting a headache.

"I don't have much time, but I did get to talk to Rachel," Abby continued.

"Her husband's in the Security Police, right?" I asked.

"No," Abby corrected. "I thought that, too. But he's actually in the OSI. That's where Thistle-whatever-his-name-is works. You know, the rude guy who suspects Jeff. She couldn't tell me anything." Abby sighed. "Look, lunch is almost over. I've got to go. I'll come by your house a little before six tonight. We can walk over to Jill's together."

I put Livvy down for her nap, then I stood a few minutes irresolutely at the kitchen door. The situation with Cass was a mess. Like a jigsaw puzzle dumped out of a box, nothing fit.

I remembered sitting on a step stool in my dad's workshop one afternoon. His tools hung on a peg board inside their outlines. Nails, nuts, and bolts rested neatly in small boxes across the back of his worktable. The air always had a warm woody smell. I'd sort the curls of wood into different piles as they spiraled down from his planer. I'd hand him a bolt from the floor and he'd toss it into the right-sized box saying, "A place for everything and everything in its place." I'd taken after my dad. I liked things lined up and in order. Nothing was in order with Cass's death. Everything was jumbled and didn't fit. I couldn't help poking and prodding, trying to make it make sense.

I clipped the baby monitor to my belt, squashing the guilt I felt at leaving Livvy alone in the house. It would take a minute to run the mail inside and look around.

At Joe's door, I twisted the key and the deadbolt slid back quietly. The only noise inside the house was the faint static on the baby monitor. Everything was still a mess, only worse now that it was covered with fingerprint powder. I had thought I might poke around, see if I could find anything, but the sheer amount of the disorder dismayed me. What was wrong with me, thinking I could find a clue in this madness that the professionals, the police, hadn't found?

I closed the door and locked it. Then I went to the kitchen and looked around. The Vernon police had finished this morning. I took my hands out of my pockets. I could touch anything now.

I picked my way carefully between the items on the floor. A bag of sugar teetered on the edge of the counter, about to fall onto the floor. I pushed it back, shoving glasses, mugs, and a stockpot out of the way. It looked as if everything had been pulled out, set on the counter, or tossed on the floor.

Why would anyone do this? The police said it was probably robbers looking for jewelry or money. I picked up the wall calendar off the floor and opened it. August's glossy photo featured a shade garden with a small koi pond. Most of the white squares were blank, but a few had hurried scrawls with a time. Every Tuesday night had "7:30" circled in red.

I looked back to the week Cass died. "Sp. Coff" was noted on Wednesday of that week. Had it only been a little less than two weeks since I'd met Cass? Then Thursday's note read: "Dr. W—9:30," but it was scratched out. She must have rescheduled because "Dr. W—10:15" was scribbled on the next day, Friday. And today's block noted, "Jill—Garage Sale," but without a time. So there had been a meeting scheduled, but Cass had forgotten to tell me. I put the calendar on top of the refrigerator and picked up cans to put them in the cabinets. I couldn't stand in the middle of the mess any longer and not do something.

The door to the backyard rattled. I whirled toward it, clutching a can of chicken broth.

Rex shot in through the doggie door and bounded up on me. "Down, Rex." My voice was breathless. He sat. I put down the soup can, a pretty ineffective weapon. "How did you get out of the backyard?" I'd left him tethered on a new steel tether, guaranteed to withstand the sharpest teeth. I rubbed his ears and then his neck. His collar was gone.

I found it attached to the tether in our backyard. After I buckled it on again, I asked, "How did you get that over your head?" There were only a few inches of space. "What are we going to do with you?" He twisted his head and perked up his ears. "You think this is a great game, don't you?" Rex grinned.

Chapter
Fourteen

Jill wrote a note and squared the edges of her stack of papers. "I'll handle the newspaper ads and put up the signs. Abby's got the bank deposit and the schedule for the checkout table." Jill swiveled toward me and demanded, "How's the pricing?"

"Well, we still have a long way to go." I thought of the jumbled boxes in my garage. All the way to go, I amended silently.

"Call Diana. She volunteered to set up. Turn her loose in your garage and she'll have a preprinted price tag on everything in there in no time. We'll make more money with everything priced. People hate to ask how much something is. If it has a price on it, they may try to talk you down, but if it's not marked, they'll just walk away." The phone rang and Jill went to answer it in the kitchen.

Abby looked at me with raised eyebrows. "I never knew people planned a garage sale. I just open the door and pull everything outside."

I stifled a laugh and wrote down Diana's phone number from the list Jill had handed me before she left.

We were in Jill's dining room. Her muffled voice continued in the kitchen. Abby asked about my afternoon and I filled her in on my cleaning session at the Vincents'. Jill returned to the table. "Now, where were we? Pricing and setup. Do you have enough tables?"

"I have a card table."

Jill made a note. "I'll have some brought over from the squadron on Friday."

We covered every aspect of the garage sale until Abby glanced out the window and noticed Jeff's blue hatchback parked at the curb. "Oh! Got to go. We're having dinner at Merdi's." Abby pulled on her coat and grabbed the cloth bank deposit envelope.

"Well, I think we've covered everything. I'll call one of you if something comes up." I suppressed a sigh as I watched Abby trot out to the car. She hopped in and it glided smoothly to the corner. No more impulsive late dinners at quiet Italian restaurants for us. We tried it once. We made it through the salads, but we had to leave with our untouched dinner in boxes because Livvy wouldn't stop crying.

I put on my coat and gathered my notes.

"Thanks for taking on the garage sale. I'm sure you'll do a better job than Cass." Jill opened the door.

I paused on the top porch step. "Did you happen to talk to Cass during the barbeque?"

Jill wrapped her cardigan around herself. "No. She was busy holding center stage with her story about her van." Her tone was as cold as the wind that sliced across my neck.

"She mentioned Gwen's name to me, but—"

"Don't believe anything Cass said." Jill cut me off. "She was spreading rumors about Gwen. It wasn't true."

"But I don't know what she was saying," I said placatingly. Jill shook her head and crossed her arms tighter around herself. "It could be very important," I argued. "Cass died shortly after mentioning Gwen and, if you know about it, she probably mentioned it to other people, too."

"Gwen's my friend. I'm not going to repeat Cass's lies. Gwen has had a hard enough time rebuilding her life since her divorce. Good night," she said and shut the door.

I walked home briskly. The sharp breeze whisked my white breath away. There was obviously no love lost between Jill and Cass. Did Cass talk to anyone else about Gwen at the barbeque? And what was Cass saying about Gwen, anyway?

I awoke with a start from the deep sleep that left me feeling like I hadn't rested at all. Heart pounding and still breathing heavily from REM sleep, I blinked in the sunlight and pushed the quilt roughly onto the ottoman. I identified the distant sound, an irritatingly regular buzz, as the phone. Blearily, I snatched it up, a reflex, and answered before I remembered why I needed to keep the house quiet. But then I remembered, all too vividly, our sleepless night with Livvy from midnight to five A.M. the night before.

"Ellie?"

I registered that Livvy wasn't crying and dropped back onto my chair, where I had tried to steal a nap along with Livvy this morning. Stifling a yawn, I replied, "Yes?"

"Oh, you didn't sound like yourself." I recognized Joe's soft-spoken tone. The connection crackled with static, making his voice even fainter, but he was speaking quickly, as if he thought we might be cut off. "I'll be back in town next Wednesday. I don't think I can face seeing Cass's things, like her clothes and her"—he broke off, then started again after a deep breath—"perfume, in the house. I think it would be better—" he stopped again. Crackling silence filled the line.

"Joe?"

"Cass told me about your organizing business. Would you go through her things? Box them up and give them to Goodwill?" I wouldn't have even described the few jobs I had done as "my business," but this was not the time to fill Joe in on my lack of resume. His voice was strained, and I realized he was speaking quickly so he could make his request before he broke down crying. Listening to someone fight back tears, especially a guy, always did me in.

"Sure. I'll do that. I'll have a cleaning service come in first. It's a mess."

"That'd be great. I'll pay whatever you usually charge."

Maybe airline tickets for the holidays weren't out of the question. I shifted to a less emotionally charged topic. "We're really sorry about the break-in."

Joe cleared his throat. "Don't be. The police said whoever broke into the garage realized the house was empty and came back. It's not your fault."

"But still, I wish we had seen something."

"It really doesn't matter. Everything could be gone and I wouldn't care. That's what got me thinking about her clothes and things. It would be too hard to come back with the house looking like she'll be back any minute." He paused, regained control of his faltering voice. "When I know she won't be. So, don't worry about the break-in. Cass was important. People are important. Things, possessions, aren't." He swallowed and let out a shaky breath. "Sorry. I'm just . . ." He started over again. "I just don't understand. This was awful enough with Cass dying, but now to know someone planned it. Someone deliberately ended her life."

"So, you talked to the OSI?"

"Yes. They wanted to know where I was after Cass left."

"Weren't you inside?"

"At the flag football sign-up table," he said bitterly. "If I'd been with her she might have made it. I might have noticed the wasps or been able to give her an injection."

Here was my chance to find out if Joe had the missing EpiPen. "So there was an EpiPen in the van? In the glove compartment?"

"Of course. Cass could never keep up with one, so I put one in the van and another one in her purse."

But there hadn't been one there when the police released the van to me. "Did the police return her purse to you? And keep the EpiPens?"

"No. They gave everything back to me. Her purse is at home in the bedroom. Just keep the pictures and her credit cards."

He thought I was asking about the purse for when I

cleaned out Cass's possessions. I didn't mention the possibility of the EpiPen being gone. I'd check first.

"Why would someone want Cass to die?" He sounded genuinely puzzled.

"I don't know." I searched for a gentle way to phrase my question. "Did anyone dislike her?"

A short huffing sound came over the line. "I've been over that with the investigators. I can't think of anyone. She was the life of the party, you know, always laughing and having fun. Everyone loved to be around her."

Maybe someone didn't like her hogging the spotlight. I kept that idea to myself. I knew of several people who didn't love her. "What about Jeff? He was awfully upset at the barbeque."

"Yeah, the hunting thing. Cass didn't like it when people interfered with nature. 'We're always messing it up,' she'd say."

"But I thought hunting kept wild animal populations under control."

"That's what hunters like to say. But I don't think that conversation had anything to do with her death."

I wasn't ready to dismiss Jeff's anger so quickly, but I changed tracks with Joe. "Well, maybe she knew something," I ventured, thinking of her gossip about Gwen.

The line was quiet, not even static marred the silence for a few seconds. "Yeah," Joe said reluctantly. "She did want to know things about people. She was curious, a real people person. Sometimes she was a little too nosy. Almost like a kid, she would ask anyone about anything. She asked Jill how long it took them to get pregnant." Joe's laughter came over the line. "Boy, that took a while to smooth over. She just wanted to get to know people and know the details of their lives. I guess she would've made a good investigative reporter. She was never afraid to ask questions.

"I used to tell her to relax sometimes. People open up if you give them time, but she didn't want to wait. She was always in a hurry for everything. It was like she tried to pack all the action and life she could into every moment. And it turned out she was right. She didn't have that long to live." Joe's voice turned even softer. "She was like a sparkler, all bright, explosive, and beautiful. But they don't last very long."

"Did she tell you anything about Gwen?"

"Who?"

"Gwen Givens, Steven's wife."

"No," he said quickly. Too quickly?

"Do you know where she went every Tuesday night?" I asked, remembering the calendar.

"I guess it won't hurt to tell you, now that she's gone. She didn't want anyone else to know. She was embarrassed."

It was a little hypocritical to want the details of people's lives, but then jealously guard your own secret.

"It was her AA meeting."

I was searching for a reply when Joe continued, cutting through the faint rustling on the phone line. "She'd had a pretty rough time. She got married young and they had kids right away. I don't know all the details, but there were problems. Her first husband was a real partyer. I guess she was, too. She told me they used to hit the clubs every weekend. Then after Chloe and Julie were born she said she lost it, thought she was falling into the pattern of her parents. You know—boring respectability. She didn't want that. I think their marriage was already shaky and the pressures of kids really added to it. When Luke lost his job, everything went downhill. Cass told me she was drinking all the time, trying to escape. Eventually, they divorced and Luke got the kids because of her drinking.

"That was her wake-up call. She checked herself into a rehab center and then moved back home to get her life straightened up. I don't think she'd had a drink since then."

"That's amazing. Quite a turnaround," I said.

"She always had such a strong will. Anything she did, she did it all the way, to the extreme. When she partied she pushed herself to the edge, and then when she realized she lost the girls because of it, she pulled herself back the other way."

"How did you two meet?" Joe's words were pouring out. I hoped talking would help him and I couldn't think of a way to ease out of the conversation without sounding abrupt.

"We went to the same high school. We knew each other but never dated. She was wild. She wanted to be out on her own and live. She told me she thought I was boring." He laughed. I could tell it didn't bother him. "We went our separate ways. I went to the Academy and she moved to Dallas and met Luke. Later, after rehab, I saw her at the mall when I was back visiting my parents for Christmas. And, well, it just grew from there." He cleared his throat. "Sorry to talk your ear off like that. You're easy to talk to."

"No problem," I said, relieved he'd wrapped up our chat. "We'll see you Wednesday." I assured him Mitch would pick him up at the airport.

Later that night, we were clearing the table after dinner when the doorbell rang.

An Everything in Its Place Tip for an Organized Move

For the final clean of your old home, arrange to borrow a neighbor's vacuum, mop, broom, and other cleaning supplies after the movers finish since your cleaning equipment will be lumbering down the street in the moving van about the time you need it.

Chapter Fifteen

What I dream of is an art of balance.
—Henri Matisse

Rex's barks reverberated in our small house until Mitch told him to be quiet.

I paused with two dinner plates smudged with spaghetti sauce in my hands. "Who could that be?"

"No one we know uses the front door." Mitch set down our glasses. Livvy's bouncy chair hummed as she kicked her feet. She was used to Rex's barking now.

"And at seven," I said. "It's so late."

Mitch grinned. "We've turned into old fogies."

"You mean people actually go places, do things, after six at night? They're not home putting their kids to bed? Or trying to?" I hurried to put the plates in the sink and returned to the living room in time to see Mitch open the door to a tall man with curly brown hair wearing a tan raincoat over a standard business casual uniform: long-sleeved oxford, khakis, and loafers.

"Hey—" Mitch began.

"Special Agent Oliver Thistlewait." The man cut him off and stuck out his hand. "Office of Special Investigations." Mitch paused and then shook his hand slowly. "Oliver Thistlewait. Nice to meet you. Come in." Mitch avoided looking at me when he turned around. Interesting. Something to ferret out later. "My wife Ellie."

"Let me take your coat," I said as I shook Thistlewait's hand.

"How can we help you?" Mitch asked over his shoulder as he led the way to our half-cleared table and sat down.

"I'm here about Cassandra Vincent." Thistlewait eyed the basket of buttered French bread. "We're looking into her death. I understand you found her body, Mrs. Avery."

"Yes. Have some bread," I said, hoping to deflect any questions.

"Thanks." He took a slice, pulled out a notebook, and began asking detailed questions, taking me through the day of the barbeque again. Good thing I got out of PR. I'm lousy at deflection.

He managed to eat two more slices of bread, scattering crumbs over the table's glossy surface and spotting his notebook with greasy fingerprints by the time we reached the break-in at the Vincents' house.

"I understand you have a key."

"Yes. We're taking his mail in for him and watering the plants."

"I'll need it to look around."

He brushed the crumbs into a neat pile and asked, "Did you know Mrs. Vincent well?"

"Not really. We just moved here. I met her the night we moved in—Tuesday wasn't it? Then I went to the coffee at her house the next night. What happened with her brakes and steering? Was it more than vandalism?"

Thistlewait continued writing in his notebook as he said, "We're looking into it."

"Well, what about her EpiPens? Have you found them? Was hers in the van?" I persisted, since he was being rude.

He looked at me this time and said each word with a faint emphasis, "We're looking into it. Now, let's go back to the barbeque. When you left did you see anyone in the parking lot?"

He leaned his elbow on the edge of the table and watched me with his dark eyes.

I ran my hand around the corner of the breadbasket, suddenly nervous. I felt like I'd just been clocked doing 75 in a 45 mph zone. "Mitch was talking to Nick Townsend, I think that's his name. I don't remember anyone else. Brent walked out with me."

"Did you see any cars on the road as you left?"

I paused. "I don't remember any."

"No one passed you going back toward the squadron?"

"I don't think so, but I don't really remember," I said with a slight shake of my head. "Gwen was the first one to stop. She was headed east to the back gate."

"Know of anyone who didn't like Mrs. Vincent? Any arguments? Rivalries?"

Mitch had been lounging at the table fiddling with a butter knife. I felt a stillness settle over him at this question. "We just moved here a few weeks ago. I don't know anyone very well, except Abby Dovonowski. We were at Hunter together," I explained. I spent the next fifteen minutes, which felt like about three hours, answering questions about how well I knew Jeff, his knowledge of bees and wasps, the confrontation between him and Cass on Friday at the barbeque, and if I'd seen him when I left. Abruptly, Thistlewait switched to a new topic. "Cass Vincent lived most of her life in Texas. You sure you didn't know her? You're from there, too."

"I never met her before two weeks ago."

"You're sure?" Thistlewait pressed.

"It's a large state." I couldn't keep the sarcasm out of my voice. I tried to ease in one more of my questions. After all, I'd answered most of his. "The Vincents' garage and house have both been broken into. Could that be linked to Cass's death?" Livvy started fussing in her seat and Mitch went to hand her a new toy.

"We coordinate with local law enforcement, Mrs. Avery," he said with a tight curve on his lips that might have been a smile. It was the faint, self-satisfied, I-know-it-all smile that did it. I'd thought I would tell him about the undercurrents at the spouse coffee, Cass's flirting and gossiping, Nick's doctor visits, and Friona's strange night car rides, but not now. He could find out on his own. He wouldn't take anything I said seriously, anyway.

"I'll get you those keys," I said.

He pocketed the keys. "I'll return these in a little while."

I shut the door on his raincoated back and turned to Mitch. "Okay, what was going on when he got here?"

"What?" Mitch tried to look blank. He quickly gathered up the empty breadbasket and our two glasses.

I followed him to the kitchen. "There was something funny. You knew him, didn't you? But you couldn't say, right?"

Mitch washed and rinsed the dishes with intense concentration.

"What kind of name is Oliver? Who names their kid Oliver? And Thistlewait! That's a made-up name if I ever heard one."

Mitch stacked the dishes in the draining board, kissed my forehead, and said, "Oliver is a nice name. In fact, it's similar to Olivia—the name you liked so much that we gave it to our daughter. I'll change Livvy."

The trials of having an honest, instruction-following husband. I wouldn't get anything else out of him. He'd never reveal anything he wasn't cleared to talk about. What was it with these close-mouthed men tonight? I picked up the phone to call Abby.

I grabbed the flimsy plastic bag handles and the diaper bag strap in one hand, then I hooked the car seat handle in the crook of my other arm. After a deep breath, I scurried through the downpour to the Cherokee, parked in the nether regions of the parking lot. I had heard motherhood described as a balancing act, but I added the literal definition to the term in my mind as I skirted the puddles and tried to keep the heavy blanket over Livvy's car seat. I jerked open the Cherokee's back door, clicked the seat into place, and tossed the diaper bag onto the floorboard. In seconds, I was in the front seat lifting wet hair off my forehead. I needed a coat with a hood since there was no way to add an umbrella to the menagerie of stuff I carried around with me.

I cranked the heater to high and reached back to remove the blanket from the car seat. Livvy had been fussy all day. In desperation, I'd called my mom. She suggested Livvy might be teething, so I'd bought Orajel, but now she sucked her thumb and stared contentedly at the primary colored butterfly toy hooked to her car seat handle. I shook my head. Babies were not easy to figure out.

I put the Cherokee in reverse and waited for a woman in a raincoat to get out of my path. Tiptoeing in her high heels, she rounded the end of the Cherokee and slid between it and the next car. I thought for a minute she was heading for my door, but she continued on to the car parked in the slot facing mine. She slid into the car's passenger side and slapped down the newspaper she'd used to shield her face from the rain.

She looked familiar. I tried to make out her features as she swiped her shoulder-length dark brown hair out of her face and turned to the man seated next to her. It was Gwen Givens. Could that be Steven? He looked too heavy, but it was hard to tell. Anyway Steven didn't drive a blue four-door Buick. I remembered him leaning out of a sporty black truck the day we moved in. Gwen drove a Camry. I glanced in my rearview mirror. A white Camry, spotted and smeared from the rain, sat one row behind me.

Chapter
Sixteen

I glanced back at them, trying not to make eye contact, but I didn't need to worry. They were completely absorbed in their conversation. He said a few words, but she cut him off. Gwen shook her head sharply and gestured with her hand, a short chopping motion.

The Cherokee was higher than the car and provided a perfect vantage point to see their interaction, although I couldn't see the man's face because his sun visor was down. I felt like a voyeur watching them, so I checked behind me again and slid out of the parking place without my lights, despite the gloom of the afternoon. Neither of them glanced at me.

Why would Gwen meet someone in a parking lot? I checked the blue car again before turning left onto the street. Still there. They didn't seem to be meeting and going anywhere. Or if they were, they weren't in any hurry. Maybe it was business related. But her work, Tate's, was on the other side of town.

How had Cass phrased her comment about Gwen at the barbeque? She had something to tell me that was so "not Gwen." Had Cass known something about Gwen that Gwen didn't want anyone to know? Her meeting in the parking lot certainly seemed clandestine, but maybe it was just the rain, the overcast atmosphere, and her raincoat.

My cell phone rang. It was Mitch. "Hey," he said. "I'm over at Nick Townsend's. His car battery's dead and I'm going to let him borrow my car this afternoon. Could you come pick me up?"

"Sure. Where does he live?"

"You're not going to believe this. A block over from us."

"I should have known. Why did I even ask?"

Mitch's laugh sounded down the line. "It's a garage apartment on the corner of Twentieth and Birch."

I found the garage apartment and pulled into the driveway behind a Mustang. My headlights flashed on the AFPILOT license plate. I hit power on my phone to call Mitch, but it responded with "Battery Low, Recharge." I unbuckled Livvy's car seat and rushed through the heavy raindrops and up the steps to the apartment.

Nick jerked open the door, greeted me while ushering me inside. "Want something to drink?" Nick asked.

"Sure. Water would be great." Nick pulled a water bottle out of the fridge while I took in the apartment. It was a typical bachelor pad with a coffee table, a single bar stool, and a worn couch that looked like the twin of the couch in the squad's break room. An oak entertainment center with every piece of high-tech sound and video equipment imaginable showed where Nick spent his money. A SportsCenter anchor detailed the latest baseball stats from the large-screen TV. What Nick lacked in the furniture department he made up for with his wall hangings. Framed posters of every type of Air Force plane covered each wall. Even the niche above the sink had a plane. Nick could check out the details of a C-5, a massive cargo hauler, while he washed dishes.

I took a sip of the water. A huffy sound came from the car seat. Mitch drained his Gatorade and stood up.

"We'd better go. Livvy's going to be hungry when she wakes up," I explained to Nick. "Thanks for the water."

Mitch took the car seat from me and started bouncing. "Call me when you get the new battery. I'll walk over and pick up my car."

"Nah. I'll drop yours off and walk back if the rain's stopped. It's only a block. Thanks." Nick smoothed down his Air Force Academy sweatshirt and opened the door again.

Back in the car, I gestured to the vanity plate. "He's a little overboard on the Air Force."

Mitch shrugged and backed out of the driveway. "He likes to fly, no big deal." The Cherokee's movement lulled Livvy back to sleep, so we could talk without shouting.

"Don't you think he's a little extreme?" I asked. Mitch liked flying, but his identity wasn't solely wrapped up in the wings he wore on his flight suit. "He had his Air Force Academy yearbooks out as coffee table books."

"Yeah," Mitch conceded with a grin. "That's a little weird, but Nick's a little hyper. He goes overboard."

I told Abby about Nick's extreme decorating style when she dropped by after school to help me price things for the garage sale.

"It figures. I set up a friend, a teacher from school, with Nick. She said all he could talk about was how great flying was and every trip he'd ever been on. She was ready to bolt by the time the appetizer arrived."

"Sorry," I said after I yawned. "It's not you."

"Did Livvy sleep last night?" Abby asked as she flicked through a pile of videos.

"No. Maybe she's teething. I bought some Orajel today." I described the weird parking lot encounter I'd seen between Gwen and the man.

Abby dragged a box across the garage floor, pulled out the masking tape and a pen, and asked, "Do you think she's having an affair?"

"What?" I asked, surprised that idea was the first thing that came to Abby's mind, but I'd wondered, too. I hadn't wanted to put it into words, even in my own mind. Leave it to Abby to put it into words. She always says what she thinks.

"Well, it sounds like it. They meet in a parking lot. Leave one car there and take one to a hotel. That way both cars aren't at the hotel, in case anyone notices."

"But there aren't any hotels close to here." I marked a beanbag chair five dollars.

"She lives down the street, maybe he lives around here, too. And downtown isn't that far from here."

"Now I really wish I'd circled back to see what happened, but it's kind of unlikely, isn't it?"

"No, it's not." Abby could tell I wasn't convinced. "Listen, when my mom and dad divorced we found out things you wouldn't believe. The finer points of sneaking around were broadcast around the house during the fights." Her voice was joking, but her eyes were serious and sad.

My own upbringing was so far from anything like that description that I didn't know what to say. Most people I knew had divorced parents. The fact that mine were still together, and happy, made me almost a freak. My family was so normal it was almost abnormal. "I'm sorry."

Abby shrugged and pulled a hand mixer out of her box. "It was a long time ago."

I shifted to another subject. "Did Cass ever say anything to you about Gwen? That she knew something about her?"

"No." Abby's forehead wrinkled together in thought. "No. I think I'd remember something like that."

"She and Steven seem very close. She doesn't seem like the kind of person who would have an affair."

"You never know."

I pushed my bangs out of my eyes and hurried to the door, shushing Rex's volley of deep barks. Late morning sunlight streamed in through the front door, silhouetting Diana's trim form and highlighting my grubbiness. The Orajel hadn't worked wonders and if Livvy hadn't already been on antibiotics I'd be making another doctor appointment for her right now. It was all I could manage to throw on some gray sweats, tuck my hair behind my ears, and rub the sleep out of my eyes this morning.

"I had an appointment cancel this morning." Diana flinched as Rex let out one more sharp bark. "I thought I could help you price things for the garage sale, but if it is a bad time . . ." Her voice trailed off. In contrast to my

slob-around-the-house ensemble, Diana wore a crisply
ironed pink oxford shirt, navy slacks, and leather penny
loafers. She looked like a mannequin from the Ralph
Lauren display. Not exactly what I would pick to work in
the grime of my garage, but Diana looked like she
buffed and waxed her garage floor, so she probably
thought she was dressed appropriately. Even though my
garage would probably shock her, I wasn't about to turn
down her help.

"No. It's not a problem. Livvy's not sleeping well. Just
let me show you where everything is and I'll be there in
a minute." I led the way through the house and down
the steps to the basement garage.

"You keep the dog inside?" She quick-stepped past
the baby gate that confined Rex to the mudroom.

"For now." I sighed, resigned to the new arrange-
ment.

Diana eyed Rex warily. "I'm more of a cat person, but
we don't have pets right now. I can work by myself if you
have other things you need to do," Diana said.

Like shower, she was probably thinking. I went to the
garage door on the right and I heaved it up and over
my head. Our older neighborhood didn't have many
two-car garages and few with garage door openers. The
left-hand side door stuck so I left it down and clicked on
the single overhead light. Digging out the box of pricing materials, I explained the different areas where we
had grouped similar things. "I left the box cutter right
here." I patted the top of a book box and looked on the
floor. "I'll get some scissors."

"Here. I have a Swiss Army knife." She pulled it out
of her compartmentalized purse and neatly lined it up
next to the black marker. I stifled another sigh. Trust
her to look perfect and be prepared. Diana, the good

Girl Scout. It irritated me that she looked composed and was prepared while I felt out of control. I was supposed to be the organized one, damn it. I rubbed my greasy bangs and said, "I left Livvy in her swing." I could see the warning sticker clearly in my mind, NEVER LEAVE CHILD UNATTENDED. "Let me put her down for her nap and I'll be right back."

"I will be fine. And really, if you need a little time, take it." She pulled a box toward her and began removing gardening tools. "I remember that—having a newborn." She smiled. "Wonderful and overwhelming at the same time."

I took her at her word and quickly showered and slapped on some makeup after putting Livvy down. When I returned to the garage, I blinked. The boxes in the corner where Diana had been working were arranged with prices boldly marked. Now she was sorting books into neat piles.

"Wow, you've done a lot."

"It always surprises me how much I can get done when there aren't any kids under my feet."

I sat the baby monitor on a box and sorted through clothes, hanging them on wire hangers. "Can I get you anything? Would you like a Coke or ice tea?" I asked.

Diana pointed at her bottled water next to her purse. "I've got water. It's all I drink, besides green tea."

"Oh." I certainly didn't have green tea, so I turned the conversation. "How many kids do you have?"

"Two. Gavin is five and Stacy is four. I just dropped her off at preschool."

A few scratchy halfhearted cries came through the monitor and I tensed, listening for more. When there were no more sounds I went back to work saying, "She's not sleeping well. I'm not sure why."

"I remember that stage. Gavin decided he did not want to sleep when he turned four months old. Just like that. From one night to the next, he stopped sleeping. We tried everything—pacifiers, feeding, music, night-lights, no night-lights." She laughed.

It sounded like our last few nights. Maybe I'd laugh like that someday, but right now I was getting desperate with sleep deprivation. "What did you do?"

"We let him learn to go to sleep on his own. There's a really good book on it. I could lend it to you."

"That would be great." I was ready to try anything at this point.

"It wasn't easy. We basically had to let him cry. He had to go to sleep on his own."

"Oh." I hated for Livvy to cry.

"Some people think it sounds cruel, but it's not. They have to learn sometime and it makes everything else go so much smoother, especially when they get older. I'd much rather teach a baby to sleep on their own than a two- or three-year-old. I know some people who still let their kindergarteners sleep in bed with them." She radiated disapproval. Her tone sounded like she was describing a person who let their kids eat raw eggs.

"I'll read the book," I said, but with some reservations. I searched for something to say, but couldn't come up with anything else, so we worked in silence. Diana seemed to be one of those people who didn't feel they needed to make conversation, but silence felt awkward to me.

"Oh, look at this," she said after a while. She flipped through a book. "*Television's First Families*," she read. I caught a glimpse of the Beav and then Lucy, her mouth bulging with chocolates. "I'm going to take this with me right now. I love those old shows. Remind me to pay for it on the day of the sale."

She set the book aside and continued until she finished with the books. I noticed her perfect pale pink nails when she pushed back her cuff and checked her leather-banded watch. "I have to go now."

As I walked to her car with her, I crossed my arms to hide my hangnail on my right hand and smothered a sigh. I couldn't keep up with women like Diana. How did she maintain her polished image, flawless hair and makeup, and outfits that matched her nail polish? And she didn't have a speck of dirt on her. I brushed at a smudge across my knees. "How do you always manage to look so perfect?"

Diana's eyebrows went up and then she self-consciously tugged at her shirt cuffs, straightening them. "Oh. I, uh, don't know. I never feel like I look that great." She quickly turned the conversation before I could protest. "Did Cass have anything else that we need to move over here?" Diana asked before she opened the door of her pristine white SUV.

"No. We moved everything over here before . . ." I faltered at the words "Cass died." Diana nodded her head and I substituted, "the squadron barbeque."

"You found her?"

I nodded, hoping she wouldn't ask how Cass had looked.

"Was she still alive?"

No one else had asked me that question. My surprise must have shown on my face because Diana continued in her even, reasonable tone, "She hadn't been gone very long before we heard the sirens. It seemed so fast." Her eyes, clear and light blue, gazed at me unblinkingly.

"No. She was dead when I found her." I said the word I had avoided earlier. Diana's unflinching translucent-blue gaze and detached approach had infected me. Since Diana seemed to be in the information-gathering mode, I asked her a question: "Did you talk to her that day?"

She tossed the book inside the SUV and hopped lightly into the driver's seat. "Not that I remember." Diana studied the trees arching over her car with leaves tinged red and gold. Her gaze cut back to me. "She talked to Gwen. Gwen looked furious. They didn't get along, you know." She slammed her door and rolled down her window.

"Did you see anyone around her van that day? Anyone that's not usually at the squadron?"

Her eyes seemed cold and remote as she studied me. "Interesting that you asked the same question as the police." The earlier rapport we'd shared while talking about our children was gone. I shifted my feet and tried to come up with a suitable response, but Diana continued, "You should leave it alone. Give her family some peace." Her window glided up, she turned toward the road, and didn't glance back.

It didn't look like she'd offer to help me again.

The next morning, Thursday, I cruised down the steep winding street of Rim Rock Road, one of the first roads cut into Black Rock Hill near the turn of the century when the town was a logging center. Commerce thrived around the river that rushed through downtown. Nearby, the residential area of lower Black Rock Hill boasted addresses of the town's wealthiest residents. Our house, located farther up the hill, had been built later. Driving through the oldest neighborhoods with the gingerbread-trimmed Victorians made me a little sad. So many of the historic homes were divided into apartments and a few looked like a good shove would send them tumbling.

Before we moved I'd read up on the history of Vernon. I always pored over maps and travel books when we were PCSing, or in civilian terms, moving. Funny, none of the information had mentioned Black Rock Hill was the hot area for Air Force personnel. If we'd picked another neighborhood I might not be constantly thinking about Cass's death. But Mitch and I had both fallen in love with the huge trees and the craftsmanship of the homes on Black Rock Hill.

Today instead of admiring the houses as I wound down the hill on my way to the bank, I hardly noticed them. I was on autopilot after another nearly sleepless night with Livvy. My gaze fixed on the double yellow stripe on the road. Resisting the urge to close my eyes, I blinked and focused on the light. The red light.

I jerked my foot over to the brake. The Cherokee screeched to a stop a foot over the white pedestrian crossing. I navigated carefully to the bottom of the hill after the light turned green. I turned into the McDonald's parking lot. I needed to hit the dry cleaner, the bank, and the drugstore, but I had to wake up first. I didn't think the caffeine in a Hershey Kiss would do it. Neither Mitch nor I were big coffee drinkers, but I needed something to keep me alert. The drive-through line had at least six cars in it, so I went inside. A blast of cold air hit me as I unhooked Livvy's car seat and I hurried inside, already feeling more awake away from the heater's warm air.

Inside, the restaurant was deserted. I sat Livvy down

on the counter and dug some change out of my bill-fold. A girl sagged to the cash register. "Yeah?"

"A small coffee," I said to the top of her purple and green hat. She took my money and slouched away. Livvy slept contentedly in her car seat. I admired her pale lashes and the smooth curve of her cheek. There's nothing more beautiful than a sleeping baby. "Fine for you to sleep all day, but some of us have things to do during the day, young lady. We're going to have to get back to sleeping at night and napping during the day."

The girl returned with my coffee. As I turned away to leave, I glanced back. She busily stacked trays and didn't look up, but she looked familiar, tall with dark brown hair tucked under her baseball cap. She sneaked a look to see if I was still there. Despite the dark circles, her beautiful eyes and perfectly arched brows gave her away, even if the polyester suit hid her figure.

An Everything in Its Place Tip for an Organized Move

Color-code boxes as you label them with a color specific to each room, such as red for girl's room, blue for boy's room, green for kitchen, etc. Sorting boxes at your new home will be a snap.

Chapter Seventeen

"Friona?" She slammed a tray into place under the counter. "Aren't you Friona? Isn't your husband in the Fifty-second?"

Her lips tightened. I thought she was about to deny it. Instead, she snapped, "Don't say anything."

I blinked. Wow. So much for customer service. She sighed like it was a burden to speak another word to me. "Curtis! I'm taking my break now," she yelled over her shoulder. She came around the counter and jerked her head toward the booths. Despite her rudeness, I was too curious to walk out the door, so I followed her and took a seat in a plastic booth across from Friona. This McDonald's was a newer one decorated in a Fifties theme with single records on the wall and framed pictures of Caddies with tailfins. A "Heartbreak Hotel" single hung on the wall between us.

I rocked Livvy's car seat to keep her asleep and waited for Friona to speak. She took off her baseball cap and her glossy hair swung down on each side of her face.

Reluctantly, she made eye contact with me. "Sorry. You freaked me out." She let out another deep sigh that would have made my Lamaze teacher proud and muttered, "Couldn't you have gotten your stupid coffee, and like, gone away?" Since it seemed to be a rhetorical question I didn't answer. "Look, don't tell anyone you saw me here, okay?" She twisted her cap in her hands. Her words were pleading, but her tone was almost angry.

"I won't. But anyone could stop in here and see you," I pointed out as I took a sip of the coffee. It needed sugar and creamer. I didn't drink it often enough to drink it black. I had decided long ago I had enough vices without adding coffee to the list. Now I wished I'd opted for a Diet Coke.

"I know." All the fight went out of her like a deflated balloon. She flattened the hat on the table. She sounded miserable.

"Why don't you want anyone to know you work here? I think it's great you've got a job." Friona looked so bored at the squadron barbeque. A job in the real world would be good for her.

"I don't want the whole squadron to know I work here, okay? I mean this is *McDonald's*," she said sullenly. I repeated my promise not to tell.

"You look exhausted. Are you trying to work two jobs? I saw you at Copeland's the other night, too." I thought her husband was a boom operator. The enlisted pay chart was stingy, to say the least. I knew either our squadron or the base had something set up to help enlisted families make ends meet.

She rubbed her forehead with the heel of her hand and muttered, "I can't *believe* this." She kept her face lowered, speaking to the tabletop as she said, "Yeah, I work two jobs." I barely caught her next words. "Not for long, though."

She checked my face, then continued. "Copeland's cut back my hours. I had to find something else." Her attitude had shifted a bit from her whiny, self-centered focus to measuring, almost calculating. "It's been tough. I mean, do you know how many people want you to be able to type? I flunked out of typing class, so there goes all those jobs."

Normally, I'm a sympathetic person, but something kept me silent. She picked up her hat and studied the stitching, then flicked a glance at me and said, "Look, my husband, Keith, is flying with your husband later this week. Don't say you saw me here, okay?" Since I hadn't joined her pity party, she'd switched back to the original topic.

I took another sip of my coffee. It was working. I was waking up, but it still took me a minute to make the connection. "You mean your husband doesn't know you work here?"

When she glanced up again her eyes were shiny. "No." I wondered if the tears were calculated, too. "He thinks I work at that telemarketing place, MultiTech," Friona continued.

"Friona, if you need help, I know there are things set up on-base for people . . ." I searched for tactful words, "in a financial bind. Or if not, they can probably refer you to an agency in Vernon that can help."

"I can't go to anyone at the base." She jammed her cap back on her head. "Just don't tell anyone." She stalked away.

Later, as I sat in the drive-through line at the bank I wondered about Friona. Was it pride that made her want to keep her job a secret? Was she in some kind of trouble? I assumed it was financial, but it could be anything.

I finished off the coffee with a grimace, replaying the conversation in my mind. Friona was upset. I kept thinking of how she had twisted her hat like she was wringing out a washcloth. There was something more. Friona's distress seemed out of proportion. I stuck my check in the tube and watched it soar up over to the teller's window, but I was thinking about the red marks I'd seen on Friona's arm at the barbeque. What if Cass knew something about Friona that Friona didn't want anyone else to know? Cass was not exactly good about keeping secrets. If Cass did know about Friona's secret employment what would Friona have done? Asked her not to tell like she asked me? Or something more?

My cell phone trilled. "Hi," Mitch said. "I've only got a few minutes. I just got us reservations for Saturday night at the Aurora Mansion."

"What?"

"Reservations. I got us reservations at the Aurora Mansion." We had talked about finding a babysitter so we could go out, but I hated the thought of leaving Livvy with a teenager who might not know what to do if Livvy started one of her crying spells. After all, most of the time I couldn't figure out what to do. And I was breast-feeding. Livvy didn't like bottles, so that didn't leave a lot of time for dates. It was a hassle and I'd never got around to planning anything. "What about Livvy? I don't know any babysitters here. And I don't think that's the kind of place that hands out crayons and paper placemats."

Mitch laughed. "It's definitely a grown-up type of place. That's why I picked it. Everything's taken care of. Abby volunteered to babysit."

"Okay. Sounds great."

"I know. See you in a little while."

We said our good-byes and I hung up. Abby probably offered to babysit. She mentioned the same thing to me awhile back and I had waved the idea aside, saying I was too busy unpacking. And what I didn't mention to Abby was that I was a little reluctant to leave Livvy. But I told myself firmly, Abby would take great care of her.

Mitch normally went with the flow, so it was unusual for him to come up with the idea and plan everything. I did spend a good portion of my day caring for Livvy. It squeezed what little time Mitch and I had together to almost nothing. Some time as a couple would be good for Mitch and me, too. On that thought, I headed home to check my closet, a little thrill of excitement running through me. I was going out on a date!

I pulled hard on Rex's leash and dragged him back from a rubber trash can to keep him walking beside me. "We have to keep moving or this won't be much exercise for me," I told him. Rex glanced back at me over his shoulder, his tongue lolling out of his mouth and his tail beating the air. Taking him with me as we circled the block had made his day. Tomorrow morning, Friday, was trash day. Trash cans squatted at the end of each driveway. Rex was in heaven with all the smells available to him. I moved out into the street and we picked up the pace, which set my pocket, heavy with my cell phone, banging against my hip.

Mitch stayed home so he could study for his check ride, an annual flying test that all pilots had to pass. I'd been surprised. "But you just got here. What's the rush?"

"Got to get it done before the end of the month or I drop dead, statistically speaking. Birth month and all that."

We'd celebrated Mitch's birthday a few days before the movers arrived. Pilots had to do a lot of box checking during their birth month, like physicals, dental cleanings, and check rides.

"Couldn't you get a waiver or something? You've flown on this airfield, what? Twice?"

"Three times. I want to get it over with. Abbots is the IP."

"Great." We'd already heard about Major Abbots. He took great pride in his reputation as the toughest instructor pilot in the squad. "Like I said, you sure you don't want to get a waiver and take it again when he's sick or on leave, or something?"

"Nope. Wouldn't look good. It'll be fine. I'll just hit the books and get it done."

A kid on a bike zipped by and I gripped Rex's leash. I never thought I would like walking, but striding through the cool twilight felt great.

As I passed Friona and Keith's house, the porch light snapped on and Friona hurried out the door and down the concrete steps toward me. I reeled in Rex's leash. "Hello."

"Hey." She'd changed out of her polyester uniform

into an oversize black sweatshirt and cutoffs. "I saw you leave." Remembering my thoughts about her possible connections with Cass's murder, I felt uncomfortable. At least I had Rex with me, who wouldn't hurt anyone, but he looked threatening. I glanced at Rex, who was peeing on a bush in Friona's front yard. Well, usually Rex looked threatening. Friona didn't seem to even notice the dog. In fact, she looked more cold than threatening. She pulled her sleeves, which had been pushed up over her elbows, down over her wrists and placed her feet close together. She bounced on the balls of her feet. I jerked the leash and Rex trotted to my side. Friona stood there, seeming reluctant to say anything, so I asked, "How's the rash?"

"What? Oh, fine. It's cleared up. No more hiking."

The silence stretched, so I said, "Did you know Cass?" I nodded toward the Vincents' house.

"Who?"

"Cass Vincent. She died after the barbeque. She lived right there."

"Oh, my God." Friona's voice held notes of surprise and curiosity as she studied the gray stucco house. "The woman who talked so much at the barbeque? No. I thought someone else lived there, but I don't know anyone around here." Reluctantly, she pulled her gaze away from the Vincents' house. She focused on me and her eyes narrowed. "I thought about what you said. I could use some help. God, it's cold out here. Let's go inside."

"All right, but just for a minute."

An Everything in Its Place Tip for an Organized Move

Avoid Snail Mail Mix-ups
- Notify the post office of your address change, but don't stop there.
- Four to six weeks before your move, create a master list of all mail received, including:
  - magazine subscriptions
  - charities
  - companies that may not send bills every month, such as insurance companies
- Call businesses with your new contact info or print a sheet of labels with your new address and stick them on the return stubs as you pay final bills.
- After you notify a business, check it off your master list.

Chapter Eighteen

One of the advantages of being disorderly is one
is constantly making exciting discoveries.
—A. A. Milne

With Rex panting at my feet, I sat on Friona's futon couch. The phone rang, interrupting the clink of ice dropping into glasses. Friona returned to the living room with the phone tucked up on her shoulder. She handed me my glass and scurried back to the kitchen.

Like the plain white frame exterior, the inside of the house was decorated in a bare, contemporary style. A black futon and a white chair sat on a red rug. A coffee table and a small glass end table with an art deco–style lamp completed the furnishings. Abstract prints in primary colors dominated the walls. I wondered if the room was sparely furnished because Friona and Keith wanted it that way or if they didn't have any money to spend on furniture. The house was tiny, probably only two bedrooms on the left and the living room and kitchen on the right.

"Rex, no!" I whispered. He pulled his nose out of Friona's expensive leather purse. She must have left it beside the coffee table on her way inside. "Drop it." He opened his mouth and several papers fell on the floor. Envelopes from Nordstrom, Bon Marche, Pottery Barn, and charge receipts from Target and Pamona Grill bore Rex's teeth marks.

I smoothed out the mangled papers and stuffed them back in her purse. All the envelopes had FINAL NO-TICE or PAST DUE stamped on the outside.

"I told you—don't call me." Friona had retreated to the rear of the kitchen and lowered her voice, but I could still hear her words and her hostile tone. "I sent it yesterday! Don't call here again."

She slammed the phone into its cradle and then sat down in the white chair.

"Is Keith flying tonight?" I asked.

"No. Gone to the store." She scrutinized her glass of water, swirling the ice.

"I like your colors in here—bright and cheerful."

Friona shrugged one shoulder. "My parents have pool houses bigger than this." She said it casually, but checked with a quick glance to gauge my reaction. She reminded me of Mitch's youngest sister, Becca. She was fourteen when I met her and tried so hard to be non-chalant, but she constantly checked my reactions to her words and attitude to see if I was impressed.

I didn't answer. What could I say? "How nice" or "Wow" seemed inadequate. Friona put down her glass, sat up straight, and said, "I love to shop." Her tone was defiant.

She was challenging me, waiting for an answer. "Well, I like to shop, too."

"But it has gotten a *little* out of hand. I realized that today after I talked to you. I mean, I work at McDonald's. I'm wearing polyester." She half smiled and then leaned back in the chair. "I used to go shopping with my mom and sisters. We went every Saturday. Since I moved here, I haven't had that much to do, so I go to the mall all the time." She heaved another sigh.

"But it really started last year when I planned our wedding. I had two credit cards and charged them up. Then offers for more came in the mail. I opened more accounts, okay? For a while the companies upped my credit limits. I'd reach a limit and it was like magic, here's five hundred or a thousand more to spend." She looked up at the ceiling.

"Keith didn't notice?" I asked in disbelief. Mitch always noticed anything new around the house.

Friona rolled her eyes. "I handle the money. As long as Keith has his Harley and SportsCenter, he doesn't care."

My surprise must have shown on my face because she continued, "If he noticed, I'd tell him my mom sent me the clothes, but he's, like, clueless about fashion, okay? I kept some of the clothes in the basement in our moving boxes."

The phone rang and she tensed. "Now I'm getting these phone calls about the bills. Like I don't know I have to pay them." The answering machine switched on after three rings and she sagged back into her chair. "It's been rough working two jobs." She checked my face again. "If I just had a little more cash this month I could make the payments on two cards . . ." Her voice trailed off. Giving money to Friona seemed like giving an alcoholic a ten and telling him to buy a meal with it. Since I wasn't going to give her cash and she'd ruled out getting help from Family Support on base, I tried another angle.

"Could your parents help you pay the bills?"

"No." She slid lower in her chair and propped her pristine Tommy Hilfiger tennis shoes on the coffee table. "I can't go to them. I'd die if they found out." Her words sounded more like a teenager than a young woman. It seemed Friona still had some growing up to do. "They didn't want me to marry Keith. They said we were too young. That Keith's job wasn't stable enough. Like working for the government isn't stable. I can't ask for their help. If I do, they'll think they were right."

"How much do you owe?" I sipped my water and braced myself for big figures.

"I don't know."

"You don't know?"

"No. Probably ten or fifteen thousand."

I gulped my water and tried to keep my expression blank. "You need to find out exactly how much you owe. And I've heard cutting up your credit cards is a good way to stop spending." She looked pained, then her expression changed, hardened. This advice wasn't what she wanted to hear. "Then you can come up with a plan to pay the bills off. You really do need to tell Keith."

She nodded, but in a preoccupied way. I followed her gaze. She stared out the window at the Vincents' house.

"Check the phone book for credit counseling services. They can help you get a plan to pay everything off." I stood up, reluctant to go. "Call me tomorrow, if you'd like to." I gathered up Rex's leash.

She stood and opened the door for me. "So she died right after the barbeque? On Friday?"

I nodded and stepped onto the porch.

Friona shivered. "Kind of freaky. I mean, like, she lived right there." She squinted over my shoulder.

I was halfway down the steps but stopped and turned back. "Oh, the other night I saw a car leave your house. Its lights were off."

"That was me. I didn't want to wake up Keith. The headlights sweep over our bedroom window. He's a light sleeper."

Such a simple explanation. I didn't ask her, but I thought she probably carried her clothes to work because she didn't want to put them on at home. Afraid Keith or a neighbor would see her. She probably kept them hidden, too. And it was Friona going to her two jobs, one a swing shift, that created the "comings and goings" Mabel noticed.

At the sound of a motor, she turned and peered down the street. "There's Keith."

Keith roared into the driveway on his Harley. I waved to Friona and left without waiting for an introduction.

I decided to walk one more block to sort out my thoughts before going home. Really, it amazed me how some people lived. I couldn't imagine keeping something like that from Mitch. In the first place, he'd notice all the new clothes. And in the second place, guilt would eat me up.

I wondered if guilt bothered Cass's killer. Apparently Friona had nothing to do with it. I shook my head at my own suspicions, remembering how I tailed her car through the night to the store. I suspected her of murder! The only thing she was guilty of was killing her credit rating. Obviously, I didn't have a good instinct for finding suspects.

I reeled in Rex's leash as we turned the corner and headed north on Ponderosa Street. I realized the backyards of these houses met the backyards of the houses on the opposite side of the street from us. No alley separated the properties, only wire or wood fences.

I wondered which house backed up to the Vincents' house. I passed a nondescript bungalow, a large red brick colonial, and then paused in front of a newer split-level. The main floor hung over the daylight basement like an overbite. It looked out of place, cheaply new when compared to the gracefully aging brick, frame, and stucco homes. The lot had probably sat vacant for fifty years. Down one of the side yards, I could see into a backyard with stubby grass and a chain link fence. Beyond it lush grass, shrubs, and flowers abounded. I didn't need to see the gray stucco and black trim to know it was the Vincents' backyard. The contemporary house in front of me was quiet. The miniblinds were tightly closed and long sprigs of grass grew around the FOR SALE sign in the yard.

Suddenly, the leash whirred as Rex sprinted after a squirrel. It sped past two trash cans, veered across a lawn, and dashed up a pine tree. Rex took the more direct route and dove between the trash cans. The cans clanged on the driveway. Trash bags and garbage sprawled across the driveway and lawn. I closed my eyes and sighed. When I opened them the first thing I saw was Rex whining and leaping at the base of the tree. I reeled in the leash with a jerk. "Bad, bad dog!" Rex cringed and returned to my side. He knew he was in big trouble because he sat down obediently and only cast a few longing glances at the tree.

I picked up a can rolling in a lazy circle and began replacing the white trash bags. I checked out the house, but no one seemed to be home. The windows were dark. In the approaching twilight, lights glowed in many houses around me. I hoped I could get everything back in without being noticed. Rex whimpered and made a small movement toward the tree. "Don't even think about it," I warned. Rex stayed where he was. I wished I could run home for a pair of gloves to pick up the rest of the trash that had spilled out of one of the bags: decomposing brown leaves, pine needles, empty plastic trays that had held boneless chicken breasts, and flattened Pepsi cans.

When I saw the DVD player I froze with the last trash bag suspended in midair. Then I let it thud into the can. I squatted down to look at the DVD player without touching it. It was a Zenith with a long scratch across the blank clock panel, just like Cass's DVD player: the one stolen item from the Vincents' house. I remembered it because we had the same brand. I'd even shown ours to the police after the break-in so the police would know what model to look for.

I stood up. No one seemed to be home at the house where the trash had come from, but ringing the doorbell didn't seem too smart. After all, it was the stolen DVD player. I was sure of it. But leaving it on the driveway covered with plastic poultry trays and other trash didn't seem like the right thing to do either. And I knew from my contact with the police in the last few weeks that I shouldn't touch it. Not that I really wanted to anyway. I stood irresolute in the growing twilight. Then I remembered my cell phone. I dialed 911 and explained my find; then I dialed our home number.

An engine purred softly past me as a white car pulled into the driveway. Gwen Givens parked near the garage and then walked back to me. Her black dress blended with the growing darkness and her russet-colored scarf flapped over her shoulder in time with the click of her low squared heels. Her husky voice sounded loud in the twilight: "I remember you from the squadron. It's Ellie, isn't it?" She surveyed the mess. "Whatever happened?"

I explained how Rex knocked over the trash cans as the phone line rang in my ear. Mitch wasn't picking up. He was probably changing a diaper or bathing Livvy and couldn't get to the phone. "Don't worry about it. I'll get a broom. It'll only take a second to clean it up. You go on with your walk. You don't need to hang around here." She pirouetted back to the garage.

"No. We can't touch anything. The police need to look at this. That's the DVD player that was stolen from the Vincents' house. Did you know they were robbed?" In my ear, our answering machine clicked on.

Gwen crossed the driveway with quick steps. "Don't call the police." She grabbed my wrist and jerked the phone away from my ear. I was so surprised I didn't even resist when she snatched the phone out of my hand and pressed the "end" button. "I won't have the police here."

Chapter
Nineteen

One man's trash is another man's treasure.
—Anonymous

I could feel Rex go on alert beside me. He growled a low, threatening sound. I didn't tell her she had hung up on my answering machine. Better not to let her know the police were already on their way, since she was so tense. She looked like a tightly coiled wire. I patted Rex's head. "Why don't you want the police here?"

"I just don't," she snapped. Her ready flow of words seemed to be drying up.

"Well, what about the DVD player? You can't just throw it back in the trash."

She looked at it and then at the trash cans, speculatively. That was exactly what she wanted to do.

"Why don't you wait here while I get Zoë out of the car. It'll only take a second."

Since she had my cell phone, I wasn't going anywhere. Gwen opened the back door and a little girl about five years old jumped out and rushed toward us with her long brown hair flying out around her head in disarray. "Can I pet your dog?" she asked. She stopped inches from Rex. She didn't touch him, but looked pleadingly at me with big green eyes.

"I don't know if he's ever been around kids. Better not," I said as gently as I could.

Gwen returned, carrying a hot pink backpack. She stopped beside Zoë. "I'm so sorry to bite your head off like that, but things have been a little stressful lately." She held out her thin, elegant hand and offered my phone back. "Please let's just let this go." She glanced down at the DVD player. "I don't want the police here, tromping over my yard and asking questions. It would be very upsetting to Zoë." Gwen's green eyes looked troubled while Zoë's sparkled with interest. I pocketed the phone. Gwen smoothed Zoë's hair down and looked at me imploringly. "We can return it, but let's leave the police out of this. It'll be so much easier. Faster, too. Last time someone rear-ended my car it took forever for the police to show up. And then there's all those forms and questions. I'm sure you have better things to do tonight than fill out forms."

What did she have to hide? Her parking lot visits with another man? A city police car cruised up to the curb. Gwen's look changed from pleading to vicious. She swept Zoë inside and left me to explain the situation.

"Ah, yes, the battle of wills." Dr. Stig said while peering into Livvy's ear. It was Friday morning and I had just described how Livvy continued to cry at night. She decided she didn't like having her ears looked at and began to cry. Further conversation was on hold until the exam was over and Livvy snuggled up with her head in the crook of my neck. I nuzzled her fuzzy head with my chin and did the gentle baby bounce to calm her. Livvy liked to be held, usually up over my shoulder, so she could see everything; she didn't cuddle much so I enjoyed the moment.

"As I was saying, about wills," Dr. Stig said as he scribbled on Livvy's chart. "Your Livvy there has a strong one. Her ears look great, so her crying at night is probably for attention. She's getting used to waking up, crying, and you feed her, or your husband comforts her, and then she goes back to sleep. Have you been rocking her to sleep?" He flipped the chart closed and stood up.

I nodded. "You basically have two options," he said. "Keep doing what you're doing or let her cry it out for a few nights. She'll sleep after that. You can do whatever you want. My wife couldn't stand to hear our kids cry, so we took the first option. It's up to you."

I could tell he had already mentally moved on to his next patient, so I said, "Well, what about the family bed and anticipating your baby's needs?"

"Two different philosophies. You decide what's best for your family and your lifestyle. Finish up her antibiotic and she'll be fine. Good luck."

"But . . ." He gave a jaunty wave and was out the door.

I mulled over his suggestions as I changed Livvy's diaper. Let her cry? Did he realize that she could cry for hours? Could I stand that? Could I stand to go on with intermittent sleep for how long? The next few months? Years? I shuddered as I finished changing Livvy and put her back in her car seat. Her cries tapered off to murmurs of protest. The nurse who worked with Dr. Stig came in as I gathered up the car seat and diaper bag. I paused at the door and turned back to the nurse. Her nametag read SHERRY. I had some questions she might be able to answer. When I arrived at the clinic and lined up to check in for Livvy's appointment, Nick had been in line in front of me, fidgeting and bouncing at the counter.

"Hi," the nurse greeted him in a breathy voice. I glanced around him and saw the same nurse from last week, only today her blond hair was in a French braid instead of a ponytail.

Nick handed over his paperwork. After some flirting interspersed with chitchat, the nurse got down to business. "Do you want your appointment for the same time next week?"

"Sure." Nick handed over cash. The nurse returned a receipt and a new appointment card to him. The phone on the counter rang.

"See you next week." Nick flung his keys into the air and caught them, then he smiled and rushed to the stairs.

I stepped up to the counter. "One moment, please." She picked up the phone. "One West."

What would bring Nick back to a civilian doctor week after week? I tried to see the diagnosis checked on the yellow form, but the print was tiny. The tall nurse walked up to the nurse who had checked me out. "He was just in, huh?"

The nurse routed the call and hung up. "Yeah, but he's never going to ask me out."

"I can't believe you! He comes in every week for his allergy shots and he talks to you every time. Just like he did today before his appointment. Maybe he's shy. You should ask him out."

I'd picked a seat in the waiting area and set up camp. Nick got an allergy shot every week. Could he do that? If Mitch took practically any over-the-counter medicine he had to go DNIF, meaning Duty Not Including Flying. He couldn't fly. What were in allergy shots anyway?

And now here was a medical professional who could answer my questions. The doctor certainly didn't have time to chat. "Ah, Sherry, I have a few questions."

She pulled a new length of fresh white butcher paper over the examining table. "Sure." She ripped the paper in a smooth motion, crumbled the used portion, and tossed it in the tall trash can.

"Well, I, ah, I'm allergic to tree pollen and I was thinking of getting allergy shots. Do you do those here?" I figured tree pollen was general enough for many people to be allergic to it.

"You must be miserable with all these pines around here. The lab handles the shots. You've been tested?"

"Umm-hum." For once, I was glad to have bloodshot eyes from my late nights with Livvy.

"You get the referral for the shots from your doctor and then you come in every week."

"But what's in the shot?"

"Oh, it's small amounts of the substance you're allergic to. Your body produces antibodies to help fight the allergen, tree pollen for you. Over time your allergy symptoms should decrease. Check with your doctor first, if you're breast-feeding."

I thanked her and left. If Nick was allergic to something natural like tree pollen or cat hair it wouldn't theoretically be going against regs to have allergy shots, but I didn't think the Air Force would like him going outside of their system to have anything done. From what I understood pilots weren't supposed to have allergies at all. And I knew Nick wouldn't want to go DNIF every week. That would cut down on his flight time.

There were too many people with secrets in this squadron. Gwen's reaction to the police showed she had something to hide even though the police only asked a few questions and took the DVD player for fingerprinting. And now it seemed Nick got allergy shots on the sly. Not a massive infringement on regs, but probably against them, nonetheless.

"Thistlewait."

"Umm, this is Ellie Avery." I fanned myself with Oliver Thistlewait's card. The kitchen suddenly seemed stuffy. "I found the Vincents' stolen DVD player last night." Gwen's fierce anger had scared me. Calling Thistlewait was the right thing to do, even though I felt a little sneaky and depressed keeping everything I'd found out from Mitch. I'd wanted to talk to Mitch, but when I returned after finding the DVD player he was "chair flying." Three-inch-thick regs scattered around him as he did a run-through of his check ride. I'd hit the highlights of finding the DVD player and let him get back to the boldface.

"I've seen the police report, Mrs. Avery," Thistlewait said and brought me back to the present.

"Oh. Well. I just wanted to make sure you knew. Gwen was so angry. It seemed out of proportion." And Nick at the clinic today. I'd tell him about that, too. Better to hand it off to him.

"Most people would be angry if they found an acquaintance sifting through their trash."

"I wasn't looking through their trash! The dog knocked it over."

"Yes, I'm sure. Mrs. Avery, someone worked very hard to make a murder look like a tragic, but natural death. Unfortunately, we don't have a lot of hard evidence to go on. Don't make anyone else angry. I know you're trying to help, but watch your step. We're pursuing everything we've got on this."

"Well." A rush of words choked in my throat.

"Thank you for your call, Mrs. Avery." He hung up. I stabbed his card into the kitchen bulletin board, thinking of what I should have said. I took a deep, cleansing breath and gulped water from my oversized cup. That would be the last time I called Thistlewait.

I folded a soft purple sweater and put it in the trash bag near my feet. Reaching back into the pile of clothes on the closet floor, I pulled out a sleek black skirt. After checking the pockets, I folded it and placed it on top of the sweater in the bag. It was Friday afternoon and I was cleaning Cass's things from her closet. During an afternoon a few days before, a cleaning crew had swept through the house and returned it to a fairly normal state. Livvy sprawled in the portable crib. I could hear her heavy breathing from several feet away. It didn't seem fair that she slept so hard during the day.

I worked steadily bagging Cass's clothes until I picked up the last garment from the floor, a woman's navy blazer. Cass's clothes ranged from stained and worn jeans and sweats, which I assumed were her gardening clothes, to expensive designer clothes, mostly in bright colors. Hardly anything matched. No pants to go with the blazer, no coordinating sweaters and shirts. Many of the clothes still had tags on them with red discount slashes. She was a bargain shopper, maybe impulsive when she found a good deal. What would Friona's closet look like? I probably didn't want to know. I wondered how Friona's conversation had gone with Keith. She hadn't called me and I debated calling her when I went home.

I slipped my hand into the pockets of the blazer and found a folded yellow paper. I smoothed it open and placed it on the desk on top of a stack of similar papers I had found in Cass's other clothes. Most were receipts for a few dollars. This one was different. In fact, it looked familiar. Northwest Family Health was printed in blue in the top left hand corner. Large looping handwriting filled in the blanks on the form: "FamPrac—Office visit/copay $12." Absently, I smoothed the fold lines. It was dated two weeks ago on Friday. Hadn't Cass said at the barbeque she'd seen the doctor that morning? Family Practice, located on the lowest level, was right across the waiting area from Urgent Care and the lab, where I had spent the last two Friday mornings. What time had she been there?

I checked Livvy in the crib. Still on her tummy, she had scooted around from facing away from me to facing toward me. Like she was on a track, she made several scooting circuits during her REM sleep. I wondered if we would ever be able to move her to a bed. Would she stop circling in her sleep? She was sleeping now, so I retrieved Cass's wall calendar from the top of the refrigerator and placed it on the desk beside the receipt. On Friday, Cass had written "B-B-Q" in black pen; "Dr. W— 10:15" was penciled above the barbeque notation.

I sat down slowly in the desk chair and studied the calendar. Ten-fifteen on Friday might put Cass in the same waiting room as Nick Townsend. For the last two weeks he had appointments between 10 and 10:30. And I heard him ask for an appointment at the same time next week.

Thoughtfully, I went back to the clothes, folded the blazer, and placed it in the pile. Had Cass seen him and realized what he was doing? If she knew, had he felt threatened? I contemplated calling Thistlewait, but cringed. I didn't want to talk to him anytime in the near future. I pulled the drawstring tight, heaved the bag down the hall, and plunked it down beside seven other bags near the front door as the doorbell chimed.

I peeked out the narrow window beside the door and saw a woman who could be Mrs. Pillsbury Dough-boy. The petite, rounded, sixtyish woman stood on the porch examining the porch light. Puffy blond hair framed her round face. She readjusted her blue wind-breaker over her ample white sweatshirt. I opened the door, hoping she had a cookie sheet with warm cookies hidden behind her back.

"Cass Vincent? I'm Isabelle Coombes," she said, extending her hand.

No cookies. Bummer. "No, I'm a neighbor, Ellie Avery," I said and shook her hand.

"Oh. Is Cass here?"

I couldn't blurt out that Cass was dead, so I said, "You'd better come in." She followed me into the living room. "You're a friend?"

Isabelle Coombes plopped down on the sofa and planted her hefty beige bag beside her laced-up rubber-soled shoes. "Not really. We're more e-mail correspondents. Cyberfriends, isn't that the proper lingo? I knew her from her newspaper column, 'Clippings with Cass,' you know?"

I was relieved she wasn't a close friend. "Mrs. Coombes, I'm afraid I have some bad news. Cass died two weeks ago."

"What?" She dropped the purse strap and pressed short, plump fingers against her lips. "She died?"

"Yes. I'm afraid so. Mrs. Coombes, can I get you something? A glass of water?"

She pulled her fingers away from her mouth and shook her head. "Please call me Isabelle. I don't need anything. I'm a nurse, after all. It just surprised me. She was quite young, wasn't she?"

"Yes. Midtwenties, I think. It was anaphylactic shock. She was stung by wasps and had a severe reaction."

"Oh, my. How terrible. I've been moving, so I didn't realize. I haven't seen the paper in a few weeks. Were you a close friend?"

"No, I'd just met her. I'm here today because her husband asked me to sort through her things. I'm a professional organizer." I realized it was the first time I'd identified myself as a professional organizer. It felt good.

"Well, I guess you're the one I need to talk to. Cass was helping me with—. Well, it's a long story. I wanted to buy back my father's land. He owned a piece of the valley." She gestured to the right, but I realized she meant the valley to the west of Vernon below the drop-off on Rim Rock Road.

"Dad sold to a neighbor down the gravel road when I finished school and moved to Portland. That finally convinced him I wasn't going to live on the land. He used to tell me it was the finest spread in the inland Northwest and someday I'd realize that. I'd told him for years I couldn't wait to get out of Vernon." She paused, then smiled a bit self-consciously. "Turns out Dad was right. I was a nurse anesthesiologist and I loved my job at the clinic in Portland. But I'm retired now and I want to move back here. To a slower pace."

This was way more information than I needed—or wanted—to know, but Isabelle was rolling along in her explanation and I couldn't cut her off and shove her out the door without being rude. She'd just had a shock, after all.

"Anyway, a few months ago I called a real estate agent and asked him to track down the current owners, so I could make an offer. I subscribed to the *Vernon Dispatch*—had it mailed—so I could see what the real estate market was like here. I was never so surprised as when the agent called back and said the property didn't belong to the Norwoods anymore and a big subdivision was going in. He said something about an easement. I wanted him to look into it for me, but he wanted a quick sale. He had several 'nifty' condos in an assisted living complex."

Isabelle sniffed. "Assisted living. 'Nifty,' indeed. I'd seen Cass's column and read in the other articles about how she protested that Wal-Mart construction, so I e-mailed her and told her about the subdivision. I just don't see how they could put a subdivision on it. Dad loved that land and he kept saying I'd want to come back to it someday. So before he sold it he put an easement on it. Cass was interested and said she'd research it. Have you seen any paperwork about that?"

"No, I haven't. But you'd need to talk to her husband, I think. He's out of town and hard to reach, but I can give him a message."

"Thank you. That is so nice." Isabelle scooted to the edge of the sofa and dug through her purse. "Here's my new phone number." She scribbled it on the back of a business card and held it out. "I've rented an apartment here until I can find out about my land. I'll be out of town for the next week or so—going down to see my grandson get married—but you can leave me a message."

Isabelle levered herself up and hooked the purse's strap into the crook of her elbow. "I surely appreciate it." She stopped at the door. "Please tell her husband I'm sorry."

I pulled out my cell phone, called Joe's parents' number, and left him a message about Isabelle Coombes, then I returned to the bedroom and sorted through shoes, belts, and a few purses. There was a gym bag, which I left for Joe, a large black leather purse with long handles and a small glittery black beaded bag. I remembered Cass's large woven bag on the front seat of her van. I found it under the bed's dust ruffle. Lipstick, sunglasses, pens, notebook, wallet, gum, hair clips, and antihistamine tablets spilled onto the bed when I up-ended it. I ran my fingers over the items, separating them. No EpiPen. Had Cass lost it? Or was it removed? Had Thistlewait looked through her purse when he looked around their house? Probably not. I couldn't see him shoving it back under the bed.

The room seemed colder. I untied the sleeves of the sweatshirt from around my waist and slipped it on before removing the plastic notebook of photos and credit cards for Joe. I sorted the things into piles—trash, donation, or for Joe to check—but I kept the spiral notebook with a plain red cover. Flicking through the pages, I saw names from the squadron, each followed with a short biographical sketch and sometimes a question or two. I tucked it in my back pocket to look at later.

Back at the closet, I sorted running shoes from heels and boots. Under a pair of cross trainers, I found a fanny pack. I picked it up and tossed it into the pile with the purses, but it was too heavy for the lightweight microfiber material. It landed with a thud. I retrieved it and unzipped the small pouch. A cell phone, a dented Walkman, and a single key fell into my palm.

I punched the power button on the phone and it beeped back at me. I wondered if I could figure out the lock code. The display lit up. No lock code. I should have known Cass wouldn't use one. Another beep sounded and the words "Two new messages" flashed on the screen. I pushed the button marked with an envelope after studying the phone and put it to my ear.

"Cass, I'm running late. I'll see you after the coffee." I recognized the quiet, steady voice as Joe's. He must have called her Wednesday.

The other message began, "Listen, Cass, this is Brent. I know you're upset." Brent? Diana's husband? Mr. Touchy-feely? "But, well," he chuckled in a way that seemed to say, "Yeah, I know I'm an ass, but I'm still pretty cute, aren't I?" The message continued, "But, if you'll just let me talk to you, I can explain everything. Look for me at the squad tomorrow." My thoughts raced. "Tomorrow at the squad" had to be at the barbeque. She might have talked with Brent at the barbeque shortly before she died. Brent had left the squad at the same time I did, but he could have placed the wasps in Cass's van beforehand.

I didn't want to, but I made myself do it. I marched over to the phone and called Thistlewait. I described why I was at the Vincents' and the voice mail message. He said he'd be there in a few minutes.

He must have been down the block because he arrived in about thirty seconds. I opened the door before he could ring the bell. "That was fast."

He smiled briefly. He pulled on latex gloves, saw my questioning look, and said, "Prints." Then he took the phone from me. It chirped and the display read, "Low battery. Recharge." Then it went blank.

Thislewait dropped the phone into a bag he pulled from his windbreaker pocket, then raised his eyebrows at me. "The messages?"

I know men don't use as many words as women, but jeez, a parrot said more words in a day than this guy had today. I described the messages while Thistlewait jotted notes.

"So have you been able to confirm anyone else's alibi besides Joe's?" If he realized I already had a little info, maybe he'd share more info with me.

"Afraid I can't say. Thanks for your help, Mrs. Avery," he said and left as quickly as he arrived.

Mitch arrived a few minutes later. It seemed the Vincents' house was as busy today as a hub airport. "I found your note saying you were over here. How's it going?" Mitch asked.

"Fine. I'm almost done with her clothes." I gestured to the pile of trash bags and boxes. "I found Cass's phone."

I described the message from Brent. "What do you think Brent did to make Cass mad?"

"Could be anything. It could have nothing to do with her death," Mitch said in a preoccupied way. He didn't want to talk about Cass. He was sticking to our avoidance policy as the best way to keep the peace between us.

"I know, but it might. Although, he didn't sound wor-

ried. Did you see him in the parking lot before he came
out with me?"

Mitch paused. "No. I don't remember anyone but
Nick." He switched gears. "Okay, here's the plan. I'll
take Livvy with me and set up a pick-up time with Goodwill. You go look for a dress for our date. I'm meeting
Jeff to shoot some hoops." He held up his hand like a
traffic cop. "Before you say anything, I'm under strict
orders from Abby. She's already on her way to meet you
at our house in fifteen minutes to go shopping. She
told you need a new dress."

I gave him a quick kiss and headed out. "I'll be back
before her next feeding." You don't have to tell me
twice to go shopping. And I knew just where I wanted to
go.

Chapter
Twenty

"I don't know." I twisted around and looked over my shoulder so I could see my back reflected in the dressing room mirror. "It's kind of revealing."

"You look great. You should get it. Everyone needs a little black dress," Abby said from her seat on the plush bench. She put a shimmery blue cocktail dress back on a hanger. We were in a dressing room at Tate's, a very expensive boutique-type store.

I turned around and faced front again. It wasn't your typical wear-to-any-occasion black dress that could be dressed up or down with the right combination of heel height and jewelry. This little black dress was little because there was little material involved and that material was cut in a cunning way so that it revealed curves. The material had a deep, almost burgundy, sheen to it when I moved. Totally impractical. "Where else would I wear this?" I studied my reflection. I really did have cleavage.

"To a nice dinner with your husband." Abby rolled her eyes. "He told you to go shopping and get something nice."

It was great to see Abby relaxed. She'd sat silent and slumped on the drive over. I'd asked if she'd heard anything about the investigation.

"No," she'd snapped, then said, "God. I'm sorry. It's just so stressful."

I checked my reflection in the mirror. "I do have that vintage handbag. You know, the black beaded clutch with the amethyst latch. But, I'll never be able to fill out this dress after I stop breast-feeding Livvy," I said with a sigh.

"How's it going?" A cheery voice called out from the other side of the door. "Do you need another size?"

I studied my reflection for a moment more. "No. I'll take this one."

I handed over my credit card at the mahogany desk that served as the checkout counter. "This dress is wonderful." The saleslady's gray pageboy fell around her face as she tilted her chin down to read the receipt over the half-glasses perched on her nose. She handed over the receipt and a pen, then straightened the bow at the neck of her plain white blouse, above a stiff tweed skirt.

I agreed with her. The door to the store opened, setting off the mechanical chime, and Gwen breezed in carrying a soft leather briefcase, a sheaf of papers, and her purse. "Hello, Alice. Gorgeous day outside." She sailed past, then paused beside a woman considering her reflection as she held a lightweight summer sweater up under her chin. "Oh, honey, that pale apple green looks spectacular on you. Did you know we've got the cardigan to match? Right here. Makes those green eyes of yours look like emeralds. Here, try it on." Gwen escorted the woman to the dressing room and then disappeared through a door at the back of the store.

"That was Gwen Givens?"

Alice put on a tight smile and said, "Yes. The manager." She handed me my dress on a hanger and I wandered back to the dressing rooms where Abby was trying on pants.

Gwen passed me on the way to the desk, but didn't look at me. "Alice. Here's the new schedule. Now about the next shipment, it's due Friday. It has some stunning suits. They're going to fly out the store, so you'd better call Mrs. Hampton. You know how fussy she is if we don't have her size in the store." Her words faded as I checked on Abby in the dressing room. A perky teenager with extremely short, curly red hair and an eyebrow ring stood next to her.

"Those look fabulous," she gushed. "Your butt looks great in those pants." Abby turned in front of the mirror again. I hid a smile. Tate's seemed to be the type of place that would frown on conversations about butts, but the young saleswoman, HEATHER her name tag read, kept raving about the fit of the pants.

Gwen passed the door to the dressing room and Heather fell silent. I sat down on a bench. Alice walked in and collected the clothes from my dressing room.

Heather said, so quietly I could hardly hear her, to Alice, "I see Miss-High-and-Mighty is back."

Alice gave a curt nod, flung the last dress over her arm, and left.

Abby said, "I'm going to try the navy ones again," and shut her door. Heather checked the other dressing rooms. Alice didn't look like she would talk about

Gwen, but maybe Heather would. I still hadn't found out what Cass knew about Gwen, but maybe her co-workers could shed some light on Gwen's personality.

"What's it like to work for Gwen?" I asked.

Heather popped out of a dressing room, more than ready to talk instead of work.

"I just met her through my husband's work, but I've heard some interesting things about her."

I raised my eyebrows.

"Well, she is a little odd. I can see why people would talk about her." Heather lowered her voice to a whisper.

"Odd?"

"She's worked here just as long as Alice and she's never once taken a day of vacation. Something like three years. Can you imagine?"

"No."

"Yeah. Alice was excited to meet someone else from Illinois, but Gwen won't talk about her family there. In fact," Heather's voice was barely audible and I had to strain to hear her, "Alice says there was some sort of scandal and Gwen won't even speak to her parents."

"Really?" It seemed Heather only needed one-word responses to keep her talking.

"They're one of those old, rich families that always had their picture in the paper for society stuff, so Alice recognized her."

"Miss High-and-Mighty?" This was more than one word, but it kept the information flowing.

"Yes." Heather nodded her head to emphasize her point. "Gwen's about to get a big promotion, regional manager. Alice works just as hard, but Gwen is more what Tate's wants people to think they'll look like if they shop here. That classy, old money look." Heather pulled up the sleeves of her orange form-fitting top.

She definitely wasn't going for that old money look. Heather obviously thought Alice was getting a raw deal. Nothing like competition in the workplace to create animosity and shake some gossip loose. "Do you know Gwen's husband?"

"The military dude? Sure." Heather fiddled with the row of pierced earrings that ranged from her lobe to the top of her ear. "He stops in sometimes."

"Have you seen her meeting with another man besides her husband?"

"No." She sorted through the clothes she held and then stopped. "But she does get these weird phone calls. A man asking for her. If she's not here, he hangs up."

"Have there been a lot of calls?"

"No, just a few in the last few weeks."

Abby emerged from the dressing room. "I'm getting the navy and the khaki."

"See, I told you your butt looked great in those," Heather said triumphantly and led Abby to the checkout.

I stood to follow them out. If Gwen was having an affair, she sure was sloppy. Jill, I was sure, would deny Gwen was involved with another man. Steven and Gwen had seemed genuinely happy at the squadron barbeque, but I guess anyone could put up a good front. And then there was the DVD player. It *had* been in her trash can.

I flicked my plastic-shrouded dress over my shoulder and stopped dead in the dressing room doorway. Gwen blocked my path. "What is it with you?" Even though her voice was the same, husky, her words were clipped. She continued without waiting for my reply. "What are you doing here?"

She kept the volume of her voice down, but she was breathing loudly and her fists were clenched at her sides. She looked like she'd been interrupted in the middle of her kickboxing workout. The dressing area was empty, making her soft words even more threatening.

"Shopping. I needed a dress," I said evenly.

"Why do you keep asking questions? Jill told me you asked about me. And now you're back here whispering with my employees." Her volume increased and heads swiveled in our direction. "Well, I won't have it. You talk to me if you want to know something." Her anger seemed to dry up her gushy, I'm-your-friend sales patter. She was strictly business now.

"Fine. What did Cass know about you that she was talking about at the barbeque?"

Gwen's anger contracted. She briefly closed her eyes and took a deep breath. "She thought I was having an affair, which is *not true*." She gouged the air with her finger to emphasize her last words.

"Well, who were you meeting in LaMont's parking lot a few days ago when it was raining? I saw you."

Gwen swallowed quickly. Her anger surged back. Her cheeks flushed. "None of your damn business. Now get out of my store."

"Feisty as ever, aren't you, Gwen?" The speaker, a man in a leather bomber jacket and jeans with intense green eyes in a tanned face, stood behind Gwen. Her face went pale and she stood motionless for a moment. Then she braced herself and turned toward the man. He slipped his arm around her waist and kissed her on the cheek. "Still as beautiful as always, too."

Gwen stiffly moved out of his casual embrace. "What do you want?"

"Just to see you and Zoë. You've been looking for

me, haven't you?" Gwen and the man had forgotten about me. I was still in the dressing room doorway and couldn't get past Gwen.

"Don't think for a minute you can walk in and pick up where you left off with me and Zoë. I knew you'd do this someday. I'm not going to let it happen."

"Gwen." He shook his head, mildly scolding, "You've always been too uptight. It's not about Zoë. It's about you keeping control. Now, don't say anything you might regret." There was a hint of a threat under his easy manner. "I think you'll come around to my way. But we're getting started all wrong. You haven't even asked what I've been doing. Don't you want to know?"

Apparently, Gwen felt the uneasiness, the vague hint of threat, because she didn't order him out like she had me. She shrugged a shoulder.

He smiled again, his white teeth contrasting with his tan skin. "I've been taking pictures. You've probably even seen some of them without knowing it." That thought seemed to amuse him. "Ever pick up *Newsweek*? *USA Today*? I'm freelance. It suits me. Hopping from one hot spot to another."

"I bet it does," Gwen said in an undertone. He must have heard her because he said, "I've been taking pictures here, too. Bet you didn't know that." His voice was completely malicious, now. "You'll probably be interested in these pictures. In fact, we should probably go somewhere and talk about them. Your office?"

Gwen hesitated and then marched stiffly to her office with the man casually striding along behind her.

Later, as Abby buckled her seat belt she said, "Did you see her face?"

"Not really. But I could sure see his. He was almost gloating," I said.

"Gwen was white the whole time. She's scared," Abby said.

I put the Cherokee in reverse. What did she have to be afraid of? Pictures, he mentioned pictures. Something related to Cass? Proof Gwen murdered Cass? I checked the parking lot for cars and backed out of the slot. I hit the gas and an irregular clunk sounded from the front of the Cherokee. I must need a tune-up. I made a mental note to find a mechanic.

If the man had proof, wouldn't he go to the police? Any law-abiding citizen would, right? I sped up and the noise faded.

Unless he wanted something—something Gwen didn't want to give, like access to Zoë. It sounded like blackmail to me.

An Everything in Its Place Tip for an Organized Move

Leave a large, self-addressed stamped envelope with your new address for the people who move into your old home so any mail that slips through the post office's automatic forwarding can be sent to you.

Chapter
Twenty-one

Science is organized knowledge. Wisdom is
organized life.
—Immanuel Kant

I dropped Abby at her door and cruised down to the
gas station to fill up before I went home. My tires
bumped over the hose and set off a bell, but I got out of
the Cherokee and removed the nozzle.

A skinny man with a thin face emerged from the under-
side of a car in one of the bays. "I'll be glad to pump
that for you. Want me to finish?" He wiped his hands on
a rough red cloth, then stuck it in his back pocket.

"Oh. No, I've got it." I pulled the nozzle out when
the numbers reached ten dollars. He picked up a squeegee and swiped it across the windshield.

"Thanks." I replaced the hose and screwed on the
gas cap.

He shrugged. "Anything I can do to keep people coming back, I do. It's the only way to compete with the big boys down the street." He swept the window clean and wiped the squeegee with a paper towel.

"Thanks." I climbed back into the Cherokee to find my cash.

"No problem." While he finished the back window, I studied the sign near the street, Bob's Repair Shop. He came around to the driver's side. I rolled down the window and handed him a ten for the gas. His cursive-stitched name tag read, BOB.

"I think my friend brought her car in here. It was a minivan, actually. Burgundy color. Her brakes were out. Do you remember?"

"No." He rubbed his hand down his face, lengthening it even more and highlighting the bags under his eyes.

"Okay. Thanks." I reached for the key, disappointed. I don't know what I'd hoped to find out, but I felt let down anyway.

"No, I mean, her brakes didn't go out. The lines were punctured."

"What? Punctured?"

"Vandalism." He pulled out the red rag and wiped his hands. "Sneaky way to go about it, too. If they'd been out or disconnected there would'a been a pool of brake fluid under the van and they'd a gone out right away when she first tried them. But with the punctures, well, there's not much fluid on the ground. The brakes would work for a little while, but the fluid would leak out. Pretty soon, no brakes. Did the same thing to the power steering fluid, too." A ghost of a smile cracked his long face. "She was hopping mad when I showed her. Called the police. They showed up and took the lines away. For evidence."

"Have you seen anything else like that?"

"Nope. Not around here. We get a few busted windshields every once in a while. Kids out making trouble or something, but nothing dangerous."

I remembered Cass's words: "Good thing I wasn't going down Rim Rock Road like I usually do."

I pulled away and heard the clunking sound again. I stopped. Bob jogged back over, leaned over the front tire on the driver's side. "You're missing a lug nut and this one just fell off. Had your tires rotated lately?"

"No." I got out and examined the bare bolts. "Could those have come off accidentally? You know, work their way off?"

"I've never seen anything like that."

I gripped the open door of the Cherokee. "Got any extra?"

"Sure thing." Bob trotted off and I walked to the back tire on the driver's side and tugged on the lug nuts. They were tight.

"I checked the rest on this side. The other tires are all fine." Bob's voice made me jump.

"Every one 'a those were loose on that front tire. Strangest thing I've seen in a while."

Not strange. Scary.

I drove the two blocks home very carefully. What could have happened? Maybe just damage to the car, but what if I'd been on the highway or Rim Rock Road with its sheer drop-off? I swallowed hard. Lug nuts didn't accidentally loosen on one tire. Porch railings didn't fall off. And Cass's brakes and steering didn't go out on a fluke. Someone was orchestrating these mishaps.

I'd just dropped Abby off at her house, so it couldn't
be Jeff. He wouldn't risk hurting her. Would he? No. He
wouldn't. Of course not. This was awful. I turned my
thoughts away from that troubling mental debate and
tried to think who else would have done it. I'd just
made Gwen furious, not to mention the details I'd un-
covered about Brent's phone call and Nick's shots.

But how would Nick or Brent know what I'd found
out? I'd told Thistlewait about the phone message a few
hours ago. Was there time for him to question Brent
and for Brent to track me down? No, not enough time
and I doubted Thistlewait would give away the name of
the person who gave him the phone. He never gave any
information away to me. Gwen was right there in the
store, but how could she have run out to the parking lot
and loosened the lug nuts while she was closeted with
the strange man who arrived at Tate's?

I pulled into the driveway and breathed a sigh of relief. I'd made it. Somehow, something I'd done or said
threatened someone. They were either trying to get me
to be quiet or silence me permanently.

I glanced around the garage. So many dangerous
things: weed killer, cleaning products, insecticides. I
suppressed a shiver as I looked at Mitch's circular saw.

I had two choices. Either run from this and maybe
this person would leave me alone or press on and figure
out who was behind the incidents, one of which led to
death.

It wasn't really a choice. I had to go on. Backing
down didn't guarantee anything.

"Where do you want these? In this cabinet?" Abby
held a cookie sheet in one hand and had Livvy propped

up on her shoulder with the other hand. Livvy let out a tentative cry. Abby bounced and bobbed.

I paused, a stack of mixing bowls weighing in my arms, and considered the cabinets. "No, put it over here closer to the oven." I dragged the box across the floor for her.

"I think we had more boxes for our kitchen than any other room in the house." I sliced the tape on a new box, pulled out the top bundle, and unwrapped a stack of china salad plates. I stacked them carefully in a high cabinet, where they would be far away from Livvy when she started exploring in a few months.

"I know. But you've only got a few more to go," Abby said in a peppy voice. It did look like we might get finished before it was time for me to get ready for my big Saturday night date with Mitch.

"Hey," Abby said, "want to come over for dinner tomorrow night?"

"Sure."

"Great. About six o'clock?"

Mitch staggered up the basement stairs. "Last one," he gasped. We'd stored some boxes with things we didn't need right away in the basement. Rex meandered around Mitch's feet, sniffing the seams of the dish-packed box. Mitch did a little two-step and dropped the box with a thud, narrowly missing Rex's tail. I cringed, hoping the dishes weren't shattered.

"Those are ready to go to the shed." I pointed to the flattened boxes we'd already unpacked. Mitch gathered them up, maneuvered out the door to the backyard, and banged against the door frame and stair handrail.

I unwrapped six delicate coffee cups before Mitch returned.

"There's a police car at Keith and Friona's house, he announced.

"I hope there wasn't another break-in," Abby said.

"Probably just another garage." He picked up his list for the hardware superstore and gave me a quick kiss. "See you in about an hour. Love you."

Livvy's huffy cries merged together and I picked up my pace. I crammed the last piece of china, a gravy boat, into the cabinet with a hurried clink and took her from Abby as her cries intensified and her face turned from pink to scarlet. In her room, I settled down to feed her. I looked around and smiled. The walls could use a new coat of paint, but her nursery looked beautiful with the white crib and dresser and the yellow crib set dotted with tiny blue and white flowers. It felt good to have it out of the box. Her mobile of flowers and birds rotated slightly and gave off a single note of "Hush, Little Baby." The window needed something, a valance maybe.

A large television truck with the number eight emblazoned on its side and a satellite lumbered past the window. I stopped rocking and watched as two women hopped down from the truck parked behind the police car at Friona's house. One woman had blond hair escaping from a scrunchie. She wore baggy shorts, a T-shirt, and that classic California fashion statement, thick sandals with white socks. I pegged her as the news photographer. The other woman had hard-looking dark hair and moved carefully in high heels over the uneven sidewalk, straightening her vivid blue suit as she walked.

A second news truck arrived by the time I finished changing Livvy. "What's going on?" I asked Abby, who was watching out the dining room window.

"I don't know. Here, I'll take Livvy. I see Mabel; she'll know. You go find out."

I headed across the lawn slowly. I didn't want to be a nosy neighbor. I'd looked down on Ed and Mabel for their snoopy ways, but I was curious, too. I merged into the little clump of neighbors gathered in Mabel's yard. I found her off to one side. "What's going on?"

"The woman who lived there was killed last night," Mabel said.

"What?" Goose bumps traveled up my arms. Another death?

"It was on the radio. Mugged in a parking lot downtown."

"She was a squadron spouse." I noticed Mabel looked annoyed that she didn't know I was acquainted with Friona. Mabel wanted to be the one giving the news, not receiving it.

"I knew nothing good was going on in that house," Mabel said.

"She was a night owl. I saw her out my back window," said another woman, a contemporary of Mabel's. "I'm Helen," she said to me. "What a welcome you're getting. This street used to be the quietest, nicest street. Now we've had a *murder*." Helen was shrunken and stooped with age. Once she'd been petite; now she was tiny. She had a thin face with lines running down to her pinched mouth and straight iron-gray hair flattened in a bowl cut.

"Never had a murder until everyone started dying or moving to Arizona, and all these young people moved in." Helen patted my arm. "I don't mean you, of course. But people like her." She pointed at the news vans obscuring Friona's house. "Snooty. Too good to come over and say hello, the few times I did see her. Kept her nose in the air and didn't even wave. But she sure kept busy coming and going at night. I don't sleep well. Never

would have guessed she was slinging burgers at McD[c]
ald's."

"Does anyone know what happened?"

"She was knifed," Helen said with relish.

"Helen you need to turn that TV of yours off," Mabel
reproved her friend. "This was a person, not some character in a cop show. She was held up at knifepoint when
she left after closing. They took her purse and then slit
her throat."

"That's terrible," I said.

"Someone at a hotel next to the restaurant heard her
scream and called the police, but it was too late," Mabel
added.

"How do you know all this?" I asked.

"I overheard Karrie Hobart talking to her photographer. Karrie's my favorite. She's on Channel Two. Unlike some people, I want to know the facts, not the
speculation." Mabel shot a look at Helen.

Helen turned and marched away with as much dig-
nity as her stooped form allowed.

"Helen gets carried away, but she's right about one
thing. This used to be a nice, quiet little street."

I returned to the house, sat down at the kitchen table,
and pressed my trembling hands between my knees. I
relayed the news to Abby.

"That's awful. Friona?" Abby's eyebrows scrunched
tighter. "From the mall?"

I nodded. I felt hot, then shivered.

Abby said, "You don't look so good, kind of pale.
You're not going to faint, are you?"

The corners of the room seemed to slip and merge.
"No." I bent over and pressed my forehead to my clenched
hands. Breathe.

It was too strange. Another spouse was dead. What kind of squadron was this? Too much stress. Breathe. Too many changes, the move, a baby, a new house, and a new squadron. On top of all that, squadron wives were dying. Dying!

Abby's voice had faded to a low murmur, but I realized she wanted me to drink some water. Experimentally, I raised my head and blinked. The sunlight in the kitchen seemed extremely bright. I didn't feel that strange hot/cold sensation anymore, so I took my large plastic water cup that Abby held out and sipped. The icy cold water felt good on my dry throat. "Sorry. It's just so scary."

Abby, who'd been hovering beside my chair, dropped into the one beside me and said, "I wonder what was she doing at McDonald's?"

It wouldn't hurt to tell Friona's secret now that it was being broadcast over the news—even Helen knew. "She worked at McDonald's. I saw her one morning and recognized her. She was embarrassed and didn't want anyone to know. Her husband didn't even know. Poor Friona. Now it's going to be all over the news."

The next night I was feeding Livvy in Jeff and Abby's bedroom while the muted stop-and-go conversation continued in the dining room between Mitch, Abby, and Jeff when I noticed a piece of paper on the floor under Jeff's dresser.

It had been a dinner of awkward pauses. Especially after I mentioned working at the Vincents' house organizing Cass's things. I mentioned it in passing, but I caught the quick look Abby shot in Jeff's direction. Almost as if—no, that was crazy. Abby couldn't be afraid of Jeff. While we ate, all I could think was that it would be a relief to go home.

But now I didn't want to go home so quickly. The folded paper tempted me. It looked like the paper that set off the argument between Cass and Jeff at the barbeque.

I scanned the rest of the bedroom as I burped Livvy. Like the rest of the house it had an eclectic flair. A patchwork spread covered their brass bed. Two different styles of dressers, one dark wood and one painted white, and an upholstered chair furnished the small room, but even with the different elements, it worked. It must have something to do with the fabrics and paint colors.

Perfume, jewelry, and a set of hand weights covered Abby's dresser. Jeff's was clean, except for a photo of Abby and a low bowl that held change and the patches off his flight suit.

I settled Livvy in the playpen that Mitch had set up at the foot of the bed. Groggy and satisfied from eating, she drifted into sleep. I slipped over to Jeff's dresser and picked up the paper.

I let out a breath that I hadn't realized I was holding. It wasn't the paper I'd seen at the squad. The paper that made Cass so mad was a check. This was a receipt for a latte and a bagel. I replaced it where I'd found it, then glanced at the drawers and the closet.

No. I would not snoop through my best friend's room. But Abby was worried and, although I hated to admit it, she was afraid. She knew Jeff was lying about something. What if he'd done it? What if Abby was living with a murderer?

I listened and heard the clink of silverware. After a since that stretched too long Abby asked about our date at the Aurora Mansion. I slid open the top dresser drawer. Sorry, Abby, I mentally apologized, but if Jeff's guilty, the sooner you know the better. I quickly felt around the edges of shirts. Nothing. I opened the rest of the drawers. Socks, jeans, underwear. Man, Jeff was neat. Nothing in the drawers except clothes and paper liners. I moved to the tiny closet and patted down Jeff's flight suits.

The door to the room creaked on its hinges and I spun around. Whisk, Abby's cat, stood on the threshold, her tail swishing slowly back and forth. The cat pranced to the bed, leapt lightly onto the spread, and settled down to watch me. I turned back to the closet. Abby had commandeered the rest of the closet. Nothing else except shoes and boots wedged next to a two-drawer filing cabinet in the back corner. I wasn't surprised to see the filing cabinet in the closet. A house with square footage on the low side made you stick things where you normally wouldn't dream of storing things. After all, I had some of my summer sandals stashed in the linen closet. I hesitated, but didn't hear any sounds in the hall, only the muted ebb and flow of voices.

I pulled open the drawer. I snuck a glance over my shoulder. Whisk still gazed at me with unblinking sapphire eyes. I tried to shake my uneasy feeling. It was absurd that a cat could induce guilty feelings. Jeff's neatness extended to the filing system, too. The top drawer contained household accounts, receipts, and tax returns. The bottom drawer had three folders. I seized the one labeled DEER LEASE, and flicked through the papers.

A letter addressed to Jeff informed him his check had been received and gave driving directions to the leased land. It went on to describe the rules: when he could hunt and regulations about guests. Jeff's canceled

check was his receipt. It was stapled to the back. It w.
deposited the Monday after Cass died. I slid the folder
back into the drawer and closed it. Jeff really did have a
deer lease. He wasn't lying about that.

But Abby knew he was lying about *something*. I scanned
the room. I couldn't stretch my time much longer. I knew
from my organizing jobs that people tended to store
items that were most important or valuable in their bedroom. I went to the tiny nightstand. The bottom was open
and lined with model airplanes. I pulled on the small
drawer at the top. It was stuck. I gave the drawer a yank.
At the same moment I heard footsteps in the hall. The
whole drawer flew out of the nightstand and the contents splattered onto the floor.

Oh no. I whipped around to check Livvy, but the rug
had muffled the crash. She shifted her feet, sighed, and
went back to deep breathing. The footsteps grew louder.
What was I going to say to Jeff and Abby? I set the drawer
down and scrambled to put everything back. A Kleenex.
I was looking for a Kleenex. I glanced over my shoulder
and saw Jeff as he walked down the hall to the bathroom
without glancing in the room.

Thank goodness he didn't see. I tossed in notepads,
pens, a mini tissue box, and a small book about weather,
one of Jeff's other interests besides hunting. I tried to
shove the drawer back, but it stuck again.

I heard the toilet flush and water run. I felt a bead of
sweat on my forehead, near my hairline. The bathroom
door opened. I shifted the drawer, jiggled it. Finally. It
slid into place.

Jeff looked in on his way back to the dining room.
"Everything okay?"

"Fine," I whispered and patted Livvy's back before I

...lowed him down the hall. Fine, if you don't count almost having a heart attack while searching your best friend's house.

I slapped the plastic tray down and slid into the booth. Back to reality, I thought, and took my paper plate with the sub sandwich and Diet Coke off the tray. Our date on Saturday night had been wonderful, a relaxing dinner served with china, crystal, real flowers on the linen tablecloth, muted music, and dim lights. We were able to talk without interruption and even dance a little. Today, Monday, it was back to real life. No slinky dress that made Mitch smile his slow smile. Today it was fast food on paper plates gulped down while I wore a sweater, jeans, and tennis shoes. After this I was off for a quick rush through the Comm. Ah well, it had been nice. And the garage sale was Saturday, five days away. I'd better get busy.

We had avoided talking about anything from the squadron during our date, except once when I mentioned Friona. "It's so sad. And weird, too. Two squadron spouses have died within two weeks. Don't you think it's a little strange?"

"Well, we know Cass's death was intentional, but Friona worked in a fairly risky place. Armed robbery at fast food restaurants isn't all that uncommon. I worked at that claim-processing unit when I was in high school. We got a lot of calls about robbery. She was in the wrong place at the wrong time. Now let's not talk about death anymore. Let's dance." He led me onto the floor, where I tucked my head under his chin and enjoyed the slow dance.

But I couldn't ignore it anymore since I wa[s]
base. Mitch rocked the car seat with one hand and held
his sub sandwich in the other. Thinking of our short
conversation about Friona, I asked, "Do you like playing
devil's advocate?"

"What?"

"You downplay my ideas, like the possibility of
Friona's and Cass's deaths being related to each other."

"Someone has to be the voice of reason in our family."

I faked a kick at his shin and he wiped the smile off
his face.

He said, "I bet you didn't know I liked debate in high
school."

"No. I didn't." Debate seemed too . . . cerebral for
my athletically inclined spouse.

"I did. I liked to argue one side and then turn
around and argue the other side. So, yeah, I like being
the devil's advocate." He waggled his eyebrows.

"Why didn't you become a lawyer?"

"Better snow skiing at the Academy. And chicks love
a man with wings."

"Please. You know I fell in love with you only because
I beat you at miniature golf."

Later in the Comm, I tossed a head of romaine lettuce into a plastic bag and put it in my cart. I dutifully
followed the arrows from the produce aisle around to
baking and canned goods. Only the military would try
to control traffic flow in a grocery store, but I had to admit
that it was a nice system when the store was crowded.

Today, Monday afternoon, was pretty slow and I didn't have to work too hard to avoid retirees. I added canned soup and flour to the basket, then I strained to remember what else was missing from the pantry. In my rush to get out of the house, I'd left the list on my desk beside my cookbooks. I checked the price on the cereal, $1.86, and dropped two boxes into the cart. The prices definitely made it worth the drive.

A slight, silver-haired woman cut in front of me in the noodle section and grabbed the last two packages of spaghetti noodles. I picked up ziti noodles instead. When we'd lived in California, the Comm had always been packed with military retirees who took their grocery shopping benefit very seriously. I'd learned to stay out of the way of frail-looking elderly folks. They could be vicious with their carts when the shelves were getting low. Today, I was too busy keeping an eye on Livvy, making sure she wasn't about to burst into one of her crying sessions, to worry about noodles.

"Isn't he a cute one! How old?" I turned to put a jumbo package of paper towels in my cart and found the spaghetti-swiping woman patting Livvy's blanket and smiling. Livvy's *pink* blanket. Despite hats with bows and pink clothing, this was the third person to stop me to look at Livvy and ask "his" age. "She's four months." I reminded myself how lucky I was to have a little baby and how much people enjoyed reliving memories of their babies when they asked about Livvy. The woman cooed and smiled at Livvy. Livvy kicked her feet and the woman's face crinkled.

On the next aisle, I tossed a package of Hershey Kisses into the cart. Then I tried to wrestle a twelve-pack of Diet Coke into a few inches of free space on the lower rack of the cart. A voice above me asked, "Can I give you a hand there?"

I looked over my shoulder at Nick Townsend. "Ah, sure." I backed out of his way. I checked out his cart. It was packed with soft drinks, jumbo packages of candy bars, Pop-Tarts, and snack bars. He stood up after shoving the box into the lower level of my cart. "I can pack a cart to the brim. I'm the Snack O."

He moved back to his cart and shoved it back and forth like a little boy revving up his toy car before it took off.

I nodded. The Snack Officer's job was to stock junk food in the snack bar, a little cubby of a room or closet somewhere in the squadron. The squad bought in bulk and resold things individually, a nice moneymaker for the squadron.

"Thanks. Hey, I was wondering, did you ever see Cass at Northwest Family Health?"

"What?" His cart stilled.

"I saw you there the last two Fridays. I know Cass had an appointment the Friday she died, so I wondered if she knew about your allergy shots."

His expression moved from blankly polite through confusion and to fury in a few seconds. He took a step toward me and I backed up against the shelves. The two-liter soft drink bottles bumped against my shoulders. Nick was about my height, so his narrowed eyes and flushed face were right in my face. "Shut up!" A wave of his onion breath engulfed me. I moved my head back further, pressing against the bottles behind me.

I glanced up and down the aisle. It was deserted. "Don't go messing in my private life." I could see little beads of sweat pop out on his upper lip. "If I hear one word, *one word,* of this from anyone else I'll know where ame from and you'll be sorry." Before I could move, he jerked away and sped off down the aisle with his overloaded cart.

I stood there for a few moments until my heartbeat calmed down a little. Then I headed for the frozen foods. Well, he didn't say it in words, but he certainly confirmed he didn't want anyone to know about the shots.

Chapter
Twenty-two

"**O**h, Rex." His head sunk nearly to the floor and hovered above the linoleum he'd shredded near the laundry room threshold. I'd pulled in the garage with the Cherokee loaded with groceries and stopped at our basement laundry room door to let Rex out. Earlier, I hadn't wanted to leave him outside with rain threatening, but he'd already chewed up two pairs of leather boots when I was home. Who knew what he'd get into if I left him alone in the house?

"Rex, no! No chewing on the floor." His head sank another inch lower. I switched the heavy grocery bag to the other arm. "Go." I gestured up the stairs. He flew up the stairs, but then ran from room to room sniffing. "Real repentant," I muttered and closed the door. I'd deal with that after unloading the groceries.

Half an hour later, the phone rang as I folded empty

brown grocery bags. I snatched it up before it could ring again and wake Livvy. My elbow hit my water cup and knocked it over. The lid popped off and water gushed into the English ivy plant I'd set in the sink to water.

A voiced shouted over the line. I jerked the phone away from my ear, but I could still hear the words. "What I do on my own time is my private business." It had to be Nick. He took a ragged breath. "Just what gives you the right to go poking around in my life? The Air Force doesn't have any say in how I live when I'm off-base and off work. You'd better keep quiet."

"Nick." Thinking fast on my feet had never been one of my greatest talents. I was lousy at verbal debates and arguments, but I tried to think of something to calm him down. The waves of hate radiating through his voice scared me. I swallowed and said, "I understand. Mitch feels the same way. When he pulls into our driveway he's done with work, too." Another reason we didn't want to live on-base was that you never left your job. Even on the way to your front door from work, you were expected to put on your hat and salute anyone higher in rank than you. Of course, Mitch would not break regs, but I needed to dampen Nick's hostility, so I didn't go into detail.

Nick didn't even seem to hear me. He stopped ranting and his voice was even, almost soft as he said, "Nosy troublemaker. You make trouble for me and I'll make plenty of trouble for you. Just understand one thing. Don't mess with me."

The dial tone sounded in my ear. I dropped into the chair at my secretary. Earlier in the morning, I had sat there making out my grocery list. I propped my elbows on the folded-down lid and rubbed my forehead.

Nick had blown up in the store, so he had a short fuse, if the situation was right. He was dangerous. His last flat statement scared me more than his threats. He was serious.

I felt vulnerable. Basically, I'd revealed to Nick that I knew he had something to hide and then asked if Cass noticed him at Northwest Health. How stupid could I be? I glanced at the back door. The dead bolt was locked. I fingered the phone and glanced at one of the tiny cubbyholes that contained my glass clock. If it was near 4:30 I'd wait until Mitch got home instead of calling the squad. This was not a conversation for the phone.

But my clock was in the bottom cubbyhole on the right, not the middle. My gaze automatically went to the middle one and snagged there on a small, framed picture of my mother and me. It shouldn't have been in the middle cubbyhole. I tried to decide if I could have switched them while dusting. Not likely. I only dusted the cubbies when they looked bad with a thick coat of dust. And besides, I didn't notice anything different this morning when I sat here and jotted down the grocery list. In fact, my list was right beside the open cookbooks, where I left it when I flew out the door in such a hurry.

But hadn't I left the Chinese cookbook on top of the pile open to the curry chicken recipe? Now it was on the bottom of the stack. The blue notebook of my mother's recipes perched on top of the stack.

I glanced around the house with an uneasy feeling. I carefully checked the rest of the house and then sat down on the bed. I wasn't imagining things. The boxes in the hall closet that we hadn't unpacked now had the tape slit. They'd been moved and put back. The towels in the bathroom cabinet were stacked differently and a few things on my dresser had been moved. Someone had been in our house and searched it carefully. I ran a shaky hand through my hair and tried to decide what to do.

Rex put his head under my hand. I rubbed his ears. "You knew, didn't you, boy? That's what you were doing, trying to get out." I smoothed down my comforter and walked restlessly around the room. I felt as if my house had been contaminated. My privacy had been violated. I felt uncomfortable in my own bedroom.

My first thought was Nick. He was furious, but it couldn't have been him. I'd left the commissary shortly after I talked with him. He wouldn't have had time to beat me home and look at anything. Besides, he was more an "in your face" type of person. He wouldn't search stealthily; he would fling things all over the place and wouldn't care if it were obvious that the house had been searched. So it had to be someone else.

Maybe Jeff *had* seen me searching in their bedroom and this was his way to get back at me. No. Don't let it be Jeff. Who else? Who else could have done it?

Gwen? I certainly wouldn't make her top ten friends list right now. A chill crept up the back of my neck and I went to turn up the heat. I'd already opened every closet and checked the basement, so I knew no one was lurking anywhere, but I still felt vulnerable. I made another circuit of the house and inspected the front door and each window. Rex tried to get in front of me at every other step, almost tripping me.

A loud banging on the kitchen door pounded through the house. My heart raced and Rex let out a volley of barks. Livvy started crying. I sidled up to the door and eased the curtain back an inch.

Abby smiled and waved. I flipped the lock and opened the door. "Didn't remember our walk?" she said, taking my jeans. Then she looked closely at me. "What's wrong?"

For a second, I tried to compose myself and act like nothing was wrong, but I couldn't do it. I couldn't hide how upset I was from Abby. "I think someone's been in our house. Oh, let me try to get Livvy back to sleep and I'll explain."

With only a few protests Livvy fell asleep and then I showed Abby the things that were in the wrong place, but I didn't mention that the thought that Jeff might have done it had crossed my mind.

"You mean you remember how your towels are stacked?" she asked.

"Not usually, but I always put the white ones, they're old and starting to fray on the edges, on the bottom. The new yellow ones go on top." Abby looked at the cabinet with white towels stacked on top of the fluffy yellow ones and shook her head.

"Okay," she said slowly. "Someone's been in here. Is anything gone?"

"No."

"Why is everything so neat?"

"They didn't want us to know. Remember when the Vincents' house was broken into? This has to be connected. It's the third break-in." I shouldn't talk to Abby about this, but I couldn't seem to shut up.

"Three?"

Don't tell Abby anything else, I mentally warned myself, but the words tumbled out. "Our house, their house, and their garage."

"But their house was trashed."

It must be the stress. I must be in shock. I kept jabbering, my thoughts racing. "I know, but right before that a few things were different—the blinds were closed and a closet door was open. I think they were searching carefully at first and then came back and weren't so careful."

"But why search carefully and then trash the place later?"

"It was taking too long?"

A creaking noise echoed up the basement stairs and we both tensed, but then I heard the familiar thud of Mitch's tread on the steps.

I shushed him like I did every day. He never remembered Livvy was sleeping and he sounded like an elephant stampede.

Abby said, "I'll go. We can walk some other time."

I convinced Mitch that someone had been in our house, then I described my encounter with Nick at the Comm and his phone call while Mitch checked the dead bolt on the kitchen door.

He stopped clicking it back and forth and stared at me. "He threatened you?"

"Yes."

Mitch closed the door, turned the dead bolt, and went to check the lock on the front door. He had a determined look on his face that I'd never seen before.

"Do you think Nick is a little fixated on flying?" I'd calmed down a bit and felt a little steadier.

"Some guys wouldn't know what to do if they couldn't fly."

Mitch loved to fly. To him it was the best part of the job, not the only reason for his existence. But to other flyers it was their whole identity. I remembered Nick's apartment with his airplane posters and Academy yearbooks. How would he react if he thought his career was threatened? He was sort of obsessed, but he didn't seem like the type of person who would use an allergic reacon to kill someone. Too subtle. Nick was all jumpy energy. He'd be more likely to bludgeon someone to death. I shook my head. Here I was speculating about how people I knew would most likely kill someone. Mitch moved to a window. He still had that determined look on his face.

"Mitch, you're not going to do anything, are you?"

"About Nick's doctor appointments? No. It's all guesswork, but about his threats, yes."

"Mitch."

"Don't worry. I'll take care of it." I opened my mouth again, but he cut me off. "I'm not going to let him threaten you. I can handle him."

Nick was several inches shorter and slighter than Mitch. "Be careful," I said.

"I will. You, too." He studied the window lock and then looked back at me. "Can't you let it go? It's not your responsibility."

I rubbed the wood grain in the trim board. "I've stumbled across lots of information that brings up too many questions. I can't trust anyone. I can't be comfortable here, live with these people, and wonder if one of them killed my neighbor."

"We don't have to do things with everyone. We can be reserved."

"I can't quit. Someone murdered Cass. We're involved." I gestured at the house. "It would be more foolish to hide and hope they go away. Because they won't."

Mitch rubbed his forehead. "I know if I tell you to back off, it'll just make you go at it harder." He sighed. "Make sure you've got your cell phone, okay?"

That's one reason I love Mitch. He understands me. "Do you see anything wrong with the locks?" I asked.

"No. No marks, nothing looks like it was forced

open." He leaned against the kitchen counter. "Eith
they picked the lock or they had a key."

"Should we call the police?"

Mitch leveled a look at me and I had to smile. "Okay,
I don't really want to call them either. They already
think I'm a weirdo since I brought them wasps in a baggie."

"We'd have to call the Vernon police."

I could imagine the reaction I'd get if I tried to explain that I thought an almost invisible search of our
house was related to a wasp-sting murder. "Ugh. You're
right. Forget it."

I went to the sink and put the English ivy back on the
windowsill. Then I ran hot water and squirted in some
soap.

Gwen didn't seem like the type of person who'd
know how to pick a lock. I could imagine her spinning
a story and convincing a neighbor to let her inside our
house, but if that had happened I was sure Ed and
Mabel, unelected captains of the neighborhood watch,
would have reported in as soon as I returned home.

No, whoever got in our house probably strolled up to
the door and unlocked it. They didn't act suspicious, so
no one noticed. But where did they get a key?

My hands went slack in the sudsy water. I *gave* a copy
away. To Abby and Jeff.

I realized the water was about to overflow the sink. I
twisted the knobs and shut off the water, then stood
there staring at the tiny bubbles as they popped. Abby
had been genuinely shocked when she arrived after I
discovered the search. She'd been acting weird lately,
but I knew her well enough to know she was acting
weird because she was worried. She wasn't faking surprise today.

at left Jeff.

I don't know how long I stood there. The slight shadow of a hope I'd had that Jeff wasn't involved in this mess evaporated like the soap bubbles laced through my fingers. What was I going to do? I didn't have an answer to that question so I shoved it aside and moved on. Why break into my house and search it anyway?

Okay, back to the beginning. I picked up a handful of silverware and scrubbed. The garage was the first break-in. Why? It was probably easier to get into the garage than the house. I washed, rinsed, and stacked the dishes. Why wait to break into the house?

I stood up straighter. Rex. Rex was still at the Vincents' house when the garage was broken into. He'd barked the night before we discovered the break-in. The day after we moved him, the house was searched for the first time. The searcher couldn't get into the house with a rottweiler guarding it.

I rinsed my large water cup, propped it up to dry, and twisted the drain open. I watched the bubbles swirl away without really seeing them. But what was the search for? I had no idea. I sighed, wiped my hands on a dish towel. It was too confusing. Maybe if I left it alone for a while my subconscious would make some sense of this mess.

Later that night, I sat in the overstuffed chair, but I wasn't relaxed. Livvy's cries sounded from down the hall. She tapered off, then after a few seconds of silence, she started up again, reminding me of an ambulance siren. She'd been crying for an hour and twenty-nine minutes. I had alternated between reassuring myself we were doing the right thing and practically wringing my hands in distress. I stopped going in her room to pat her back and tell her it was all right after the third time. It seemed to

make her furious instead of comforting her. With
cry I felt like a spring wound tighter and tighter. I watched
the minute hand on the clock sweep around to twelve.

"Okay. That's it. I can't stand it anymore. I'm going
to get her."

"Ellie. She's fine. She's dry, she's been fed, she's been
burped. She just wants you to rock her to sleep."

"I know."

"And if you go in there and rock her to sleep now,
she'll want you to rock her to sleep again at midnight.
And again at two. And—"

"I know. But I can't stand it anymore." I hopped up
out of the chair, but stopped before I crossed the room.
Silence.

And the house stayed quiet as I tiptoed down the hall.
I could hear her heavy breathing from the doorway. Her
plump arms were flung out, relaxed. I heard a tiny snore.
I leaned my head against the door frame. "Oh, Livvy.
It's not easy growing up, is it?"

I slipped back to the living room. "She's asleep!"
Mitch and I exchanged high fives.

"Six-thirty is such a civilized time to get up," I said to
Livvy as I gathered up my cereal bowl and juice glass.
Livvy kicked her feet and the rattles over her bouncy
chair jangled. I was rejuvenated after almost seven hours
of sleep last night, even with a nighttime feeding for
Livvy. Amazing what a few uninterrupted hours of sleep
could do. If we could stay in this routine I just might
survive until preschool. And it was a good thing, too,
because I had a lot to do today.

Joe had returned my call about Isabelle Coombes

...ked me to look for her papers and give her anything I found. I needed to run by the grocery store. And I had the charity pickup at the Vincents' at two o'clock. I loved the variety of being a stay-at-home mom. Every day was different and none of them were boring. I jotted down a list.

Then I dumped the dishes in the sink, grabbed the dishcloth to wipe the table. What was wrong with my ivy? I leaned over the counter so I could see better. I'd watered it yesterday before I left for the Comm.

Could I have overwatered? The stalks were brown and they sagged as if they couldn't support the weight of the leaves, which had an odd transparency. I pulled the pot down off the windowsill. A little water caught in the saucer sloshed on my hand. But it wasn't water. It felt greasy.

Then I remembered. I'd knocked my oversized water cup into the sink yesterday when Nick called and doused the ivy with water. I looked at my water cup, freshly washed last night and resting with the clean dishes.

But it couldn't have been water. I didn't have much of a green thumb but, wow, I'd never managed to kill a plant overnight. I rubbed my oily fingers together. Some of my optimism that had arrived with the new day seeped away. I picked up the phone to call Mitch, but put it down when I glanced at the clock. He'd had a six A.M. show time for his flight. He was gearing up, practicing for the check ride. He was in the air by now. I sighed and went to shower before I called Thistlewait.

Thistlewait poked his finger in the soil, then in the liquid in the saucer. He smelled his fingers and wiped them on a paper towel. "I'll take this in and checked, but my guess is antifreeze."

"Antifreeze?"

"It's colorless, odorless, and can be lethal. Dogs or cats that lick it off garage floors die all the time."

I felt lightheaded. Poison in the water cup that I chugged water from every day. Someone had gotten in my house, searched it, and poisoned the water I drank.

Why had I given a key to Abby and Jeff? I mentally kicked myself. Why didn't I hide a key somewhere around the outside of the house in case I locked myself out? How could Jeff do something like this? I realized Thistlewait was speaking, but I couldn't take in what he was saying.

I held Livvy propped up on my shoulder. The dizziness went away, but a wave of revulsion swept through me and I thought for a second I might throw up. Whatever I ate, Livvy ate, too. I passed everything on to her through the breast milk. She could have been poisoned, too. I gritted my teeth together and waited for the queasy sensation to pass. I rubbed my cheek against Livvy's fuzzy head. We were okay, nothing had happened. But whoever was doing these things was evil and ruthless.

Even though I vowed not to share anything I'd found with Thistlewait, I couldn't avoid it. Things were too serious. I put Livvy in the swing and went back to the kitchen table where he was seated. Then I told him everything: the loose porch railing and lug nuts, Friona's jobs, Gwen's parking lot meeting with a man, Nick's doctor visits and threats, how I thought our house had been searched. Everything.

When I finished he leaned back. "You've managed to gather a lot of info on your own."

"Well, I interact with these people every day. I'm bound to see and hear things that you won't."

Thistlewait nodded, then ran his hands down over his face. "I'm sure if I tell you to stay out of this you'll follow my directions," he said in a resigned tone.

"I'm involved. Someone got in my house and tried to poison me! How can I stay out of it? I'm in danger in my car, even at home. I don't think hiding out will make it go away."

Thistlewait didn't reply, just sighed and picked up the ivy. "I'll send someone out to fingerprint your house and your car."

As he walked down the porch he gave the railing an experimental tug. It held fast. Mitch was handy around the house. Thistlewait said, "Thanks for the call, Mrs. Avery." His manner was different. Instead of his usual faintly amused tone, his voice was serious.

An Everything in Its Place Tip for an Organized Move

Three ways to "recycle" your stuff:

- Ticket stubs—line several in a row and laminate for bookmarks.
- Pictures—cut out, place magnets on the back, and use as refrigerator magnets.
- Clothing—give outdated items to kids for a dress-up box.

Chapter
Twenty-three

Making the simple complicated is commonplace;
making the complicated simple, awesomely
simple, that's creativity.
—Charles Mingus

The danger in my life seemed to be escalating and I wasn't going to sit around and wait for Thistlewait. So far my discoveries had been more accidental than purposeful. It was time to focus and do some serious digging.

I called Abby. When her answering machine came on, I was relieved. It gave me more time to figure out a way to subtly ask what Jeff was doing yesterday afternoon.

I still had unanswered questions about Gwen, too. Next I drove to Tate's. On my way in from the parking lot, I spotted Alice. I had a feeling she might know something about Gwen. They worked together and the other saleslady said they were from the same place. And she had mentioned a scandal. If I could get Alice to talk to

me maybe I could find out something more ab
Gwen.

"Excuse me, do you mind if I ask you a few questions? You sold me a dress a few weeks ago."

Alice placed her tuna sandwich on the square of plastic wrap and wiped her mouth with a napkin. "The black sheath. I remember you." She gestured to the empty chair at her table. I sat down and placed Livvy's car seat on the ground between the chairs. We were on the terrace of Hailey's Deli, a chic little spot for expensive lunches just down from Tate's. It was warm in the sun and sheltered from the wind.

Alice leaned down and peered under the sun hood covering the upper half of the car seat. "She's beautiful." My opinion of Alice went up a few notches. One, she could recognize the visual clue of a baby wearing a white hat with pink flowers as a girl. And, two, she realized Livvy was beautiful.

"Have you worn the dress yet?" She picked up her paper coffee cup and leaned back in her chair.

"Yes. I love it. I didn't want to talk to you about that." I considered how much to tell Alice. "My husband is in the same squadron as Gwen's husband out at Greenly. Several people from the squadron live in my neighborhood, up on Black Rock Hill. We've had some break-ins. And I've received a threatening phone call. I think Gwen may be involved."

Alice sipped her coffee and looked at me for a moment with her eyes squinting against the sun. She crossed one arm over her stomach, propped her elbow on her hand, and let her coffee waver in the air as she studied me. It was the pose of movie stars in black-and-white films, except those women usually held a cigarette instead of a caramel macchiato. "I think there's e a bit you're not telling me, but I will tell you what I know about Gwen. It isn't much."

"You're both from Illinois?" I asked to get the ball rolling.

"Springfield. Her mother's picture was in the paper often, in the society pages. Hosting gala dinners and fund-raisers, that sort of thing. I didn't move in those same circles, but I'm very active with the cancer society, so I knew her mother slightly from dealing with her for our fund-raisers. If I remember right, her mother was a widow, something about her father dying in a car accident, I think, when Gwen was young. After Gwen married, I saw her pictures occasionally in the paper, but she wasn't involved in charities like her mother. And it took me quite a while to realize it was her husband next to her in the photos. She kept her own last name, so I didn't know Gwen was married until someone on the Winter Ball Committee told me."

She sipped her coffee and glanced down at the car seat. "I don't remember seeing a birth announcement for her daughter, but I don't usually read those." I wondered if Alice was a thorough reader of the newspaper with a good memory or if she was lonely and kept tabs on slight acquaintances through grainy photos and lived vicariously through those photos.

Today Alice wore a serviceable navy pantsuit and a plain white shell. Basic, generic clothing that would last forever, but frumpy. Her clothes combined with her gray bob with Mamie Eisenhower bangs made me think she led a rather isolated life, but her relaxed pose with the coffee and the way she'd critically studied me before saying anything suggested Alice wasn't quite a gullible, lonely old lady.

Alice set her coffee down and smoothed the plastic

wrap around her sandwich. She seemed reluctant [...]
on. "There was some sort of scandal? Her divorce?" I
ventured.

Alice made an "um-hum" noise for agreement. "Her
husband left her. He was in medical school and most
people spoke highly of him. I didn't know him. There
had been"—Alice tossed her hand out and looked disapproving—"whispers, rumors, whatever you would call
them that she drove him away from her. I found that
hard to believe. After all, they had a new baby. A few
months later Gwen moved to California. Her mother
said Gwen moved there to reconcile with her husband.
But it must not have worked out because she showed up
here at Tate's two years later on her own."

"Why did you move here?"

"To be closer to my grandkids after my husband
died."

I murmured my sympathies and my thoughts of her
as a lonely old lady evaporated when she pulled out her
photos to show off her four grandchildren. After admiring the children and asking ages, I returned to
Gwen. "Was she surprised to see you?"

Alice laughed briefly. "We both started work the
same day at Tate's. The HR people said we should have
a lot in common since we were both from Springfield.
She didn't know me, but I knew her. I mentioned her
mother and the cancer society and she got quiet. Later
that day, she told me she didn't want to talk about
Springfield and she would appreciate it if I didn't mention it again. As far as I know, she's never been back
there. In fact, she hardly ever takes off work."

"Does she bring any of her friends by work?" When
Alice shook her head no, I pressed, "Any men friends?"

"No." Alice looked faintly amused.

...es she ever talk about her husband's work, the squadron, or the people in her neighborhood?"

"No. She's strictly business."

"She never mentioned a friend named Cass?"

"No." Alice's reply was quick. She didn't even have to think about it.

"Has she ever been involved in anything . . ." I searched for an innocuous way to say illegal since the stolen DVD player had turned up in her trash can, "unethical?" I finished.

"Let me explain." Alice looked a little exasperated. "Gwen Givens is focused on getting to the top. She doesn't distract herself with friends or gossip at work. I've never seen her do anything questionable, but with her drive to succeed . . ." Alice's voice trailed off. "You just never know how far some people will go."

I didn't know if I should believe Alice. After all, Gwen was being promoted above Alice. Maybe Alice was just jealous. "That's a big promotion Gwen is getting," I said.

"She can have it and the headaches that go with it. All I want is a nice little job for some extra income. I've got plenty to do."

Alice stood up and tossed her sandwich and empty cup in the trash. "That's all I can tell you." I thanked her for talking to me. Gwen kept her business and personal life separate and I'd already offended Jill, her best friend, by asking questions about Gwen. Where else could I find out more about Gwen?

I checked my watch and jumped up. I had ten minutes to get back to Cass's house to meet the people for the Goodwill pickup.

I hurtled into the Vincents' driveway at two o'clock on the dot. No van in sight. I took a deep breath, pulled

Livvy's car seat out, and strolled to the door. I
transferred Livvy to the BabyBjörn front carrier an
made a quick circuit of the house. I'd finished packing
Cass's things on Sunday afternoon and I didn't see anything I'd missed. My work combined with the cleaning
crew's labor had left the house presentable. I might
have to call the cleaning crew back to my house to clean
up the fine fingerprint powder that now coated every
surface.

I checked my watch. Ten after. They were late. I sat
down on the couch, but Livvy was getting sleepy and
she sensed the interruption in the constant motion that
was lulling her to sleep. She huffed and geared up for a
crying jag.

"Okay, shush. I'll walk." I bouncy-walked through the
house and Livvy sighed contentedly before drifting into
deep REM. I knew better than to sit down again.

I wandered over to the snack bar and restacked the
mail into neater piles. There was something I was supposed to do. I'd had a plan that morning, but my dead
ivy had blown my concentration. I dug my to-do list out
of my purse. Of course, Isabelle Coombes. I bobbed down
the hall to the master bedroom. Livvy snored, music to
my ears. Bundles of paper drifted over the desk, like a
mini–mountain range. I hadn't tried to organize the papers, I'd just stacked them.

I flipped through the first stack and found home
loan paperwork, bills, and receipts. It reminded me of
the box I needed to return to Brent and Diana. I
worked my way through the other mounds. Eventually, I
came across Cass's notes about the Wal-Mart protest.
She'd found a watershed regulation that prevented
streams from being piped or rerouted when an area was
developed. Wal-Mart had applied for a variance to

e stream that flowed smack-dab through their
proposed site, but Cass's protests and media campaign
had an impact. Wal-Mart opted for a less troublesome
plot of land.

I turned the last paper over and frowned. Nothing
about Isabelle's valley. I pressed the button on the
dented hard drive. Nothing happened. If Cass's notes
were in there, it would take someone more expert than
me to retrieve them.

I bounced back to the front door, peered out the
window. Still no truck. I called Goodwill and the woman
who tracked down the schedule said, "You're scheduled
for between two and three."

Okay. What now? At least fifteen more minutes to
burn. I decided to clean out my purse. It wasn't like I
could sit down and relax. I tossed a bunch of old receipts, then pulled out the spiral notebook, Cass's notebook with her Squadron Spotlight column notes. I'd
forgotten about it until now.

Jeff, Nick, and Brent wouldn't be listed, but Diana
and Gwen were. Diana's entry read:

From Southern California, only child
Tennis scholarship to Central California University
Kids: Gavin (5), Stacy (4)
No pets
Still plays tennis twice a week, likes to watch Nick at
Night
Remote. Perfectionist.
One of Vernon's top realtors, Million Dollar Club
As cold and as perfect as a cemetery statue

I assumed the last line was Cass's private summary
that didn't make it into the final version.

I paged through the notebook, amazed at th[...]
of info Cass found and recorded about the spouses. Sh[...]
had an insight into personalities and was sometimes just
plain funny. Like Jill's summary: "Practical, great organizer. So good, in fact, she never leaves anything for
herself to do!"

I found Gwen's entry.

Born and raised—Springfield, Illinois
Mother widowed, no siblings
BS in Business Ad, Retail Business
Daughter, Zoë, from previous marriage
Moved to California (Sac) after divorce, then Vernon
Pet—goldfish (Squiggy)
Likes golf, sailing, and classical music
*She may look like a trust fund baby, but I think she's
had a tough time in the past. Won't talk about it.*

No help there. Idly, I flicked the page over, then
frowned. Cass had jotted down two phone numbers and
a string of letters and numbers on the back of Gwen's
entry. I picked up the phone and dialed the first number, a local one.

"Assessor's office. This is Ginger."

"Hi, Ginger. I've got a number here—I think an account number." I read it to her.

"Oh, that's a parcel number." I could hear her clicking away on a keyboard. "Here you go. Taxes are current." She rattled off an address and I wrote it down in
the spiral notebook.

"Where's that?"

"The billing address and the parcel number sound
like it's out in the valley. You know, east of Black Rock
Hill."

"Thanks." This was Isabelle's land.

I dialed the next number.

"Trinity County auditor."

"Hi. I've got a parcel number here. Could you tell me—" What did I want to know? Who owned it? Where it was? What would Cass want to know?

The doorbell rang. "I'll have to call you back."

I opened the door for two guys in jeans and T-shirts. They loaded Cass's belongings into the Goodwill truck while I paced around the porch. Auditor. I'd seen that recently, but where? One of the guys wrote me a receipt and I placed it on the snack bar next to Joe's stack of mail.

The mail! That's where I'd seen it. I shifted through the piles and found an envelope with Trinity County Auditor, Recording Department. I slit the envelope and pulled out several papers, a deed. Lots of legalese, but it boiled down to a Mrs. Norwood selling her property to Tecmarc Corporation. I checked the parcel number and it matched. So Isabelle's father sold to Mrs. Norwood, the neighbor down the road. And Mrs. Norwood sold to Tecmarc. What is Tecmarc? I searched the paperwork. Tecmarc was represented by—Friona Herrerras?

Friona? Friona seemed like the least likely person I knew to be involved in buying land. Buying a new wardrobe, yes, but land? I couldn't see her caring about land. And she'd been broke. What was Tecmarc?

Livvy wiggled, sighed, and opened her eyes. I found Cass's phone book, but there wasn't a listing for Tecmarc. Where could I find out information about Tecmarc? Would Friona's husband, Keith, be able to tell me anything? I didn't feel too confident that he'd be a great source of information, considering how much

Friona hid from him. Friona had told me she didn't have any close friends in Vernon, either.

I looked back over the paperwork again and read a yellow sticky note attached to the first page. "Mrs. Vincent, I'm still researching the other easement. Do you want me to continue? If so, another search fee is required." It was signed with the name Debbie and a phone number.

Livvy nuzzled around the fabric of the front carrier, gave out a halfhearted cry, then gnawed on her thumb. Okay, time to head home for a diaper change and a feeding. A little later, I was settled in Livvy's room feeding her. I checked Mitch's recall roster and dialed Keith's phone number.

An answering machine clicked on after a few rings and gave the standard, "We can't come to the phone" spiel. I didn't leave a message. I dialed the squadron next.

"Orderly room. Airman Jones."

"Hi, Tessa. It's Ellie."

"Hey, girl. How are you?"

"I'm all right and Livvy's doing great."

"What's up? I haven't seen Mitch lately."

"That's okay," I said. "I'm actually looking for Keith Herrerras. Is he in today?"

"No, he's gone back to New York to bury his wife."

I knew Tessa would have the latest info. "Then that's a dead end," I muttered to myself.

But Tessa picked up on my words. "What's a dead end?"

"You know I'm sorting through Cass's things, right? I've got some papers. Business paperwork with Friona's signature, like she worked for a company, but I can't see her involved in corporate business deals. I mean, she told me she didn't have any office skills. She couldn't even type."

"Hold on," Tessa said to me. Then, to someone else she said, "Thanks. See you tomorrow. Okay, I'm back. Yeah, I think she would've had a hard time squeezing in an office job between her mall runs. That girl. I couldn't believe how many shoes she had. Our own little Imelda. And she wanted the jewelry to go with her fancy clothes, too. One day she was in here talking to Keith. She wasn't paying attention and forgot I was here. She described this pair of diamond earrings she wanted. I'd about tuned her out, but then she said, 'I will be able to afford them. After this deal, I'll be able to pay for them in cash.' I couldn't hear what Keith said, but she got defensive. She said something like, 'Give it a rest. You could at least be glad for me.' She looked really surprised when she saw me sitting right here at my desk, not two feet from her. Oops, gotta go."

"Okay. Thanks."

I finished feeding Livvy, then put her on her play mat with her noisiest, brightest toys. I shook a black and white ball dotted with red. She kicked her feet out and squeaked, delighted.

I grabbed the phone and the public records I'd brought back from the Vincents'. I figured Joe wanted me to hand these off to Isabelle Coombes so I might as well bring them home with me.

I dialed the number on the sticky note. "This-is-Debbie-how-may-I-help-you." She ran the words together in a flat, no-nonsense tone.

This was a woman who didn't have time for a rambling explanation. I tried to be succinct. "I'm following up on some paperwork for a friend, Cass Vincent. I've got a deed. Your note says you need another search fee to keep looking for the rest of the documents?"

"Give me the number on the top right-hand corner." I read it to her. After a few moments of silence, her voice exploded, "Right. Norwood. Easements. I remember your friend." A note of exasperation crept into her voice. "She was on her cell phone the whole time she was in here, carrying on a conversation with me and someone else at the same time."

"Was there more research she wanted?"

"She said there was another easement from way back. I didn't find it." Her voice said she doubted it was there. "But I did run across a recent easement, filed, let me see, this year. I pulled it because I figured your friend would want to see it. Basically, it amounted to a company, Tecmarc, granting Forever Wild, that sounds like a nonprofit, the right to maintain and preserve open space. Restricted development of part of the property allowed."

"Well, if there's another easement, wouldn't it be filed with that one or the deed?"

A sigh. "Not necessarily. Sometimes they're filed separately. They're a pain to find, let me tell you."

"I'll pay another search fee." Debbie gave me directions for paying the fee, then I asked, "Where can I find out more about Tecmarc and Forever Wild?"

"Let's see. They'd have to file a business license— that'd be with us. And you could check with the secretary of state. I know they've got business records there, too. Articles of incorporation and all that. They've got a good Web site."

I added business licenses to Debbie's search and then checked on Livvy. She was fascinated with the crinkly sound a toy elephant's ears made as she crushed them. I turned on the computer, waited for the right screen, and typed in the address for the secretary of state.

They had an online database. Sometimes I loved technology, especially when it didn't make me wait. I found Tecmarc with Friona listed as registered agent and the same address as Mrs. Norwood's property listed as the business address. I typed in Forever Wild. I came up with the Norwood address again. Popular place. Automatically, I scrolled down and opened my eyes wide. I leaned closer to the screen, but the words didn't change. "Registered agent: Jeff Dovonowski."

Why hadn't I asked whose signatures were on that easement Debbie had found?

I sat back, stunned. The other registered agent in this strange mix of companies and legal paperwork was dead. This *wasn't* good.

I chewed my lip. Could I ask Abby about this? No, better not to. If she knew about Jeff being involved in a land easement, she would've told me. At least, I think she would have. No way was I going to bring this up until I knew more.

I glanced at the play mat and jumped up. It was empty. Where was Livvy?

I scurried around the end of the bed. She'd scooted around until her head was tucked under the dust ruffle. I picked her up. "You're quite the tricky one, aren't you." She squealed and grinned her toothless grin. I kissed her cheek. "Come on, let's go for a drive. Mommy's got to get food for tonight. And I want to see that land."

I turned onto the steep switchback road and reached out to brace the grocery bag of tortillas, cream cheese, green onions, and pimentos on the passenger seat, but I removed my hand after a few seconds. Despite the steepness, the smooth road between the pines was easy to navigate.

At the bottom of the hill the road swept through an ornate gate of black wrought iron set in red brick. A modest home was under construction inside the gate. Maybe Wilde Creek Estates wasn't totally out of our price range. Then I saw the sign with a map of the lots plotted around the future golf course. I glanced back at the building under construction. It was the gatehouse, not a future residence. If that was the gatehouse, then the homes here would look like the country homes of British royalty.

Livvy made some tentative squawks, so I pulled a toy out of the diaper bag. Mitch and I called it "Thing One" because it looked like something out of a Dr. Seuss book. Livvy grasped the contraption of circles, sliding balls, and clear rattles filled with tiny, noisy pellets that drained from one chamber to another. Livvy shook it. I couldn't see her face, but from her contented mumblings I assumed she liked it.

I coasted down the empty street. The fresh blacktop branched off at intervals, then ended abruptly at patches of dirt and gravel. Along the road, thick tubes sprouted occasionally from the ground like some alien plant life. I could see four mansions under construction with men balancing on roofs or working inside the partly framed walls. The main street ended at a fringe of trees.

Livvy jabbered as the rattles swirled. She seemed happy enough, so I left her in the Cherokee. I locked the doors and walked a few steps to the edge of the trees. A crow called sharply and took flight in a flurry of wings.

Isabelle's father had been right: it was a beautiful valley. Below me a meadow gently rippled down to a thin ribbon of silver that twisted lazily through the valley floor. I thought for a moment I could hear the river, but then I realized it was the wind sweeping through the pines. A movement in the valley on my right caught my eye. A yellow excavator gnawed at the earth and then dumped its claw into a dump truck.

A shiny red pickup rumbled down the road and stopped next to the Cherokee. "That's the ninth tee box. Quite a view," said the man who climbed out of the pickup and slammed the door. He had on a crisp long-sleeved white oxford, khaki pants, and a tie. The office casual look ended at his ankles. Muddy hiking boots provided a realistic counterpoint to the rest of his slick image. I moved back to the Cherokee, unlocked the door.

"Sorry to startle you there. You looking for a lot? This road'll be residential." He smoothed his shiny yellow tie and nodded down the hill where the machinery labored. His black hair was as dark as the feathers of the crow that just flew away. "All these lots will be directly on the course. Can't get much better than that. Walk right off your porch onto the course. Close to the clubhouse, too." He squinted his eyes in the sunlight as he circled around to study the view. "Wilde Creek will be the premier area in Vernon. You should get in now. Value here is only going to go up."

"I'm just looking today." I bet this guy could tell me a few things about Wilde Creek, but I'd probably get more out of him if he thought I was a potential customer. "It is nice out here right now, but with a whole development going in, I don't know, I don't want to be packed in next to my neighbors," I said, trying to do my best snotty, rich girl impression. I thought of the junior high clique that I hadn't been part of. Barri Carslow was the eye in the center of the popularity ring. Others moved in and out, but Barri, with her disdain and supreme self-confidence, remained firmly at the epicenter of the "in" group.

He crossed his arms, planted his feet, and shook his head. "No. Not here. This is an exclusive development. High end. Lots'll be at least two acres. The golf course and tracks around Wilde Creek are preserved as open space with a conservation easement. It'll be wide open out here with a country feel to it. But you'll have the best golf course in the county in your backyard, and shopping and downtown only minutes away."

Barri could look down her pert nose and dismiss you with a sharp comment. I tried to imitate her. "Easement. Whatever. Anything can be changed. There's no guarantee about what will go in all around. At least if we buy on Black Rock Hill I know what will be a few blocks away—the houses that are already there."

"We're lucky to be under a conservation easement here. It allows only restricted development."

I raised my eyebrows skeptically, I hoped.

He swept his starched oxford cloth arm around. "All this land, the whole valley, is covered under the easement. It's a legally binding document. Property's got a bunch of rights, like water rights, logging rights. Well, the owners of Wilde Creek signed an easement with Forever Wild to conserve the open space and natural beauty of this valley. No way another development or strip mall is going in here." Somehow I didn't think nature and environmental groups had a golf course in mind when someone said, "open space." He continued, "Good little tax break for the owners, too." He winked.

"And you are?"

"Cody Jenkins. Jenkins Custom Homes." So he was a builder. He whipped out a card from a silver case. I must be a better actress than I thought because the poor guy thought he was close to making a sale.

I took the card. "The lots are how much?"

"Eighty-five thousand and up. But most of the prime lots are sold. I own about a third of them, some on the course, some with a wildlife view."

I pointed to a real estate sign posted across the street. "Diana McCarter. She own some, too?"

Jenkins laughed. "Nah. She's the little real estate lady that handled most of the lot sales in here. There are still a few left, but you'd be better off looking at my lots because I can give you the whole deal, the lot and a house designed specifically to maximize the terrain and the value of the location."

"I think I know her. She handled the whole development? Why?"

Jenkins shrugged. "Wilde Creek hired her. Did a great job. Of course, these lots sell themselves."

"Doesn't seem like you'd want to waste your time on someone else's development. I bet you've got your own subdivision going somewhere in Vernon."

"Three subdivisions, to be exact." He named a few subdivisions that Mitch and I had visited, but left as quickly as we could because the houses looked cheap and boring. "But I'm not wasting a minute of my time," he continued. "Wilde Creek is going to change the way folks here think about homes. It's going to be the standard and I'll be associated with that standard. Connections are what it's all about." So Jenkins was using Wilde Creek to move into the luxury home league.

"Who do you work with from Wilde Creek? Are they local?"

"They're out of state, but you know how it is with fax and e-mail. I didn't catch your name."

I ignored him, just like Barri ignored two-thirds of the school population. "I'll think about it." I climbed in the Cherokee, slammed the door, and gave Jenkins a brief wave before I did a quick three-point turn that would've made my driver's ed teacher proud. On the way out, I spotted a white clapboard house with outbuildings tucked at the foot of Black Rock Hill, probably either the old Norwood or Coombes homestead.

I inched my way down the buffet and added cheese and crackers to the fruit salad on my plate. I grabbed a tortilla roll-up, my contribution to the spread. I'd raced home, mixed the chives and pimentos with the cream cheese, and slathered it on the tortillas. Then, I'd rolled and sliced the stuffed tortillas. It wasn't gourmet, but it was the best I could do after the day I'd had. I turned from the buffet with a weird sense of being in a replay. It had only been a month ago when I first met the other spouses at the coffee at Cass's house. I felt tense and on edge as I scanned the faces. Did one of these people murder Cass?

"Ellie." Abby touched my arm and I jumped, nearly dumping my plate.

"Sorry. You're holding up the line."

"Would you like something to drink?" Diana poised near the kitchen door. "Green tea or coffee?" she asked.

I hid a grimace. "Just water for me."

"I'll try the tea," Abby said from behind me.

I felt awkward with Abby. I couldn't just blurt out, "I think Jeff tried to kill me." I didn't want her to let Jeff know what I suspected. Abby and I had scurried through the cold to Diana's red brick colonial. It was a small mansion with a lofty balcony over a portico that extended out to cover the circular driveway. The questions I'd asked as we walked over must have been casual enough because Abby told me what I wanted to know without asking why I wanted to know. She said yesterday Jeff worked in the squad, except for a trip to the gym around lunchtime, which would have been about the time my house was searched.

I picked up a napkin and moved into the kitchen. Diana was hosting the coffee this month. Of course, I should have expected it, but I was surprised to find her address one block north of ours. I wondered who else from the squadron lived close to us. I made a mental note to buy a pooper-scooper.

Diana's home was decorated in the country home look: hardwood, chintz, florals, plaids, and leather furniture mixed in an eclectic blend that looked haphazard, but I'd bet there was a decorator involved somewhere in the casually elegant surroundings. Something felt odd about the house, too. But I couldn't figure out what it was.

In the blue and white country kitchen, cows, pigs, and ducks ornamented everything from the towel rack to the curtains. Diana handed me a tall glass of ice water with a lemon slice. She straightened the turtleneck on her sweater with fall foliage and returned to serving drinks. I propped myself up near the sink. Gwen was in the living room and I didn't know if she'd be civil to me, so I figured avoidance was the best policy until the formal part of the coffee started. Surely she wouldn't make a scene with Jill going over old business. And I needed to sort through the info I'd found out. Friona and Jeff were both connected with Wilde Creek.

Abby edged over to me and interrupted my thoughts. "Wow. Did you see the pool in the back?" she asked.

I peered out the French doors and saw leaves snagged on the edges of a large rectangular tarp.

"Who knew the military paid so well?" I asked.

"It's a huge house. How do they afford it?" She lowered her voice. "And everything is so perfect. I feel like I'm in a furniture showroom."

I nodded and realized that was it. There wasn't anything personal in the rooms. No magazines, books, or family pictures.

Something moved at the edge of my vision. I hadn't realized anyone else was beside me in the kitchen, but a petite, plain woman stood beside me and had, apparently, been absorbing our conversation. Her long reddish-brown hair, pulled back in an untidy French braid, revealed her bland face. Small brown eyes surrounded by stubby lashes darted from me to Abby. She looked vaguely familiar. I glanced at Abby for help.

"You're Penny, aren't you?" asked Abby. "You're arranging the children's Christmas party, right?" Then I remembered her from the last coffee. Thank goodness, I could always count on Abby to remember faces. Penny nodded and sipped her tea. She wore an oversized gray turtleneck with a black broomstick skirt that sagged down to the tips of her scuffed black boots. "Did you bring your daughter with you?" she asked me.

"No. She's at home with my husband," I said, surprised she even knew I had a daughter. I wondered how

Livvy was doing. Would she cry as long as she did last night?

"Oh, I hoped you'd bring her. I saw her at the squadron barbeque and she was so precious. I wanted to hold her." She finished her tea and set it in the sink. "Do you ever need a sitter? I like kids and would love to babysit her. We live just around the corner."

"Don't we all? Thanks for offering. I might give you a call sometime." She studied the brick floor a moment and I wondered if she could tell that I wouldn't call someone I didn't know to watch Livvy. I regretted my casual reply, but she said, "Thanks. I'm looking for a new job, so I have a lot of time on my hands right now."

Abby said, "I've just found a job myself. I hate the want ads. I hope I never have to do it again. But, of course, I'll have to since we'll move again in a few years." She said the last with a grimace. "I teach. What do you do?"

"I'm an archivist. Archeological conservation. I'm hoping for an opening at one of the universities, but nothing so far."

I was surprised. Her unassuming personality and sloppy appearance didn't look like university material, at least not tenured material. I mentally scolded myself for my prejudices. I slid over to the phone and called Mitch to see if Livvy was asleep.

"Forty-five minutes. She's out like a light." There was a note of triumph in his voice.

"Really? That's better," I said.

"Ladies, let's get started," Jill commanded from the living room. I hung up the phone, put my glass in the sink, and looked around for the trash can. I noticed a built-in desk and stopped to look at it. My dad's part-time hobby of making desks and other furniture always made me curious when I saw unusual furniture. Made of golden oak, this one had cubbyholes and small drawers across the back. A snapshot was propped up in one of the cubbies behind a small blue bottle. I stopped because it was the first picture I had seen in the house. We have so many pictures I don't know where to put them. Diana's house seemed barren without smiling portraits in the hall and candid snapshots on the fridge.

This snapshot captured two women. Diana wore a black cap and gown. She looked the same as she did now, except her hair was longer. The other woman was older, probably early forties. Frizzy bright red hair surrounded a tan face with heavy black eyeliner and mascara circling her eyes. The two women stood stiffly beside each other. No hugs or arms around each other. Something about their faces, the noses or something, seemed similar.

Diana entered the kitchen, carrying coffee cups. "Diana, is this your mom?" The cups clattered into the sink and she hurried across the kitchen.

She snatched it out of my hand and removed my paper plate from the other hand. "They're starting in there."

As I left, Diana shoved the picture in a drawer and slammed it shut.

Chapter
Twenty-four

I slid into a dining room chair near the back of the room. The clipboards were already circulating as Jill reminded people of their assignments for the garage sale at the end of the week. She quickly moved on to up-coming events, like the next spouse coffee and the Christmas party. When she launched into the next fund-raiser, a weekly sale of sandwiches and snacks at the squadron, "Monday Morsels," I tuned her out, thinking of Joe's arrival a few hours ago.

I couldn't really tell any change in him. He was quiet and withdrawn. I wondered if the time away had helped at all. Maybe it had just delayed the awful reality of his empty house. He murmured something about picking up Rex in a few days after he got settled, which I thought was odd. Wouldn't he want some companionship in that quiet, dark house?

I glanced around the room. Diana's house was quiet, too, except for Jill's voice. Had Brent taken the kids out for the night? I couldn't picture him eating a Big Mac and guarding the Happy Meal toys at a McDonald's playland while his kids climbed in the tunnels.

Jill finished up the business portion of the coffee. "Remember everyone, the garage sale is this Saturday. Show up fifteen minutes before the time slot you volunteered to take," she commanded sternly. Then she announced, "We didn't have time during the last coffee, but this month we will have a craft." I checked out the supplies. Baby food jars and votive candles, aka candleholders. Across the room, Abby crossed her eyes and I suppressed a smile. Why we had to incorporate craft time in the coffee like preschoolers, I had no idea. I was inherently uncrafty and had no use for a baby food jar with hot-glued gingham ruffles. I went in search of a bathroom. The half bath downstairs was occupied, so I climbed the stairs, hoping the rest of the house was empty.

I found the kids' bathroom, decorated with a Mickey Mouse theme. I dried my hands on the red towels and walked quietly back down the ornate runner in the center of the hall. The open doors revealed the kids' rooms, blue spaceships for the boy and yellow sunflowers for the girl. A closed door stood between these rooms, probably a closet. I decided to take a quick peek before I let myself wonder what I was looking for or mentally talk myself out of it.

Brent's raised eyebrows and icy blue eyes met mine. It wasn't a closet; it was a tiny office. Unlike the rest of the house, which had a hotel-like neatness, the office was a mess, with stacks of boxes covering most of the floor and papers scattered over the desk. No decorator's touch in this room. In a glance, I took in the locked gun display case, a gray metal desk and file cabinet, the uncurtained window, and the plain white walls. He cocked an eyebrow and said, "Looking for something?"

"Just the bathroom," I stammered and mentally told my heartbeat to calm down.

"Well, you've found my hideaway. Care to join me?" He slipped one paper under another, then grabbed his beer and pointed with it toward a small refrigerator tucked beside the file cabinet. "No one will miss you for a few minutes."

"I'll pass on the beer, but I did want to ask you a question." I sat down in the metal folding chair to get a closer look at the paper he'd covered so quickly, but the Nevis bank statement hid all but a thin edge of the paper underneath. I could see part of a logo, a leaf or vine, on the bottom paper. "I want to know why you told Cass you were sorry. What did you do?"

His bottle paused in midair for a beat, then he took a swallow and set the bottle down. He smiled and brushed his golden hair off his forehead. "We just had a little misunderstanding." He stood up and came around the desk, then leaned back on the front of it. He angled his long legs out, blocking my way to the door. Even though I'd left it open, I felt a trickle of unease nudge my heartbeat faster. He looked directly into my eyes and asked in a low voice, "Did she tell you about it?"

I swallowed. There was something about his directness and his sense of pent-up energy that made me nervous and aware of him. "In a roundabout way," I hedged. "Has the OSI asked you about it?"

"The OSI?" He snorted and folded his arms across

his chest. "Why would they ask me about it? It was a little misunderstanding. She was a beautiful woman." He shrugged as if that explained everything.

He must have made a pass at her and she rejected him. "Did you talk to her at the squadron barbeque?" I eyed the distance to the door and listened for someone else in the hall, but the women's voices were faint, barely floating up the stairs in bursts of chatter and laughter.

"No, I never got to talk to her." His smile was still there, but it looked a little forced.

"She rejected you," I said, pushing a little.

His tension seemed to evaporate and he shook his head. "She wasn't interested in what I wanted. Fine by me. There are lots of beautiful women out there."

"What about Diana? How does she feel about your beautiful women?" I bet there was a long line of women in Brent's life.

He shrugged again, leaned back over the desk, and picked up his bottle of beer. "We have an understanding. She knows I admire women. She leaves me alone and I leave her alone. We don't interfere in each other's lives."

I tried to keep the disgust off my face. After all, Cass rejected Brent before she died. Could he have been angry enough to kill her? Or maybe Diana was tired of being cheated on and killed Cass. But if there was a long line of women, why would Cass be the one to die? Diana couldn't take it anymore? I would have thought that if Brent's affairs upset Diana, she'd have killed him.

"That is the saddest thing I've ever heard someone say about their marriage." I jumped up, skipped over his ankles, yanked his door shut, and flew down the stairs.

When I entered the living room, Abby raised her eyebrows, as if to ask where I had been, but she didn't move from the card table with craft supplies. Her jar was painted with wildflowers and now she was gluing lace around the edge. I was about to make the first move to leave when the doorbell rang. Since I was closest, I opened it. Who would arrive an hour late?

A woman in her fifties stood on the porch. Cigarette smoke drifted in the door. When she saw me her smile faded. "Di?" She asked hesitantly, then looked past me into the house and said with relief, "Oh, a party." She took a last drag on her cigarette, dropped it, and crushed it with the heel of her purple tennis shoe before stepping inside.

Her short, flaming red hair extended in every direction around her face, but the back was flattened against her head. She had that artificial dark tan that makes me automatically think tanning bed. Her lined face showed her smoking and "sun worshipping" were not recent activities. Small eyes, rimmed in thick black liner, scanned faces as she chewed the remnants of scarlet lipstick. She adjusted her fuchsia wind suit trimmed in gold braid, then gripped my arm and said in a wave of cigarette and alcohol breath, "I'm Di's mother Vera. Where is she?" She smiled, revealing yellow teeth. This had to be a joke. The thought of Diana and Vera being even loosely related was too far-fetched to be true. I realized the room had gone quiet.

"Diana," I called as I turned around. Diana froze in the door of the kitchen, a dish towel knotted in her hands.

"Di!" Vera flew across the room and enveloped Diana in a hug. Diana stood as motionless as a fence post.

When Vera released her, Diana said in a low voice, "What are you doing here?"

"Just dropping in for a visit."

"But you live in California." Diana's voice was angry and what else? Annoyed, embarrassed?

"I sold the mobile home and bought a Winnebago!" Vera grabbed Diana's arm and pulled her to the front window. "See, there it is. Since you never come visit me, I figured I could see the country and come visit you. You won't have to worry about anything. I'll stay right there in Winnie! That's what I call it. A thing that big needs a name, like a ship."

For a moment I thought Diana might pass out, but she seemed to remember there were people vividly watching the reunion. She smiled and said in a tight voice, "The kids are spending the night at a friend's house, but let me go find Brent and tell him you're here. Help yourself to something to eat." She hurried up the stairs and the room suddenly seemed too quiet. At once the wives went back to their crafts and food, talking a little too loudly and shooting covert glances at Vera, who went to the buffet and filled a plate with her shoulders drooping. I can't stand to see someone with their feelings hurt, so when Vera sat down on the couch, I sat down beside her and asked her what part of California she was from.

"Everywhere." She smiled, but her eyes were shiny. "I've never much liked to stay in one place. Diana. She likes to be called Diana now. I'd forgotten that." Vera shook her head. "I can't call her anything but Di." They must not have been in touch for a long time if Vera didn't remember what name her daughter liked to use. Jill arrived with coffee for Vera.

"What kind of gig is this? One of those parties where you try to sell crap like baskets or candles?"

Jill explained about the spouse coffee and the activities connected with the squadron.

Vera said, "I remember when she met Brent at a tennis tournament. She was so excited. An officer! She thinks she's so different from me, but look at her life. Moving around every few years, just like her ma. She's not so different." Vera patted her pockets and pulled out a worn quilted cigarette case and a lighter. She looked around for an ashtray, but didn't find one, so she used her empty plate instead. She blew out a long stream of smoke toward the ceiling.

Diana and Brent clattered down the stairs and I stood up with relief and moved out of the cigarette aura. Brent gave his mother-in-law an awkward air kiss near her cheek. Diana waved away the cigarette smoke and strode off to the kitchen with the ash-filled dish. The meeting broke up and Abby and I escaped. No one seemed to want to linger, but I didn't think the family reunion was going to be that pleasant after the company left.

We crunched quickly through the piles of leaves on the sidewalk. "So where did you disappear to?" Abby asked.

"I went upstairs to find a bathroom and ran into Brent. There was something . . . I don't know what it was, but something about that conversation with Brent tonight that bothered me," I said.

Abby snorted, "Brent's smarminess?"

"No, it was something else, but I can't figure it out."

"Did you know he latched onto me at the barbeque after you left The Hole?" Abby made a face. "I couldn't get away from him. Finally, I told him to back off."

I wished I could be so bold. "What do some women see in him?" I asked.

Abby shrugged. "Irene, you know, the fluffy blond one, I saw her at the Comm. She couldn't stop talking about him. She says he's the squadron heartthrob. 'It's his energy. The tension vibrates off of him.' You can stop laughing. She did say it just like that."

"In that same breathless way?"

"Yes." Abby's defensive face broke into a smile. "It cracked me up too, at the time. I think he's a jerk."

"You weren't with him when he met me in the hall at the parking lot door," I said to Abby.

"No, I don't know where he went after I ditched him."

So there was a window of time he was unaccounted for. Maybe alone in the parking lot before Mitch went out there. "What about Diana? I wonder if she stayed in the squad."

"I don't know, but I did see her while Brent was hanging around me. She didn't say anything, just stood on the other side of the room and gave him the evil eye over the rim of her Coke."

At that moment, a rumbling sound came from the darkness beside me, then I collided with a dark green trash can. Helen's tiny, stooped form emerged from behind it. She clutched her flat chest. "Oh, it's just you girls. You gave me a fright. I thought you were the Peeping Tom."

"What?"

"Well, you see, I forgot to put my trash can out before dark, and I've been inside fretting about it. The truck comes at different times. I'm afraid I'll miss getting it out. So I finally decided to run it out here as fast as I could and get back inside. So sorry I bumped you. Are you all right?"

"I'm fine. Helen, this is Abby, a friend of mine." I performed the introduction and crossed my arms to keep warm in the frigid air.

"What Peeping Tom?" Abby asked.

"That man over there. He's been parking there for days. He leaves in the middle of the night and comes back early in the morning." Helen flapped her hand at a gray Ford parked a little up the street. "In fact," her voice stopped quivering and grew stronger, "I'm getting damn tired of worrying about what he's going to do next. I'm going to tell him to get out of here, or I'm calling the police."

"Helen, don't. That's not a good idea," I said.

"You girls are here. He won't do anything with witnesses." Helen was spry for her age. Before I could grab her arm, she trotted off across the street and banged on the driver's window. "Get out of here or I'm calling the police," she shouted.

We crossed the street. "Helen, let's go inside," I said.

"He's ignoring me. Won't even look at me!" She jerked on the handle, the door opened, and a bundle thudded into the street at our feet. A human bundle.

An Everything in Its Place Tip for an Organized Move

If a moving company is packing your household goods, find out what items they will not pack. Banned items usually include
- Fertilizer
- Batteries

- Candles
- Nail polish
- Certain cleaning fluids
- Propane tanks

Plan to move these things yourself, give them away, or dispose of them.

Chapter
Twenty-five

Abby put her arm around Helen and pulled her back. I tentatively touched the pale wrist a few inches from my ankle. Cold. I jerked my hand back and said, "Let's go back to your house, Helen. We need to call the police."

She nodded and leaned into Abby as they crossed the street. In her living room, she collapsed into her threadbare rocker-recliner. "You call." She pointed to an early cordless phone. "I'm too shaky."

I picked up a phone the size of a brick and dialed. Abby watched out the window until the first flashing light disturbed the still street and then she went to make coffee.

An officer arrived, took our names, got the basic facts, and said he'd return. In the kitchen, Abby opened and closed cabinet doors. "Did you see his face?" I asked. "The man that fell out of the car?"

She paused with a coffee filter in her hand. "No."

"I did when I checked for a pulse. It was his profile. I think it was the man who talked to Gwen in Tate's."

"Oh, boy. We're a few houses down from Gwen and Steven's." She added two more scoops of coffee. "It's going to be a long night."

I moved a rusted push mower over an inch to make room for a wheelbarrow brimming with water hoses and decrepit gardening tools. It was Friday, one day until G-Day, garage sale day, and I was in my garage trying to make room for the old baby strollers, knickknacks, and beat-up furniture that had been dropped off during the last few days in preparation for the garage sale. I knew some early bird bargain hunter would knock on my door at six tomorrow, asking to look around "real quick." I paused to rub my eyes. I was still tired from my late night with the police two nights ago. They had more questions than I could answer.

Today was overcast and chilly, so I'd kept one of the garage doors closed. Livvy snoozed limply in the compartment of the front carrier. She jerked at the screech of tires in our driveway but didn't wake up. I went outside. Jill slammed her car door and hurried down the sloping driveway to me. She said a breathless greeting and dropped two grocery bags inside the garage. "Last minute donations," she explained on her way back to her car. I stood still in her flurry of motion. "It took me forever to get up Rim Rock Road. Some sort of accident had traffic backed up for miles. I'm behind schedule now." She pulled two card tables from her trunk and carried them inside. On her way back she paused beside me, pulled a tiny notebook from her fanny pack, and checked her watch. "I was supposed to pick up some more dishes from Gwen for tomorrow, but I'm not going to make it to the bank if I do that. Run over there and pick them up for me, will you?"

It was more a command than a request. Jill, already walking backward to her car, flung instructions as she went. "It's third from the corner on Twentieth. Brick, red door, black trim, and shutters. Everything is in boxes on the back porch. No one's home. Just grab it and go. Thanks." She hopped in the car and roared out of the driveway, barely missing Mabel, who was on her walk. Mabel waved to me, never breaking her stride, which sent her orange poncho fluttering out behind her.

I set up the tables and arranged the last-minute items, muttering under my breath the whole time. I need to learn to say "no" more often. Of course, Jill hadn't given me a chance to get a word in edgewise.

I was too polite. I need to learn to interrupt. I sighed and went to get my keys. "Two more days," I muttered, "and this will be over." I gently transferred Livvy from the carrier to her bed with only a few grunts and a half-cry. A miracle.

On my way out, I leaned over Mitch's shoulder. "I'm going to pick up some last-minute donations. Livvy is sleeping." He was off this afternoon: no flying and no paperwork to be done in the squadron. One of the benefits of being active duty was that he had a lot of time off from the squadron, which helped to balance his weeks-long TDY trips and his ever lengthening deployments. In the middle of paying bills, he dropped his pen on the open checkbook and turned to me. "Where are you going?"

"Just up a few blocks. Then I'm going to run by the grocery store. We're out of milk again." I didn't want to mention Gwen's house. He probably wouldn't want me to go there by myself, but no one was home. I wanted to get everything for this garage sale done and over. And a little time to myself would be great. Leisurely shopping at the store sounded heavenly. I never thought I would think of going to the grocery store as a relaxing escape, but that's motherhood for you. I gave Mitch a quick kiss, said, "I love you," grabbed my funky patchwork tote bag, and shrugged into my hooded coat in case it rained.

Cruising up Twentieth Street, I passed Brent and Diana's house. The Winnebago was gone. I wondered if Vera had decided to keep touring the country after the limp welcome from her daughter, or if house-proud Diana had found her somewhere else to park the monster. I found Gwen's house, backed in the driveway of the detached garage, and quickly loaded the boxes into the back of the Cherokee. I didn't want to spend any more time here than I absolutely had to. I shoved in the boxes between the box I needed to drop off at Diana's and several packages of bulbs and seeds I'd wanted to plant. I'd meant to give Brent's box to Mitch to take to the squadron, but I kept forgetting. I'd drop it off at Diana's on the way home from the store. I slammed the hatchback door, rounded the corner of the Cherokee, and ran into Gwen.

"Oh, Ellie, it's you." She grabbed the door handle to steady herself. "I didn't recognize the Cherokee and I came out to see what was going on." She made no move to let me get to the driver's door, but she looked just as startled and uneasy as I felt. "I was expecting Jill. As long as you're here why don't you come inside and have a cup of coffee? I'd like to talk to you." She glanced inside the tinted windows of the Cherokee. "Your daughter's not with you?" she asked as she turned and headed back to the small porch at the back of the house.

"No, she's with Mitch right now. In fact, I'd better call him." I whipped out my cell phone from the console in the Cherokee and dialed home. If Gwen wanted to talk, I wanted to hear what she had to say, but I didn't want to go into her house alone, especially after she checked to make sure I was alone. And I wasn't going to mention the body in the street.

Piercing screams sounded in my ear before Mitch said hello rather loudly.

"Hi, how's it going?"

"Livvy's mad. She got tangled up in her blanket."

"Well, I'm at Gwen's. I'm going to run in for a minute. Just wanted to let you know."

He muttered something then said, "Where's the extra package of diapers?"

"Hall closet, bottom shelf. See you in a little bit." A distracted mumble sounded in my ear before he hung up.

I followed Gwen into her kitchen and took a seat at a table topped with white ceramic tiles. She moved back and forth between the knotty pine cabinets as she made coffee and set out mugs. In her powder blue sweatshirt, gray sweatpants, and low ponytail she didn't look nearly as commanding as she did in her power suits. The kitchen and what I could see of the living room were furnished simply with cheap furniture. Not what I expected of Gwen. Maybe her polished professional image took all her time and money.

"Zoë's sick today. I had to pick her up from school at noon." Gwen carried the mugs to the table and sat down.

"Just a cold, but I'm glad Livvy isn't here. I wouldn't want to expose her to it. Zoë's upstairs asleep. She always sleeps when she gets sick."

I sipped my coffee as the wall clock ticked loudly in the silence. I searched for something innocuous to say to break the tension. "I like this table." I ran my hand over the smooth ceramic tiles. A hand-painted fruit motif decorated the center and corners.

"Thanks. I found it at a yard sale. Fifteen bucks. I talked them down from twenty-five dollars."

Gwen took a sip of her coffee and glanced around the kitchen. She's nervous, I realized. Her breezy confidence had vanished. "I don't really know how to begin," she said as she traced the square grooves on the table. She leaned back in her chair and smoothed back her already perfect ponytail. I wondered if her friendly, chatty side was her sales persona and this more reserved demeanor revealed another, more private, side of her personality.

Finally, she looked at me. "You've been asking questions about me and I'd hoped you would stop, but I can see now you're not going to. You're persistent. So instead of rumors, I want to tell you the truth.

"Cass was spreading lies about me. She said I was having an affair, but I'm not." Her voice became firmer and her hesitancy disappeared. "It's not true. I'm not having an affair. Of course, some people would say I was, if you're going by the letter of the law." Her tone turned bitter. "But I'm not. I'm married to Steven in my heart." She took in my confused look and said, "God, this is hard. I'd better start with my marriage to Colin.

"After college, I worked at Hayden's part time in women's casuals. This was back in Illinois, where I'm from. Colin worked part time in ladies shoes. He was premed, following in his father's footsteps to become an ophthalmologist, but his dad didn't want to give him the spoiled-rich-kid free ride through college and med school. His dad was determined Colin would have to work as hard as he did to get through school, so Colin sold shoes. Or, I should say, charmed women into shoes they didn't need, but could certainly afford. Hayden's is very upscale. He was a great salesman, all subtle flattery and friendliness, but never too aggressive."

She finished her coffee and then continued, "I fell for him. Hard. He was spontaneous. Outrageous, even. We married after a few months. That marriage was probably the only thing I've done in my whole life that pleased my mother. Colin's family was on the right rung of the social ladder, at least for my mother. I was so happy. I thought he was, too." Gwen traced the outline of a tile. "Looking back, I can see that it was probably too much pressure and too many changes. We married and had Zoë about a year later. I guess being a new husband, a new dad, and medical school were just too much for Colin." Now that she'd started talking, the words poured out of her.

She sighed. "At least, that's what I tell myself." She picked up her coffee mug and set it back down. She absently studied the empty interior, turning it a quarter turn again and again, rotating it.

"He left and didn't come back." She gave her head a little shake and said, "He left for class on Thursday morning and never came back. I was frantic by midnight. By Friday, I was almost insane with worry. I was sure he had been carjacked or mugged and left for dead, but the police never found any leads. It was like he drove out of town and never looked back.

"Now I'm pretty sure that's what happened. I hired a

private investigator when the police search slowed down, but he couldn't come up with anything new. Everyone seemed to believe Colin checked out of our life. But how could he leave Zoë?" She quickly wiped the corners of her eyes and went to get a tissue. She came back, cleared the mugs off the table, rinsed them, and sat back down, composed again. "I'm sorry. I don't talk about this very much.

"After a few months, I couldn't stand it anymore. Being reminded of him, constantly wondering what happened to him. And everyone asking *me* what *I* did to run a nice boy like that off. Like it was my fault! So I moved. There was an opening in Hayden's in California. I took it. A fresh start." She ran her hand over the tiles of the table. "I bought this and our other furniture at yard sales because that's all I could afford. I didn't want any help from family. I wanted to do it on my own." The pride was evident in her voice, her straightened posture.

"And I did. We made it. When the opening came for Tate's here, I moved. I missed the change of seasons but didn't want to go back to Illinois.

"My job was great, Zoë loved preschool, we had friends, this little house. Everything seemed perfect. Then I met Steven and everything wasn't perfect." She smiled as she gazed out the window, not seeing the view. "I had a flat tire on the way to work one day. He stopped to help me change it. That's how I met him. How many people are there who actually stop to help when someone needs it? We got to talking and realized we had some friends in common. Anyway, we started dating. Zoë fell in love with him, too. So, we got married a year later."

I smiled. "I'm really happy for you." This was interesting, but hearing a story of true love finally found was

low on my priority list today. Gwen must have sensed my
impatience because she said, "There was only one problem. I never divorced Colin."

What? Why not? Gwen a bigamist? Could a woman
be a bigamist or was there another word for women
with multiple husbands? The questions formed so fast
in my mind that I couldn't get even one of them out.

She rubbed her forehead and slumped down over
the table again. "I know it's crazy, but, well, everyone always assumed I was divorced and it was easier to let
them think that. So when I met Steven, I let him think
the same thing. At first, I convinced myself there was
nothing serious between us, just friends and all that, because I was the big career woman on the fast track and I
didn't need or want to be married again, but then one
day I realized how foolish I was being, deluding myself. I
needed Steven like I'd never needed anyone in my life."

"So he still doesn't know?"

"No."

"Why don't you tell him now?" It would be a difficult
subject to bring up, but if it was causing her this much
anguish, then wouldn't it be better out in the open?

"I can't. You don't know Steven very well, do you?"

"No, I've only met him a few times."

"He's honest." Her eyes were bleak. "Above all, he
prides himself on his honesty. If someone gives him too
much change at the grocery store, even if it's just a few
pennies or a nickel, Steven gives it back. He never lies.
Not even to Zoë to get her to do something. I used to
promise her a Popsicle or a trip to the playground if she
would straighten up when she threw a fit. When she was
younger she'd usually forget about the treat and I'd
skip it, but Steven would never do that. If he says he's
going to do something, he will. He'll go to work when

he's sick to get paperwork finished before a deadline because he gave his word it would be done." Her eyes were glassy. "He's so honest. I'd lose his trust if he knew." She swallowed. "I'd lose him."

An Everything in Its Place Tip for an Organized Move

Sift through your keepsakes and consider why you value certain items.

- Don't keep things out of a sense of duty. Just because your Aunt Dot gave you a ceramic cat statue doesn't mean you have to keep it, especially if you don't like it. Give it away to someone who really appreciates it.
- If you stash things because of their sentimental value, ask yourself if the physical presence of the theater program makes your memory of the play more vivid. Can you keep the memory and let go of the program?

Chapter
Twenty-six

Gwen grabbed a tissue, wiped her eyes, and then squared her shoulders. "So I hired a P.I. to find Colin. I wanted to serve the divorce papers. That's who I met in the parking lot, the detective. It had gotten to the point where I couldn't sleep at night, wondering if Colin was going to show up again, or call while I wasn't home. And I knew that's what he *would* do. And I was right. He waltzed into Tate's that day and expected everything to be the same. I couldn't live with the stress, so I decided to find him first."

"Did Cass know about this?"

"Of course not, no one knows."

Except me. Not good. The house was very quiet. Maybe Cass had found out. Gwen would certainly say Cass didn't know anything. Cass wasn't around to correct her.

"So can you do that? Divorce Colin without Steven knowing? But then you still wouldn't be married to Steven."

"I know," she snapped. "One problem at a time. I'll divorce Colin. Then I'll convince Steven to renew our vows on our next anniversary. But it will be a real ceremony not just a walk-through."

I was speechless. Was I the only person in the entire squadron with a normal marriage? My suggestion of coming clean with Steven died on my lips. If she was planning this convoluted divorce/marriage scenario then she wouldn't listen to my feeble attempt to get her to tell the truth. Was I the only person who didn't lie or hide things from my husband? Well, almost everything. I thought of the Hershey bar I had stashed in the cabinet over the fridge.

I combined this new information with the death I'd seen the night before and murmured, "Of course, now that he's dead that solves a lot of your problems."

She looked puzzled. "What?"

Oops. So much for not mentioning the dead body. She was trying to pretend she didn't know Colin was dead? I knew the police were on their way to question her after they talked to us that night. Since I'd already slipped up I might as well see if she'd talk about Colin's death. "You're not a very good actress," I said with more assurance than I felt. *I'm probably a terrible actress and I need to get out of here right now.*

She covered her face with her hands. When she looked at me again her eyes were red and desperate. "How can you know? Please don't tell anyone. Please."

"Calm down." I pushed the tissue box to her. "Abby and I walked home from the coffee. We ran into Helen and were with her when she found him. We called the police. I told them he looked like the man I saw talking to you at Tate's."

She blew her nose, wiped her eyes, and sighed. Her shoulders slumped. "I thought I could confide in you and convince you to keep quiet about me. You're sympathetic. Easy to talk to. I thought if I told you what was really going on, you'd see I had nothing to do with Cass and leave me alone."

"But what about the police?"

"I told them he was an old family friend. Steven's on a trip so I hoped it would be cleared up before he got back. He wouldn't even need to know."

"Gwen, they're going to find out. You'd better tell them."

"No," she said sharply. "It's going to go away." Her viciousness surprised me.

"Mommy?" a weak voice called from the back of the house.

I hopped up from the table. "You need to go." I eased toward the door.

Gwen gripped the table. "I had nothing to do with Cass. I didn't like her or what she was saying about me, but I certainly didn't kill her."

With my hand safely on the doorknob, I asked, "What about the DVD player? Why was it in your trash?"

"I don't know. Someone must have dumped it there to get rid of it. We're just a few houses down from Cass on this side of the street. Someone probably went out her back gate and came through the neighbor's side yard onto this street. It's really overgrown where the backyards from the two streets meet."

"They have a back gate?"

"Sure, lots of these yards do. People use the gates to cut through to the next street, so they don't have to walk around the block. We have one, too."

I checked her yard on my way out. She did indeed have a gate that opened directly into the backyard opposite her house. Tall pines shaded thick bushes that grew in a solid wall down the wire fence. It would be easy to slip though a gate, stay in the shadows, and emerge unnoticed in the next block. Maybe in Gwen's mind her story exonerated her from wanting to harm Cass, but if she was lying and Cass did know Gwen wasn't a divorcée, then it just gave her an even greater motive than I'd realized.

I batted a strand of ivy out of my face and headed to the Cherokee. I cruised slowly past Joe's house. His car wasn't in the driveway, so I parked and walked around to the side of the garage. If he was home, I could always say something about looking for extra food for Rex. I lifted the latch and paced slowly around the chain-link fence to the section that marked off the divided backyards. About a third of the way down the fence in the shade of tall pine and maple trees, I found a honeysuckle-covered gate. The vines wove in and out of the openings and draped over the top of the gate, but around the frame and the gate's latch the vines were neatly cut. I lifted the latch and pushed. The gate swung open on silent hinges.

"Will you take a dollar for this?"

"Do you have a bathroom we can use?"

"Any more lawn equipment?"

The questions were coming faster than I could answer them. Livvy, strapped into the BabyBjörn carrier, flailed her arms and started to fuss. I bounced faster and readjusted her little hat. "Sure we'll take a dollar," I told the bald man and directed him toward the checkout table. "No bathrooms and everything is already out." The two bargain hunters turned and quickly walked to their cars, on to the next garage sale in search of cheap, overlooked treasures. Livvy's soft whining rose in pitch and fervency. I bounced more energetically. It was only ten and the garage looked pathetically picked over.

The scent of rain mingled in the cool air as I stood full in the weak sunshine, warming Livvy and myself. Despite the NO EARLY BIRDS sign posted on the garage, the first knock on our door came at six-twelve. For the first two hours, Mitch had taken care of Livvy, but then Jill sent him to the store for more change.

A bearded man in a flannel shirt over a dirty T-shirt held up an electric edger. "Does this work?"

"I have no idea. There's a plug and an extension cord over there. Help yourself," I shouted over Livvy's operatic attempts to shatter the remaining crystal in the vicinity.

I left the garage sale in the hands of the other spouses on duty and escaped up the steps into the house. In Livvy's room, I sank into the rocking chair and got Livvy latched on. Then I leaned back and closed my eyes. They could get along without me for a while. She gulped down the milk like she hadn't eaten in days, instead of barely two hours ago.

I rocked gently and listened to the hum of the edger. It cut off abruptly. Other snatches of conversations drifted up through the open window that overlooked the backyard. "Nothing here. Let's go. . . ." and "Oh,

Stan needs a hat like this." I drifted, flirting with sleep as the hum of conversation and the thud of car doors receded.

Livvy, of course, picked that moment to lean back with a sigh and a smile. I wiped a drop of milk off the corner of her mouth, burped her, and settled her on the other side. One of the advantages of breast-feeding was that it gave me the ability to escape and spend some time with Livvy. And no bottles to wash either.

Compared to the last week, I felt better and she did, too. Since we'd decided to let her learn to go to sleep on her own, she'd cried for a shorter time each night. Last night, she cried for about ten minutes and then went to sleep. Score one for the parents.

I propped Livvy up on my shoulder and patted her back. Her head bobbed as she strained to take in every detail in that corner of the room. I prodded the floor with my toe and set the rocking chair in motion as I thought about my last conversation with Gwen. It had felt more like a confession. I rocked faster as I considered my options. If she didn't kill Cass, I didn't feel I had a right to say anything about her nondivorce. But if she did kill Cass to conceal her past, then I had to go to Thistlewait. Especially if she'd killed a second time. I shivered, remembering Colin's body falling from the car onto the ground at our feet.

The problem was I didn't have any proof. There wasn't any proof she'd killed twice and there wasn't any proof she was innocent. She'd been at the barbeque, but so were about fifty other people. Anyone could learn how to trap wasps if they did an Internet search.

Livvy let out a very unfeminine burp and I stood up with a sigh. I had to keep Gwen's secret until some physical evidence connected her to either death. I tuned into the sounds from the driveway when I heard Gwen's husky voice. "Sorry, I'm late. The traffic was horrendous. Have you ever tried to get across Vernon on a Saturday? It's insane. Who planned this town? Did they have something against turn lanes, or what?"

A chorus of voices agreed with her. Gwen's grave, reserved attitude yesterday was almost the opposite of her usual wordy, extroverted side that showed today. Everyone has different aspects to their personality, but the contrast made me wonder. Did she really have a calmer side or was yesterday's confession an act? But why would she make up something like that?

I put Livvy down for her nap and returned to the garage sale, where I slid into my chair at the checkout table with Diana. In between waves of customers, the conversation centered on the tabloid-like events in the neighborhood.

"They don't know how he died." Irene Innes pushed her blond hair out of her face and stacked some books. "I'm a news junkie." She looked slightly embarrassed, but then she dove right in again. "At least, they aren't reporting it." Gwen became absorbed in picking up some clothes that had fallen off hangers.

"Were there injuries? Obvious wounds?" Diana asked as she recorded a sale. I watched her form the perfect sweeps in her cursive letters with a mixture of horror and admiration. Her exact strokes looked like they could be posted in Abby's elementary school for students to copy. My scribbles, a mixture of cursive and print, looked terrible. But you're supposed to make your handwriting your own, distinctive and unique, I thought defensively.

"I don't remember anything like that," I said.

Irene said, "It's so violent here. Friona gets her throat cut and then that man dies in a car on our block."

Everyone was silent. Gwen's fingers slipped and a coat fell off the hanger she held. A few people looked at Irene disapprovingly.

"Well, I'm sorry!" She stood up and dusted her hands. "It's true. It may sound shocking, but that's exactly what happened."

"And don't forget Cass," Penny murmured. Gwen re-hung the coat and smoothed the other clothes.

"Right. So that's three people dead from this neighborhood. Maybe there's a serial killer." Irene looked more excited than scared.

"Those deaths aren't connected in any way," Diana argued.

Irene said, "I bet they are. We just can't see the connection yet."

An Everything in Its Place Tip for an Organized Move

Keeping Collections under Control
- Evaluate—Do you have duplicates or items that aren't as rare as they were at one time? Moving time is a great time to thin your collections.
- Display—Choose the best format to show off your collection:
  - Books need bookshelves.
  - Kitchen collectibles might fit in a corner cabinet or on a baker's rack.
  - Shadow boxes are a great option to display small items like buttons or rocks.

- Set limits—Allow a reasonable space for your collection and don't let it expand beyond those boundaries.
- If your collections are delicate or require special packing steps, be sure to let the movers know a few days ahead of your pack-out date, so they can bring the appropriate boxes with them.

Chapter Twenty-seven

The ability to simplify means to eliminate the unnecessary so that the necessary may speak.
—Hans Hofmann

I climbed out of the Cherokee and the drizzle hit me in the face, making my vision fuzzy. I scurried to the squadron door with Livvy's blanket-covered car seat banging against one hip and her diaper bag thumping against the other. Low dark clouds had fooled the light-sensitive parking lot lights into glowing. The cold bite of the air on my hands and face told me fall was almost over. With my head down and drizzle-impaired vision, I didn't realize someone else was hurrying across the parking lot until we collided at the heavy door.

"Oh." Nick Townsend. I felt my heart speed up, unsure of what he would say or do. I hadn't seen or heard from him since he threatened me. I gripped the slippery door handle and tugged, wanting to get around other people. It was too far back to the Cherokee. I yanked on the door again, but it remained shut.

"Here, let me get that for you." He punched in a code on a number pad above the handle. I blinked the water off my lashes and looked at him. He didn't look angry. His face wasn't flushed and he smiled over his shoulder when he opened the door. "Someone forgot to unlock it this morning."

He held the door and I went in. We walked down the empty hall in an awkward silence. "Look, I wanted to apologize." He fiddled with his Air Force Academy ring. "I'm sorry for overreacting. I've got a short fuse and you set me off asking about . . . well, the uh . . ." He didn't even want to say the word "shot" inside the squadron. He pulled the ring down and spun it around his finger.

He continued, "I want the Air Force to stay out of my personal life, that's all. Anyway, I don't need them anymore. Season's over and I'm going to a new assignment next month." He'd ended his allergy shots. I wondered if he was lying. Medical records were sealed pretty tightly. It would be my word against his. His chunky ring flashed as it circled his finger.

"Well, good luck. I hope you get a good base," I said.

He studied my face for a moment and then nodded. "Thanks." He turned and walked down the hall. At least I'd told Thistlewait about Nick. I was sure the OSI could keep track of him.

"Hi." Mitch had walked up behind me. He picked up the car seat and pulled back the cover. Livvy gurgled and smiled. "Let's go down to The Hole," Mitch said.

Once I was settled on the earth-tone couch, I pulled the paper bag with our hamburgers out of the diaper bag. I'd picked them up on the way to the squadron as I ran errands, tidying up loose ends that had been piling up as I focused my attention on getting ready for the garage sale and thinking about Cass. Livvy was in a great mood, stringing "aah" and "ooh" together. Apparently, falling asleep on her own suited her as much as it did us.

"Do you want a Diet Coke?" Mitch asked as he got a Dr Pepper from the refrigerator behind the bar.

"No, I brought some water." I pulled a bottle from the diaper bag and twisted the cap. It made a satisfying crack. Since the antifreeze incident I'd taken an instant liking to bottled water and I was especially fond of the safety seal caps. Mitch poked fifty cents into the money box for his drink and then dropped into the couch beside me. I thought about Nick moving to a new base. Allergy season was over for him now, but what about next year?

"Hey, are you going to eat that burger or just look at it?" Mitch asked.

"Sorry. I'm a little preoccupied." I focused on Mitch. "Are you busy today?" I asked.

"Nah. Just trying to look busy until lunch time."

"You government employees are such slackers." Civilian friends often kidded Mitch, saying he had a cushy job because he had times when he didn't have much to do and was able to be home for part of the day. And I had to agree with them, at times. He had a great job with flexible hours, except for the deployments that could endure for months.

"We're working hard. We just got out of a class, IRC. It starts up again at twelve-thirty. I'm free until then."

Mentally I translated Mitch's acronym of IRC into civilian language. It stood for Instrument Review

Course. "Well, I've got some work for you and whoever is lounging around. I have some folding chairs in the Cherokee that need unloading."

"We'll get them after lunch."

The guys from the squadron picked up the tables after the garage sale, but they left the folding chairs. I'd brought them in myself this morning to get them out of our garage. The sale had been a success and all traces of it were gone.

"So what else is going on?" I asked.

"Not much. Wade just got back from the Caribbean. St. Kitts."

"Really?" The image of vivid blue waters of St. Thomas popped into my mind. We'd gone there on our honeymoon.

"It would be great to go back, wouldn't it?" Mitch asked.

I thought of the gray drizzly day. "It's just going to get colder here."

We looked at each other. Then he smiled, slowly. "What about January or February? Let's plan a trip and go."

I couldn't help smiling back when he looked at me like that. "I did want to go to St. John, too, when we were there. Remember? But, we ran out of time."

His smile widened. "I remember."

I had to laugh at his mock-leer, but then I sobered. "What about Livvy? How many hours would that be on a plane?"

"You know both our moms could literally be here overnight if we asked them to keep Livvy for a few days."

"Leave Livvy? I don't know, I've never been away from her."

"Let's just check into it, right now."

"Okay. I'll stop at the travel office and get some brochures." I picked up my purse and water, then heaved the diaper bag onto my shoulder. Mitch carried the car seat as we climbed the stairs.

"See if you can find something on Grand Cayman, too. I think there's good diving there." Mitch opened the heavy door to the parking lot. "I'll go round up some guys to carry in the chairs." In a few minutes, the chairs were unloaded and my list of things to do was reduced to leaving the box for Brent. After my conversation with Gwen, I'd forgotten about dropping off the box.

I pulled the box out of the front seat of the Cherokee. I wanted to avoid Brent, so I'd hand this little task off to Mitch. A spotlessly clean white SUV pulled into the open parking space beside us. I wondered how Diana kept it so clean, even in the rain. Mitch and I squeezed against the Cherokee and I tried to avoid touching its mud-spattered side.

"Oh, that's Diana. We can just give it to her."

We met her around the back of her SUV. "Hi, Diana. I've been meaning to return this box." She zipped up her coat halfway, paused to study the box, and then yanked the zipper up, enclosing her cardigan and oxford shirt.

"Ah, sure."

"I was going to have Mitch give it to Brent. I figured you'd be at work today and I didn't want to leave it on your porch with the rain."

"I had a dentist appointment." Diana studied the box, but didn't move, like she didn't recognize it.

"It was with the garage sale donations, but it must be a mistake. It's files and stuff. I've had it in the back of the Cherokee for weeks, and I kept forgetting to drop it off." She fumbled with her keys as she unlocked the back portion of the SUV. Mitch placed the box in the back and slammed it shut.

"What are you doing today?" Her voice was hoarse. She pulled a water bottle out of her purse and unscrewed the lid. "Are you going to lunch?"

"No, we just ate and Livvy's getting fussy. I'm heading home." I glanced at the sky. "I wanted to plant some bulbs and seeds. I don't think I'm going to make it before the heavy rain starts, but I might."

"Well. Maybe we could have lunch another time." She tilted the water bottle up for a drink as she hurried across the parking lot.

"What's wrong?" Mitch asked.

"I don't know. Something's bothering me." I shrugged. "I'll think of it later, I'm sure. She didn't sound very excited about going to lunch," I said.

"Maybe she had a cavity filled and she's not feeling good." Mitch clicked the car seat into its holder. We said good-bye and Mitch gave me a quick kiss on the cheek. He jogged off toward the squadron and I headed for the travel office.

I pulled up to the U-shaped building. Old train tracks crisscrossed the parking lot, evidence of the building's prior use as a loading dock and storage facility. It had been converted into offices and painted the ever-popular bland yellow.

My purse, a fallish red, cream, and green plaid drawstring tote, trilled as I parked the Cherokee.

"Mrs. Avery, Thistlewait here. Just wanted to let you know it was antifreeze."

I leaned my head back against the headrest.

"Just a minute," he interrupted. He must have put his hand over the phone because I could hear muffled voices, then he came back on the line. "Mrs. Avery, I've got to put you on hold." He didn't wait for a reply, just pushed a button.

I expected Muzak, but instead I heard a different voice say, "Thanks. I've only got a few minutes." The voice was deeper and rumbled more than Thistlewait's. I opened my mouth to tell Thistlewait he hit speakerphone instead of hold. The man continued, "I wanted to brief you on it since it involves Captain McCarter." I closed my mouth.

"Just got off the phone with Drummy. IRS. You met him yet?"

"Yeah. Good guy," Thistlewait confirmed. A chair squeaked and I covered the mouthpiece of the phone. A cry from Livvy would let them know they were on a party line.

"He is." The first man said. "Anyway, Drummy's checking out McCarter for money laundering. Looks like McCarter's using his old recall roster to contact families from his previous squad and pose as a representative of Serviceman's Group Life Insurance. He tells them their relative didn't elect the death benefit clause on their policy, but if they'll FedEx him a five-hundred-dollar money order they can activate it and get a ten-thousand-dollar benefit to cover funeral expenses."

Thistlewait said, "What an SOB."

"I know. Especially since the Air Force already pays a death benefit to family members of anyone who dies on active duty, and that's over and above any insurance coverage whether or not they've got McCarter's fake form guaranteeing them funeral coverage. Not to mention the casket, the remains prep, and interment provision."

"Jeez. What a slimeball."

For once, Thistlewait and I were in agreement.

The rumbly voice continued, "Apparently, McCarter's favorite targets are family members of people currently deployed."

I hoped I wouldn't fall for a ploy like that if Mitch were deployed to Iraq or some other hot spot. But did I really know all the ins and outs of our insurance coverage? Not by a long shot.

"All right," gruff voice said, "Just wanted to let you know. I gave Drummy your phone number. Told him to contact you when he gets the info. How's the Vincent investigation going?"

Thistlewait said, "We've been able to confirm Mrs. Vincent's ex-husband was in Cancún with wife number two. Lieutenant Townsend says he was at the Shopette, but the security tapes have been taped over and no one remembers him. And most husbands and wives, like the McCarters and the Givens, alibi each other."

"It'll break. I gotta run."

Thistlewait picked up the phone and said, "All right, Mrs. Avery, I'm back. Have you considered going out of town until this blows over? Your family's in Texas, right?"

I sat up straight. "I can't run from this." A warm getaway had a lot more appeal when it came from Mitch instead of Thistlewait.

"No interest in a suntan, then?"

What was this? Thistlewait making a joke? "No. I'm not leaving."

Thistlewait said, "Then be careful." He ended the call.

As I walked to the travel office my mind spun with the new details from Thistlewait. Nick didn't have an alibi. He didn't seem threatening today. And the Givens were together the whole time. Or, at least that was what they were saying. I didn't think Gwen would think twice before lying to cover for Steven, but if he was as honest as Gwen said I doubted he'd lie to protect Gwen. Then there was Brent running a scam. No wonder they had such a nice house.

I pushed open the glass door to the travel office. The only occupant was a skinny woman with a corkscrew perm. The other two desks were empty but covered with papers. The woman continued to bang away at her keyboard, so I searched the racks and grabbed anything I saw about the Caribbean.

"Sorry. I had to finish that." The woman ripped off a headset that her bushy hair had hidden and pranced over to me as fast as her tight leopard print skirt allowed. "What are you looking for, honey? Sun and fun? A cruise?" Then she noticed Livvy in the car seat. "How about Disney?"

"Anything in the Caribbean."

"Aren't you the smart one. Book early. Come January this place will be overrun. Let me see what you've got." She pulled a few more glossy packets out and tossed them at me.

"Do you have anything on St. Kitts or Grand Cayman?"

She cocked an eyebrow. "You looking for a vacation or an offshore account?"

"What?" Maybe this office was empty because the help was kind of loony.

"Obviously not. Just joking, honey. Take a look at those. Here's one on BVI. The British Virgin Islands." She translated for me when she saw I didn't understand.

"Sorry. I can only keep up with so many acronyms."

"Tell me about it. Here's my card. Call if you've got questions. I'm here every day but Thursday."

Back in the Cherokee, I fastened a dozing Livvy in the back and climbed in the driver's seat. I might as well take time to look through the brochures now. After Livvy woke up I wouldn't have a chance.

I skimmed pictures of beautiful people frolicking in sand and surf and read the destination descriptions. One brochure had a foldout map that I spread across the steering wheel so I could study the islands. St. Kitts, St. Thomas, Grand Cayman, Nevis, Cozumel, the Bahamas. Just the names made me think of sand between my toes, lush flowers, and turquoise water. Too many destinations to sort out now. I refolded the map and put the Cherokee in drive.

I crept down the main road. The speed limit on the base is a whopping twenty-five miles an hour and the Security Police hand out tickets like they're giving away candy on Halloween. The sky seemed darker than it had an hour ago. I flipped on my lights and edged the heater up a notch. Grand Cayman, St. Thomas, Nevis. I savored the tropical names and the thought that we might escape part of the coming winter.

Nevis. Where had I heard that before? A memory merged with a conversation. I understood the travel agent's little joke that I'd missed earlier. I eased off the accelerator when I saw the red needle hovering at 45 mph. I switched lanes and headed back to the squadron with thoughts percolating. Nevis, an island in the Caribbean, famous for unspoiled tropical beauty and offshore banking. I knew where I'd seen the name Nevis and I was pretty sure most folks I knew in the Air Force didn't have, or need, an offshore account.

I cruised into the same parking space and looked at the white SUV still parked in the same slot beside me. I reached for my water bottle and took a drink. Then it clicked. I sat still for a few moments. I checked the clock and pulled out my phone. After what I was sure would be an exorbitant call to directory information, I was talking to Abby's school. "Abby Dovonowski. She's subbing for a few weeks. I have to talk to her. It's urgent. Can you get her out of class?"

"She's right here, checking her mail. Hold on." Abby came on the line.

"Abby. It's Ellie. Remember when you said Diana was staring at you and Brent during the barbeque?"

"Yes. What's going on? You sound—weird."

"You said she was holding something."

"Yeah. A Coke," Abby said.

"How did you know it was a Coke?"

"Well, I guess I didn't really know. I just assumed because that was what it said on the side. Are you okay?"

"Thanks." I punched END and cut off her questions.

Now I knew, but I also knew it wouldn't be enough for Thistlewait. He had an irritating habit of wanting the details and proof. Why did I have to pick today to give that box back?

I took a deep breath, then said to Livvy, "Just a little peek and I'll be back." I left the Cherokee running to keep Livvy asleep, but I put the parking brake on. Then I slipped out and tried a door handle on the SUV. The back door clicked open and I crawled in.

I hesitated. If I found what I was looking for, I'd call Thistlewait, but if it wasn't there, I'd save myself a whole lot of embarrassment. Leaning over into the cargo area I pulled the box toward me and flicked the flaps back. File tabs marched from front to back.

A quick glance out the window showed an empty

parking lot with the Cherokee still idling beside me. I turned my attention back to the box. My fingers skimmed over the folders.

Past the tax returns and pay stubs I found the folder labeled NEVIS BANK and opened it. The top paper was a bank statement. An ornate font beside a crest headed the paper and proclaimed Bank of Nevis, Charlestown, Nevis, W.I.

W.I.? West Indies? I scanned down the list of deposits and withdrawals. There were many, many deposits of three-, four-, and five-hundred dollars. Along with much larger, but more irregular deposits ranging from a few thousand dollars up to the hundred thousands. Filed behind the statements were incorporation documents complete with copies of Brent and Diana's passports and driver's licenses, along with a copy of a money order for a security deposit to open the bank account in the name of MC Corp. An envelope, the large brown kind with a flap and a brad to keep it closed, followed the statements.

I checked the parking lot again. Empty, except for the gray sky and the blacktop shiny with drizzle. My breath had fogged the windows and my heartbeat pounded inside my head. Calm down. There's no one out there.

I returned to the folder and emptied the envelope, which contained a stack of debit card receipts. Diana's perfect handwriting noted on the bottom of each receipt what the cash was for: attorney's fees, recording fees, office products. The McCarters were big fans of cash transactions, it seemed.

A large paper clip secured the next set of documents. I waded through the text until I had the highlights. Brent and Diana hadn't incorporated one company; they'd incorporated two more, Tecmarc, which bought the property from Mrs. Norwood, and Forever Wild. And it looked like Forever Wild was more about protecting money than protecting wilderness.

The papers trembled as my hand sent out little shock waves. This box was at Cass's house. Did she find these papers? Did she know the truth about who owned these companies? I couldn't imagine that she'd give the box to me if she'd known what was in it. Were the possibility that she might have seen the documents and the fact that she was delving into the real estate records what led to her death?

I needed to take the file and get out of there. I jammed the papers into the folder. I wiped a clear spot on the window and checked the parking lot, but it was deserted. As I scooted around to replace the folder in the box, my foot slipped and I kicked a small plastic trash can, sending crumpled tissues and bits of paper flying over the floorboard. I bit my lip. Diana would notice if anything was out of place in her immaculate car.

I dropped the folder on the seat, righted the trash can, and grabbed a handful of trash. I shoved it back in the trash can while I plucked gum wrappers from under the front passenger seat. I squished the wrappers down and gave the carpet under the seat a quick sweep with my hand. My fingers connected with a light, round object in the groove between the floor mat and the metal fixture that held the seat in place. I pinched it between two fingertips and pulled. It was a marker inside a tube. I held up the amber tube to read the writing on the thick marking pen inside. The pen had double caps, a small black one on one end and a larger gray one on the other end. "O.3 Epinephrine Auto-Injector."

I twisted the amber tube and the words on the pen jumped out, EpiPen. I swallowed. Unless Diana was also allergic to bee and wasp stings, this had to be one of Cass's missing EpiPens. My hands felt sweaty. Fingerprints. I pulled out the edge of my coat pocket with my left hand and dropped the amber tube into the pocket with my right hand. I snapped the pocket flap closed. I wanted out of the SUV, now! I picked up the folder from where I'd dropped it on the car seat. I tried to straighten the fanned papers with trembling fingers.

The pages ruffled in the breeze as the door opened.

Chapter
Twenty-eight

Our life is frittered away by detail. . . .
Simplify, simplify, simplify!
—Henry David Thoreau

Brent McCarter blocked the opening. His golden hair, wet with drizzle, sparkled above gray-blue eyes. Today his eyes didn't look icy, just empty. My heart skidded to a stop, then resumed beating, double time. I stuck the papers back in the folder.

He touched my shoulder lightly. "El. You really are a troublemaker. You should have left everything alone." His tone was half-regretful, half-joking. I couldn't move. I almost expected him to give my shoulder a playful squeeze and then tell me it was all a practical joke.

"I'll just take these." He pulled the folder out of my stiff fingers. "Why don't you go back to your car? That would be best, I think." I scrambled out of Diana's SUV and surged into the Cherokee's driver's seat, but he was there before I could close the door with my clumsy, fumbling hands. He leaned across me to unlock the passenger door. I recoiled instinctively. "Ah, here's my wife. She'll take care of everything," he said.

Diana opened the Cherokee's passenger door and climbed in. She lifted her folded coat off her arm, placed it carefully across her lap, and revealed a gun in her right hand. I don't know much about guns, but this one was small, sleek, and modern. Its short barrel gleamed even though the day was overcast. She held it low, pointed at my hip.

"This is crazy." I took a shaky breath.

She checked her watch, then tucked her hair behind her ears with her left hand. Her fingers trembled slightly, but the gun in her other hand never moved. "Give me fifteen minutes. Then leave. Pick me up at home," she ordered Brent. Her eyes narrowed as she scanned the ceiling of the Cherokee. "Yes, that should be enough time. We'll have lunch somewhere in town. Somewhere crowded. Then you can run me back here to pick up my car." Diana spoke to Brent as if I wasn't even there. This woman was talking about my murder. Figuring she could squeeze me in between her eleven o'clock dental and her twelve-thirty lunch.

"Are you sure? I mean . . ." Brent wheedled.

"Brent," she snapped, "I know you're attracted to her, but get over it. She knows. She's seen everything. She had it in her car. For weeks!" She gouged the air with the gun toward her car. I moved back, brushed up against Brent, and then scrunched away from him, but tried to not get any closer to Diana. I checked the rearview mirror, but the parking lot was empty. I felt a sinking sensation in the pit of my stomach, like I'd just swallowed a rock.

"This really isn't a good idea," I said.

"And on top of that," Diana continued, as if I hadn't spoken, "she's asked questions nonstop. We don't have any choice. Stop arguing. I need to think." She rubbed her temple. "It would be best if it happened at her house. Can't do anything with the car. That might look suspicious." She talked to herself in a low tone.

"Diana, maybe we should . . ." Brent began.

"Shut up!" She licked her dry and cracked lips, then chewed on her index fingernail. "We have to do it now. I hate this!" She tucked another stray hair behind her ear. "No time to plan."

Brent opened his mouth to argue, but Diana pointed the gun at him. "Get in there. And don't forget to pick me up!"

"All right." Brent slammed the door and Livvy started to wail. In my rearview mirror, I watched him quickly cross the parking lot. I'd hoped they would forget Livvy was in the back, but no such luck now. She never had been one to let anyone forget she was around.

I automatically reached back to jiggle Livvy's car seat. Diana jerked and raised the gun. "I'm just trying to calm her down." I tried for a soothing tone, but my voice came out squeaky. Diana lowered the gun slightly, back out of view of anyone passing the car. Not that there was anyone out there anyway.

"Drive," she commanded and then rubbed her head again with quivering fingers. "Go the back way."

Livvy's cries subsided to murmurs of protest when I hit the road. We passed the point where I had found Cass. The noises changed to grunts. Oh no, not now. We sailed through the back gate. The Security Police on duty glanced our way and then returned to their paperwork. Diana seemed to relax a little once we were on the highway.

There was a squishy, splattering sound from the backseat, a momentary silence, and then Livvy started crying again, full-force screams. Within seconds, the whole interior of the Cherokee smelled like a combination of stockyard, moldy socks, and rotten eggs.

"Good grief. Do something about that. It smells awful."

I jerked the wheel and brought the Cherokee to a stop on the shoulder of the road. I hopped out and grabbed the diaper bag.

Cars whooshed past. The air of their wake pressed the back of my jeans to my legs. With my shaking fingers, I struggled to release Livvy's seat belt.

"Hurry up," Diana demanded.

"It takes a while to get her out." I gently placed Livvy on a blanket on the backseat to shelter her from the drizzle and the gusts of wind. I checked Diana. She leaned over the seat, watching me intensely.

Stupid. Stupid, I cursed myself. Why hadn't I waited until we were in Vernon, or at least at a gas station? There would have been people around; maybe I could have signaled someone I was in trouble. I unsnapped Livvy's outfit and pulled out a diaper and the box of wipes. I'd been so anxious to get out of the car that I pulled over too soon. I glanced at the flat terrain. Even if I picked up Livvy and ran we wouldn't be able to get far. Nowhere to hide. No trees, rocks, or buildings, just patchy grass. I should have at least waited until the land started to rise and the road cut a passage deeply through rock, making steep "walls" on each side of the road. Livvy continued to cry. I can't believe this is happening. I fought down a spasm of laughter.

Diana's voice was steadier than it had been earlier. "Don't even think about it. I'll shoot. I want this to look like an accident, but if you run, I'll kill you and cover it up."

I opened the diaper's tape fasteners with jerky fingers. It was happening, all right. Diana pulled back when I opened the diaper and cleaned up Livvy. I toyed with the idea of tossing the whole thing in Diana's face and running, but where would we go? Instead I put the diaper in a plastic bag and sealed it. I quickly taped on the clean diaper, my hands moving smoothly through the rote motions I'd already performed thousands of times in Livvy's short life. I refastened the snaps on her outfit and scooped her up in my arms. I hummed in her ear with my chin pressed against her wooly hat. She hiccuped, sighed, and began sucking her thumb. A car surged past, ruffled my hair, and made my jeans flap against my legs.

If fear had a continuum like grief, my fear seemed to morph into cold, hard anger. Diana would probably kill us both without a second's hesitation, but I was determined to fight with everything I had. Livvy needed me and Mitch needed me. There was no way I was going down without a fight. I took a deep breath and put Livvy back in the car seat. My hands were steadier and I'd lost the feeling of sheer panic. I'd settled into determined anger.

I pulled back onto the road, but kept under the speed limit. Diana shifted around in her seat. "Go faster." She bit her thumbnail.

"I can't. The roads are too slick. It's the drizzle."

We drove in silence for a while.

"You must specialize in 'accidents,'" I said. Diana twisted toward me. We entered Clairmont, a tiny assemblage of gas stations, check-cashing businesses, and pizza places that clung to the side of the freeway leading to the base. Maybe I could distract her.

When she didn't reply I went on, "Cass's death was almost perfect. No one suspected you planned it." Flattery couldn't hurt. "But why did you leave the cup in her car?"

"I'm not stupid enough to talk to you." The tires schussed through the thin layer of water on the road as fat drops of rain plopped on the windshield. I turned the wipers on intermittent and slowed a little more.

"It won't hurt to tell. I'm not going to be around." My heartbeat seemed to thunder in my ears for a moment and I thought I might pass out, but then I managed to say, "You must have planned to be the first person to reach her after the attack."

Diana sighed a sigh of pure exasperation, like a parent discussing their difficult teenager. "She wasn't even supposed to leave the squadron. She should have stepped on it when she first accelerated and that would trigger their defense, stinging. Repeatedly, you know. Bees can only sting once, but wasps sting again and again. I'd have said I was calling for help, but delayed. In the confusion, I could have gotten the cup and thrown it away."

I glanced down at my pocket. The EpiPen made a faint bulge, but to me it seemed to pulsate. Diana probably took the EpiPen out of the van when she put the wasps in it. Maybe she removed the one from Cass's purse during the barbeque. It wouldn't have been hard to take either one, since Cass left the van unlocked and her purse probably sat in the pile of unattended purses and bags near the door of The Hole during the barbeque.

Joe had mentioned Cass's allergic reaction last year at the squad's pool party. Everyone at the squad would have known about her allergy and where Cass kept the EpiPens. And even if Cass was able to inject herself with a spare EpiPen, Diana had the variable of time on her side since the base didn't have an emergency room.

"Know much about bees and wasps? Are you allergic, too?" I asked.

Diana snorted. "No. The Internet is wonderful for research," she said condescendingly.

"How did you get the wasps in there in the first place?"

Diana waved the gun in an off-handed gesture. "I made a trap. Used some soft strawberries to attract the wasps. Then I cooled them in the refrigerator so I could move them. Before the barbeque, I put them in the cup and left it in a small cooler in the basement." She shrugged. "Not that difficult."

No one would have noticed a cooler at a squadron during a barbeque. And I did remember seeing Diana in the hall on my way out of the squadron with an armload of picnic supplies, including a small cooler.

"But that wasn't your first attempt. You had something to do with the brakes and steering failing on Cass's van, didn't you?"

She was silent, so I continued, "The Internet again?"

"Hardly. One of mom's many, many boyfriends worked on his car while I played. Mom was off on one of her jobs. Was it waitressing? Or maybe that was when she was checking groceries? It didn't matter. Ted thought I was playing while he showed his greasy friend how to 'fix' the brakes and steering on his wife's car. She'd been fooling around on him."

We reached the main highway. I moved into the lane that arched to the east and merged with the traffic on the interstate. Only about ten minutes until we reached my house. My hands were slick on the steering wheel and my mouth felt dry. Could I use the EpiPen on her? I discarded the idea. It would be too hard to get it out of the amber tube and I didn't know what it would do to her, if anything. Better to keep her talking.

"Where's your mom?"

Diana shrugged. "Took off for Canada. She's always been like that." Her voice turned bitter. "She's never been able to settle down. Make a home, a life. We moved eighteen times when I was in school. Can you believe that? What kind of mother would do that to her child?" I murmured sympathetic noises and she continued, "I certainly wouldn't. I know what my kids need. Security, a stable home." Her breathing went raspy. "I'm a good mom. I'm not about to lose everything I've worked for. Not for them and not for me."

"But how was Cass a threat to you?"

Diana looked at me like she thought I was the biggest imbecile she'd ever seen. "I wasn't about to let Cass blab that there might, *might,* be an earlier easement that completely restricted development."

"How did you know Cass knew about that easement?" I asked.

"She was stupid enough to call me and ask about it while she was at the county requesting copies of everything she could get her hands on about the land."

I remembered Debbie, the clerk at the county records office, and her irritation that Cass wouldn't get off her cell phone. I reviewed the past weeks and a few things fell into place.

"So it was you searching Cass's house and garage." She lifted one shoulder in acknowledgment.

"Why did you trash their house?'"

"I couldn't find the box. The box that was in your car." Out of the corner of my eye I saw her hands tighten on the gun. Livvy started crying. Diana raised her voice. "It could have been *anywhere*. It was just a bundle of paper."

Anger seemed to radiate from Diana. I gripped the wheel tighter and tried to distract her from thinking about that box in my car, so close, but just out of reach. "You took the DVD player to make it look like a burglary. Nice touch. It threw the police off."

She took a deep breath, sat up straighter, and regained control of herself. "Of course it did." A tiny smile turned up the corners of her lips. "I dumped it in the first trash can I came to. Pure luck it was Gwen's."

When Diana couldn't find the box at Cass's, she assumed it was at my house with the garage sale things and searched there. "How did you get into our house?"

"I took the extra key off your key holder while you thought I was setting up for the garage sale," Diana said.

I decided not to bring up the failed attempt to poison me. She probably added the antifreeze to my cup while she was searching.

After a few beats of silence she spoke again. "Cass was infuriating. She wasn't about to let it go." Diana was still thinking about Cass. The break-ins had been minor things to her. "She would have told everyone. You know how she was, couldn't keep a secret if her life depended on it." Diana rolled her eyes, like how childish can you be? "One little thing and she couldn't keep from talking about it. I've kept secrets all my life. It's not that hard."

I raised my eyebrows in a silent question. Diana didn't look like the type of person who had secrets in her past.

"Do you think I always dressed like this, acted like this? You've met my mother." Diana's attention focused on the drenched trees that formed a corridor on each side of the interstate. She gave a little half-laugh and shook her head. "We were classic trailer park trash. I hated it and was *not* going to keep living that way." She watched the trees for a few miles. I tried not to break the reminiscent spell. Diana was distracted and if I could get to the turnoff for Rim Rock Road, there were businesses, gas stations, and a convenience store. Maybe I could do something there. I said softly, "But your mom said something about tennis." Tennis matches brought to mind country clubs, not trailer parks.

"It was part of P.E. in middle school. I was good, so I got on the tennis team. My coach knew where I came from and told me I could get a scholarship, if I worked at it. So I did. I played in high school and during my junior year I got a job at the local country club working in the locker room. For the first time, I saw another way of life. Those women could lose a diamond tennis bracelet and not even care because they had another one at home. They looked spectacular, even if they weren't beautiful.

"Security and stability, that was what they had. I didn't put it into words then, but I knew I wanted to be like them. It's funny. I haven't thought about this in a long time. It seems almost like I'm talking about another person, not myself.

"I remade myself. I paid attention to how those women dressed, did their hair, their makeup. I got my scholarship."

I concentrated on the road while I ran over my impressions of Diana. She always seemed perfect, exact in her words and her appearance. At times, she even reminded me of a mannequin, a flawless exterior, but inside she was plastic and artificial. She was too perfect to be real. Her nail polish never had a chip, her shoes never had a scuff mark. At least now that I knew Diana's perfection was a carefully maintained act, I didn't have to feel like I fell short. She was an impersonation.

But that realization didn't help me now. I mentally kicked myself for not exploring her flawlessness. It made me uncomfortable, but if I'd pursued it, I might not be chauffeuring a killer. I focused on Diana again to keep her talking. "How's Jeff involved in this?"

"Not at all."

"But he's your registered agent for Forever Wild."

"Oh, that. Whatever. He's just on the paperwork. We paid him five hundred dollars, a one-time fee, to file the paperwork." Diana rolled her eyes again. "But, of course, Brent had to go and screw that up, too. I told him always use the debit card. Cash. *Cash.* But no, he forgot to make the withdrawal, so he just wrote a check. No big deal, he said. But, wouldn't you know—Jeff took the check to the squad, Cass saw it, and it set her off."

So the check had Forever Wild printed on it. That's what Cass was so upset about, not a hunting lease like Jeff said. But if Jeff was only peripherally involved, why did he lie?

I hit the blinker and slowed for the exit ramp. Diana shifted in her seat, more alert and watchful. It only took a few minutes to drive the climbing, winding road to my street, but it seemed to pass in seconds. What am I going to do? I searched frantically for options, but couldn't think of anything. I couldn't wreck the Cherokee or make a run for it, not with Livvy strapped in the backseat.

I pulled into the driveway and searched the sidewalks for a walker, a jogger, anyone. The neighborhood was quiet except for the rain pounding a steady rhythm on the Cherokee. I turned to her. "You can't do this. You know three deaths in the squadron within a few weeks won't be overlooked. It will be investigated."

"Three?"

"Cass and Friona."

"Oh, Friona." She flicked her hand. "I'd almost forgotten about her. That was tedious. It was so boring waiting for her. And messy. I don't want to have to do that again," she murmured to herself. "No blood this time. I don't have time to change."

I tightened my grip on the door handle, so stunned that I couldn't move. She'd just admitted to killing Friona. Her precise, analytical assessment of why she wouldn't kill me with a knife chilled me. To Diana, killing wasn't wrong, it was just too messy with a knife.

Lost in thought, she gnawed on her fingernail. Then she seemed to come to a decision and roughly nodded her head. "Suicide." My look of disbelief must have shown on my face. "You'll leave a note," she said. "You're distraught, exhausted, overwhelmed with the responsibility of raising your daughter. All that, on top of the move—it was too much for you. They'll conclude postpartum depression."

"I would *not* do that. Mitch will know. I'd never do that to him or Livvy." Diana's face was hard, her eyes stony. I tried another approach. "We don't own a gun. I hate blood, so I'd never slit my wrists, and there aren't any drugs in the house because I'm breast-feeding."

Diana stopped chewing on her thumbnail. "Stop it!" she shouted. "Stop talking. You're making me nervous." Great, I was making a crazy woman holding a gun on me nervous. "I need time to think and to make a plan. Pull in the garage," she ordered. She seemed to calm down a bit. "There's other ways."

"The garage door is broken," I lied.

"All right. Get out. Get the car seat. I'll follow you."

Chapter
Twenty-nine

The rain splashed my face as I opened the back door of the Cherokee. I could hear Rex's barks and whines. He was ready to get out of the basement. We were going to buy a kennel, but hadn't done it yet, so he was back in the basement since the weather was too bad to leave him outside. Diana awkwardly climbed over the console and got out the driver's side. She kept the gun on me the whole time. She stood with her back against the Cherokee and watched the street while I struggled with the releasing mechanism of the car seat. "What's taking so long?" she asked. Out of the corner of my eye, I saw she was drenched. She had to use her coat to cover her gun, so her hair was plastered to her head and her cardigan, soaking up water, hung heavy from her shoulders.

"There. It was stuck." I flipped a thick blanket over

the car seat and slammed the door. A car swept down the street, splashing water. Diana stuck the gun into my lower back around the vicinity of my kidney and pushed me toward the house and away from the street.

She marched me to the door. I started up the steps. It's now or never. If I go in that house, I'm not coming back out. Excited barks sounded and Rex, a furry, wet, black shape, rounded the corner of the house. He had escaped again. I was only slightly surprised. We didn't seem to be able to keep him confined anywhere. I looked back over my shoulder and saw Diana glance at Rex.

I raised the car seat and rammed it into Diana's chest. She clutched at the car seat, missed, and landed with a hard splash on her back on the sidewalk. The gun arched through the air and plopped into the grass a few feet away. I dropped the car seat and ran down the steps. Rex danced back and forth between us, unsure how he could join us in our game. Diana grabbed my ankle and I fell. Stinging pain exploded from my right knee and radiated through my leg. I heard Rex growl behind me.

Diana made a wheezy, hollow sound as she tried to get her breath back. She rolled over into a crouch and looked for the gun. Water from the grass soaked through my jeans to my knees as I scanned the ground. I concentrated on the fresh, earthy smell and tried to ignore the sharp pain that stabbed from my knee up my leg. I saw the dull glint of the gun and scrambled for it. A rumbling growl sounded behind me. Diana roughly shoved me away from the gun.

Before I could get up, Diana half-wheezed, half-screamed. She writhed, trying to get away from Rex. He gripped a corner of the sleeve of her cardigan in his teeth. With his paws planted, he used his weight to pull Diana away from me. He twisted his head back and forth and I heard a muted ripping sound as the material tore at the shoulder seam. Diana shrugged out of the cardigan and Rex lunged for another bite. Angling across the yard, Diana grabbed the lowest branch of one of the pines in our yard and scrambled up.

Rex danced around the base, delighted with this giant squirrel he'd treed. I heard footsteps splashing up the driveway and I focused on plaid rubber boots coming toward me. Mabel pushed back the hood of her orange poncho and calmly asked, "What's all the fuss?"

I realized Diana was screaming at me to call off my attack dog. She yelled she was going to sue me for not keeping my dog restrained.

I pointed at Diana. "She tried to kill me."

Mabel lifted her poncho, unzipped her fanny pack, and punched three numbers on her cell phone.

I made my way on noodlelike legs to the Cherokee. I opened the door and Livvy's screams filled the air. I gripped the door as a wave of relief surged over me. She was crying; she was fine. I was thankful that the rain had covered the noise when I left her there. Mabel reached in, picked Livvy up off the floorboard, and handed her to me. Too shaky to stand, I climbed into the backseat of the Cherokee and cuddled Livvy until she popped her thumb in her mouth.

A car screeched into the driveway. I assumed it was the police or an ambulance until Mitch elbowed Mabel out of the way and leaned into the Cherokee. "What's going on?"

I glanced at the tree. "It's a long story." My voice quavered. It was as shaky as my legs. "What are you doing home? I thought you had a class."

"Canceled. The instructor's wife went into labor, so he dismissed us. I didn't have anything else to do at the squad, so I thought I'd come on home."

"Slacker," I teased in a more steady voice. "Taking off in the middle of the afternoon. I'm glad to see you, though. You can explain this to Thistlewait. I'm sure he'll show up here soon."

"He opened the basement window." Mitch took a bite of his double chocolate ice cream and waited for a reaction.

Abby's voice was incredulous. "A basement window? Those are at least six feet off the floor."

"We're changing his name to Houdini," Mitch joked. He'd passed his check ride that morning and was in a good mood.

I put my fork down beside my chocolate raspberry torte. I liked my Hershey Kisses, but this was serious chocolate. "Don't keep them in suspense any longer," I said. "Rex jumped up on the dryer, and, well, you know how the dryer vent in our basement is fixed to go out one of the windows?"

"Just like ours," Abby said. The basement windows of the bungalows in our neighborhood opened at an angle and had three horizontal panes. With one pane removed, the dryer vent went in the opening and plywood filled the rest of the pane.

"He jumped on the dryer, pushed the plywood out, the vent tube fell off, and then he wiggled out the opening," I said.

Abby took another drink of her cappuccino and said, "He's never liked that laundry room in the first place."

"Considering he shredded the linoleum the other
time we left him in there, I guess not." I laughed. "He
won't be staying down there anymore."

"Joe's not taking Rex with him?" Abby asked. Joe'd
put in for a transfer to a new base.

"No, he didn't want to take Rex. Too many memories. Looks like we have a dog for good." Mitch smiled.

I stretched my leg under the table. Even after twenty-
four hours my knee ached and it wasn't going to stop
anytime soon. It was Tuesday evening, one day since the
showdown in my yard. After dinner, Mitch and I had
walked to the neighborhood café and bakery, Cobble-
stone, with Abby and Jeff. It was the perfect place because it had something for everyone: ice cream for
Mitch, chocolate for me, and coffee for Abby and Jeff.
It was a relief to talk freely to Abby and Jeff. The ten-
sions and undercurrents were gone.

"The whole thing was so bizarre. I can't believe it
happened," Abby said.

I took my last bite of the torte and said, "I can't either.
I feel like it was a dream. No, a nightmare." But the ache
in my knee reminded me it was real.

"What's going to happen to Brent?" Abby asked.

"The police found him at his house yesterday afternoon, right on time to pick up Diana per her orders.
Apparently, when he realized that Diana hadn't killed
me, he started talking and hasn't stopped. Of course,
he's saying Diana planned everything and did it all herself," I said sarcastically, which basically backed up what
Diana had told me, but what else would he do? He'd
never admit to any of it.

"What's going to happen to Diana?" Abby asked.

"They're untangling the jurisdictions, but everyone
wants her," I said.

"Why?" Jeff asked.

"Cass died on-base, so the OSI wants to interrogate her. The Vernon police want her because of Friona. Brent says Friona tried to blackmail Diana. Get this, Friona saw Diana in the Vincents' house while Joe was out of town for the funeral. Diana was there searching for the box they mistakenly gave to the garage sale."

"But Friona worked for them, too?" Abby asked. "This is too confusing."

"It is," I replied. "They drafted Friona, just like they drafted Jeff, to be the official name on the paperwork to hide their involvement in the corporations that were buying land and granting easements."

I left the statement hanging. I knew Jeff had talked to the OSI again and they'd released him, but I didn't know if he was cleared or still under investigation.

Jeff wiped his hand over his face. "Yeah. I didn't know what I was getting into. Brent asked me to be Forever Wild's registered agent. He said his brother-in-law lived in Seattle and was a developer who wanted to expand his business over here in Vernon. Brent said there'd be a huge hassle if his brother-in-law found out Brent and Diana were involved in a development here. He wanted to keep the whole thing quiet. He said I'd be doing him a favor. I've known Brent since the Academy. He was in my squad." Jeff shrugged. "Not one of my better investment decisions, let me tell you."

"But your argument with Cass. Why did you say that there were different ways to do things?"

"She saw Forever Wild on the check and lost it. I tried to calm her down. You were there and saw the whole thing. A few months after I filed the paperwork for Brent, I asked him how things were going. He said there was some opposition. People, like Cass, who didn't want any progress. He described how the development would preserve open space. It sounded good to me. But I knew she opposed any development and I tried to tell her there were other viewpoints besides hers."

"Did you cash the check?" Mitch asked.

"No. Couldn't do it. After she died, I started to wonder if everything with Forever Wild was really on the up and up. Then the OSI started asking questions and I panicked. I said it was about a hunting lease. I'd just mailed the check for the lease the day she died, so it could have been that check that set her off. She didn't like hunting either. I hoped the OSI would buy that and leave me out of the rest of the investigation. I put the check Brent had given me in my wallet. Never cashed it. It was a relief to give it to that Thistledown guy and explain everything."

"Thistlewait, that's his name, not Thistledown," I said to Jeff. I felt myself flush as I remembered my search of Abby and Jeff's bedroom. No wonder I couldn't find anything. He'd had the real check on him all the time. Risky, if he was arrested, but I could understand how he wouldn't want to let it out of his reach. I checked Abby and Jeff's faces. Abby leaned back in her chair, her face relaxed, and Jeff looked relieved if a little shaken. He'd come so close to getting involved in a dark scheme with people who wouldn't hesitate to take him out if he caused problems. Apparently they didn't know about my snooping. Hopefully, they'd never know I suspected Jeff of murder, either.

Abby sipped her coffee, then said, "But I still don't understand what they were doing wrong. Besides murder, of course. What is this conservation easement thing?"

"I did a search last night on the Internet and found

out there's nothing wrong with a conservation easement," I said. "It's a way to protect or limit development
on a piece of land. It depends on how the easement is
written. Cass thought this easement gave a cursory nod
to environmental issues while basically allowing the
builders free reign on the land. Brent and Diana fun-
neled the profits from the land sales to their offshore
account, where they also deposited money he'd scammed
from military families. Evidently he used the insurance
scam to grease some palms in the city and the county.
That's why the development went in so fast. The real
problem was that Brent and Diana also owned Forever
Wild, which oversaw the easement. Most conservation
easements are set up with an independent foundation,
a nonprofit, or a government agency. Their job is to en-
force the easement. Essentially, they were checking up
on themselves.

"What really set the whole thing in motion was the
original landowner's daughter, Isabelle Coombes. She
said there was a prior easement that prevented *any* further development of the valley."

Mitch took a bite of his waffle cone, wiped his mouth,
and said, "Can you imagine the litigation if they found
that easement? The original owner could sue Forever
Wild for allowing development."

"And people who'd bought lots and started to build
would sue Forever Wild," Abby chimed in.

"Not to mention that the legal dealings of Forever
Wild and Tecmarc would be scrutinized and their sweet
double ownership deal would be exposed," I said.

"They owned the land so they profited from selling
the lots and they also owned the company that held the
easement, so they controlled the development," Abby

summarized with wide eyes. "So *is* there another ease-ment?"

I shook my head. "I talked to Debbie this morning. She works in the county offices and she's been search-ing for the easement that Isabelle said her father put on the land. Turns out that there isn't one. Her dad talked about it, but never did it."

Abby nodded her head. "That would explain why it never showed up in the title searches for all the other real estate transactions in Wilde Creek Estates. Boy, I'm glad we couldn't afford to live there. It's crazy. Cass and Friona got in their way. Can they prove Diana killed Friona? Do they have anything else besides what she told you?" Abby asked.

I said, "There were traces of blood on Diana's Swiss Army knife. It's being tested to see if it was Friona's blood."

Jeff raised his eyebrows. "If she used it to kill Friona, why would she keep it?"

"And the EpiPen?" Abby added.

"I think the EpiPen slid down between the seats and she didn't realize she hadn't thrown it away. Brent says she trashed them on the way home from the barbeque in a Dumpster behind a dry cleaner off the highway. I don't know why she kept the knife."

"Arrogance?" Jeff speculated. "Maybe she thought she'd never get caught? No one had connected her to Cass's death."

Abby put down her mug. "Okay, now explain that strange phone call about the cup."

"After we gave Diana the box she took a drink from a water bottle. On the way back from the travel office I re-membered you said that Diana had a Coke at the barbeque. But the drinks at the barbeque were served in clear plastic cups. I needed to know if you'd seen a cup with the words "Coke" on it or if you'd seen her drinking from a clear cup and assumed it was a Coke because of the dark color of the drink."

"It was a red and white cup with Coke printed on it, just like I told you. But why does it matter?"

"Because that was the kind of cup that I found the wasps in. Diana told me she only drank water and green tea. You must have seen her before she went to get the wasps and put them in Cass's van." I ran my fork through the raspberry drizzle on the edge of my plate. "But I knew it wouldn't be enough for Thistlewait. And I knew those papers were going to disappear. I was kicking myself for giving them back to her that day. I had to do something."

I felt Mitch shift and I knew he was giving me that disapproving look. But what was done was done and I couldn't change it. I didn't want to rehash what we'd been over too many times already, so I said. "Look at Livvy." She cooed and clutched a rattle. "She couldn't do that a few weeks ago," I said. Now she completed the motions with ease. I looked at Mitch. "She's growing and changing every day." I nudged the butterfly toy suspended from her car seat handle. It jingled and Livvy's gaze fastened on it. "I know I'm kind of a control freak. I'm beginning to realize I can't control everything, put it in a box and label it."

The tension in Mitch's face eased and he squeezed my hand. "Kind of a control freak?" he asked, grinning.

"Okay, I'm a huge control freak," I allowed. We stacked our plates and mugs in the center of the table as Gwen and Zoë walked in the café. Mitch buckled Livvy into her car seat while I went to talk to Gwen.

"Go pick out which kind of cookie you want," Gwen said. Zoë scampered to the front of the café and planted her nose on the glass display case.

"How are you?" I asked as Gwen set her expensive leather purse down and unwound her red scarf.

"We're as okay as we can be when our life is falling apart. I told Steven. Everything." Her eyes were puffy. "The medical examiner said Colin died from an aneurysm." She fiddled with her scarf, adjusted it on the chair. "Steven's gone."

"Where?"

"I don't know. He said he was going away to think and he'd be back. Then he left. It was awful. He was so quiet. He wasn't even angry. Just hurt."

"What will you do?"

"I don't know. I'm trying to keep things as normal as I can for Zoë." She sighed. "I told her Steven's on a trip."

"He said he would be back."

"I've heard that before."

Mitch met us in the aisle. I told Gwen to call me if she needed anything and tossed a blanket over Livvy's car seat to protect her on the short walk home. We pushed out through the glass door into the brisk air and swirling snowflakes.

"Oh, Livvy's first snowfall," Abby said. Jeff and Abby took the lead. I linked arms with Mitch and we strolled behind them, or actually lurched along, overbalanced by the car seat.

We waved to Abby and Jeff and turned onto our street. "Well, now we can get back to a normal life," Mitch said. "No more chasing down leads and questioning possible suspects." I agreed and we paced along. It was good to have our easy, companionable silence back.

"You know that I didn't want to suspect Jeff," I said finally.

"I know."

"We're different. You supported him by believing he didn't do it. I supported him by proving he didn't do it."

Mitch sighed with exasperation. "Some way to show your support." His tone went from playful to serious. "You gave me a scare."

"I know. I was scared myself."

At the top of our driveway, I paused, picturing next spring when the flower bed that lined the house would blaze with white tulips and red poppies. I'd planted them this morning despite my sore knee. It had been good working in the ground, turning over the thick, moist clumps of dirt. The poppies were for Cass. She loved flowers and these poppies even reminded me of her. They were bright and showy with leggy stems and flamboyant blooms, but within the beauty lurked dangerous seeds.

Rex trotted around the side of the house, his mouth open in his doggie grin, tongue lolling off to the side. A frayed tether rope attached to his collar trailed behind him.

"You were talking about change tonight, but some things stay the same." Mitch wound the frayed rope around his hand. "We can be pretty sure you won't have to worry about stumbling across a murder again."

I almost agreed, but then a strange, almost dark, feeling assailed me. Mitch hadn't realized I'd stopped at the foot of the steps. He called for Rex, opened the door, and flicked on the kitchen light, creating a glowing rectangle in the night. I shook off the strange feeling and hurried home through the swirling flakes.

An Everything in Its Place Tip for an Organized Move

On moving day itself remove everything from your home you don't want packed and sent on the moving van. A safe place to stash items is the trunk of your car. Don't forget:

- Packed suitcases
- Travel documents
- Moving paperwork

Otherwise, you may find your toothbrush and jammies boxed and loaded on the moving van!

Acknowledgments

Writing a book is an intensely solitary pursuit interspersed with periods of collaboration, so I must thank many people who helped get this book onto the bookshelves. A big thank you to Faith Hamlin, Rebecca Friedman, and Katherine Darling for loving *Moving Is Murder* and being persistent. Kudos to my wonderful editor, Michaela Hamilton. Thank you for making a dream come true. My cybersisters (and cyber-brothers) from the Internet Chapter of Sisters in Crime supported and encouraged me as only other writers can. Mark Berman, Steven Kerry Brown, Dr. P. D. Lyle, Mel Savoie, Mary V. Welk, and Sharon Wildwind graciously helped with research. Any mistakes are mine, not theirs. First readers, John and Edwyna Honderich, Trish Carruth, and Emilie Davis gave great suggestions. Thanks to Mom for those Saturday trips to the library and to Grandad for giving me my first thesaurus. Look what you started! And last but certainly not least, thanks to Glenn for endless support and encouragement and to Lauren and Jonathan for supplying me with ideas, hugs, and smiles.

Glossary

AAFES—Army and Air Force Exchange Service, organization that operates Base Exchanges

AFB—Air Force Base

AR—Air Refueling

BDU—Battle Dress Uniform, camouflage

Blues—Uniform of light blue shirt and dark blue pants

Boldface—Portions of text in Air Force publications set in bold type, information that is mandatory to know

BX—Base Exchange, small department store on-base

Check ride—Flight test pilots must pass annually to maintain flying currency

Currency—Flight status; all tests and requirements are met and pilot is allowed to fly sorties

DNIF—Duty Not Including Flying; military member is ill but can perform duties except for flying

DV—Distinguished Visitor

HQ—Headquarters

IP—Instructor pilot

IRC—Instrument Review Course

Lodging—Motel on-base (previously know as Billeting)

O Club—Officers' Club

OSI—Office of Special Investigations

PA—Public Affairs

PCS—Permanent Change of Station (PSCing means moving)

Pubs—Air Force publications about aircraft (flight manuals)

Regs—Regulations (rules)

Shopette—Convenience store on-base

Sim—Flight simulator

Sortie—A flight

Squad—Squadron

SWA—Southwest Asia

TDY—Temporary Duty (a short trip)

UAE—United Arab Emirates

Turn the page for a sneak preview of
Sara Rosett's new Mom Zone mystery
STAYING HOME IS A KILLER,
available in Kensington hardcover in April 2007!

After a quick lunch with Mitch I drove home, pushing the speed limit to reach our house before Livvy went to sleep in the Cherokee. Once she was asleep, even if it was for five minutes, that was it, no more naps for that day. I turned onto our street and crept through the scattering of pickups, vans, and cars in front of the Wilsons's house. Our neighborhood of arts and crafts bungalows from the '20s and '30s had plenty of charm and character. Gorgeous maple and pine trees towered over the homes, each with its own special touches, but modern conveniences like dishwashers and garage door openers were in short supply. The Wilsons had tackled a complete modernization and had a different set of contractors and work crews clogging the street every day. I edged past an oversized shiny pickup, an ancient blue van with a mountain landscape painted on the side, a van labeled "Buzzard Electric," and a dented Ford Tempo. Finally, I pulled into the driveway in front of our basement garage.

Despite the inconveniences, I loved our house. Its honey colored brick looked cozy even on this cold day and the graceful Tudor-inspired lines and the leaded glass gave it a uniqueness that we'd never find in modern tract housing or in base housing, either. Our house sat on a corner lot. The lot sloped down at the rear of the property and the builder had taken advantage of the drop. He'd burrowed into the slope to create a two-car attached garage at the basement level.

With Livvy's head tucked under my chin to shelter her from the frigid wind that made my eyes water, I crunched through the snow and ice that rimmed our driveway. Inside, I peeled her out of her snowsuit like I was peeling a banana and changed her diaper.

"Dogs. Woof, woof," she said, her face serious as I carried her to bed. She held her eyes wide open to keep them from shutting.

"Yes. There were some very loud dogs today at the vet." I snuggled her in bed, positioned Pink Girl on the night stand, sang a lullaby, and tip-toed into the hall. I left the answering machine blinking "three" and went to get Rex, our mutt, a mix of lab and rottweiler, out of his kennel in the Cherokee. Since we didn't have another of suburbia's staples, a completely fenced backyard, I put him on his long tether in the backyard. He galloped through the snow, dug his nose into the powder, and flung it into the air while I dragged the kennel inside and put it in the kitchen.

I shut the kitchen door and stood still trying to absorb the warmth of the kitchen. I worked my boots off and padded across the golden oak floorboards to turn up the heat another notch. Then I hit Play on the answering machine and scrounged in the pantry for hot chocolate packets.

A languid voice stated, "Hello, Ellie. This is Clarissa Bedford. You said to call you about a consultation. Next week, either Tuesday or Friday morning works for me." I heard a trace of an accent in the message that I hadn't noticed in person. Southern? Or more of a Southwest drawl? I'll have to ask her where she was from. The machine stated the date and time, then beeped.

"Ellie. Jill. Call me. It's urgent." I smiled as I pulled out the cocoa and marshmallows. The staccato commands from the squadron commander's wife couldn't have been more different from Clarissa's slower, deeper voice.

I picked up the phone and dialed Jill's number, but my cell phone trilled, so I hung up the kitchen phone and dug my cell phone out from under a sippy cup in my purse.

"Ellie. Where are you?" Abby, my best friend, sounded breathless and shaken.

"I'm at home."

"I just got a busy signal," she said sharply.

"Hey, can't I listen to my messages? I was returning a phone call." The wonders of technology. Now when someone is too impatient to wait for the phone not to be busy they can call my cell phone.

"Sorry," Abby rushed on, "Jill's trying to find you. You remember that form, the one we filled out at the Spouse Coffee? With all the info? Penny never filled one out. They don't know who to call."

"Slow down. What's going on?" I was used to Abby's scattered conversations, but I felt a finger of cold that had nothing to do with the weather trace itself along my neck. Her trembling voice held a note of fear. Something was not right.

"I'm doing this all wrong." Abby took a deep breath. "Penny's dead."